Empire of the Senses
General Editor: Mike Mitchell

Abbé Jules

Octave Mirbeau

Abbé Jules

translated by Nicoletta Simborowski
and with an introduction by Adrian Murdoch

Dedalus

Funded by
THE ARTS COUNCIL
OF ENGLAND

Dedalus would like to thank The Arts Council of England and the French Ministry of Foreign Affairs for their assistance in producing this translation

Published in the UK by Dedalus Ltd, Langford Lodge, St Judith's Lane, Sawtry, Cambs, PE17 5XE

ISBN 1873982 37 2

Distributed in Australia & New Zealand by Peribo Pty Ltd, 58 Beaumont Road, Mount Kuring-gai N.S.W. 2080

Distributed in Canada by Marginal Distribution, Unit 102, 277 George Street North, Peterborough, Ontario, KJ9 3G9

First published by Dedalus in 1996
Translation copyright © 1996 Nicoletta Simborowski
Introduction copyright © 1996 by Adrian Murdoch

Printed in Finland by Wsoy
Typeset by Datix International Limited, Bungay, Suffolk

This book is sold subject to the condition that it shall not, by way of trade or otherwise, be lent, resold, hired out, or otherwise circulated without the publisher's prior consent in any form of binding or cover other than that in which it is published and without a similar condition including this condition being imposed on the subsequent purchaser.

A C.I.P. listing for this book is available on request

THE TRANSLATOR

Nicoletta Simborowski read Modern Languages at Oxford and then worked in publishing and as a teacher at Westminster School in London. She has translated several books from French and Italian, including *The Late Mattia Pascal* by Luigi Pirandello for Dedalus.

She combines a career as a lecturer in Italian at Christ Church, Oxford with freelance interpreting and translating for television and video. Her current projects include translating Octave Mirbeau's *Sebastien Roche*, which Dedalus will publish in 1997.

THE EDITOR

Adrian Murdoch was educated in Scotland and at The Queen's College, Oxford. He works as a journalist in London. He collaborated with his father, Brian Murdoch, in translating material for Geoffrey Farrington's *The Dedalus Book of Roman Decadence* and has edited several other works for Dedalus. He is currently editing *The Dedalus Book of Central and Eastern European Literature: Storm from the East*.

French Literature from Dedalus:

French Language Literature in translation is an important part of Dedalus's list, with French being the language *par excellence* of literary fantasy.

French books from Dedalus include:

Séraphita – Balzac £6.99
The Quest of the Absolute – Balzac £6.99
Episodes of Vathek – Beckford £6.99
The Devil in Love – Jacques Cazotte £5.99
Les Diaboliques – Barbey D'Aurevilly £6.99
Angels of Perversity – Remy de Gourmont £6.99
The Book of Nights – Sylvie Germain £8.99
The Weeping Woman – Sylvie Germain £6.99
Days of Anger – Sylvie Germain £8.99
The Medusa Child – Sylvie Germain £8.99
Night of Amber – Sylvie Germain £8.99
La-Bas – J.K. Huysmans £7.99
The Cathedral – J.K. Huysmans £6.95
En Route – J.K. Huysmans £6.95
Monsieur de Phocas – Jean Lorrain £8.99
Abbé Jules – Octave Mirbeau £7.99
Le Calvaire – Octave Mirbeau £7.99
The Diary of a Chambermaid – Octave Mirbeau £7.99
Torture Garden – Octave Mirbeau £7.99
Smarra & Trilby – Charles Nodier £6.99
Tales from the Saragossa Manuscript – Jan Potocki £6.99
Monsieur Venus – Rachilde £6.99
The Marquise de Sade – Rachilde £8.99
The Mysteries of Paris – Eugene Sue £6.99
The Wandering Jew – Eugene Sue £9.99
Micromegas – Voltaire £5.99

forthcoming titles include:

The Experiences of the Night – Marcel Bealu
The Dedalus Book of French Fantasy – editor Christine Donougher

Anthologies featuring French Literature in translation:

The Dedalus Book of Decadence
　　　　　　　　　　–editor Brian Stableford £7.99
The Second Dedalus Book of Decadence
　　　　　　　　　　–editor Brian Stableford £8.99
The Dedalus Book of Surrealism
　　　　　　　　　　–editor Michael Richardson £8.99
The Myth of the World: Surrealism 2
　　　　　　　　　　–editor Michael Richardson £8.99

Introduction to Octave Mirbeau's *Abbé Jules*

"I speak . . . of the presbyterate. Such men think of nothing but their dress. They use perfumes freely and see that there are no creases in their shoes. Their curling hair shows traces of the tongs; their fingers glisten with rings; they walk on tiptoe across a damp road not to splash their feet."
St Jerome

By rights, Octave Mirbeau should have become a pillar of the establishment. His family were dyed-in-the-wool middle class members of that establishment, and his education was what one would have expected.

But then at the age of 11 he was sent to boarding school at Vannes to be educated by Jesuits and just like the Abbé Jules himself, Mirbeau came to hate the Church. In his letters he calls religious schools "a disgrace" and a "permanent danger" and his novel is one of the high points of anticlerical literature.

Abbé Jules is the second novel – written in 1888 – in an unconnected trilogy that began with *Le Calvaire* in 1886 and would be concluded with *Sebastien Roch* in 1890. In the first the radical that Mirbeau had become railed against the army, in the second against the Catholic Church and in the third against society.

Whereas *Le Calvaire* is a fairly straightforward tale of love – however perverted it might become – in the following two years Mirbeau had become an angry social commentator.

Although Jules himself is a grotesquely exaggerated caricature of a fallen priest – indeed the passages about his childhood show an utterly loathsome man – Mirbeau wants him to be seen as a victim of society. He has been corrupted by his environment. By this time Mirbeau had become a close friend of Jules-Amadée Barbey d'Aurevilly, whose collection of short stories, *Les Diaboliques* were a considerable influence on him. That book explored how outward respectability conceals moral depravity.

Mirbeau can be particularly direct in his commentary, and lack of subtlety is a fair charge often levelled against him by detractors. His use of rhetoric to expose the hypocrisy he saw and felt is frequently a case of over-egging the pudding. The aged Jules teaching his nephew Albert rants:

"Religions – and the Catholic religion above all – have set themselves up as the great pimps of love. Under the pretext of softening the brutal side of love – which is in fact its only heroic aspect – they have developed the perverse, unhealthy side, by the sensuality of music and perfumes, by the mysticism of prayer and the moral onanism of adoration . . . Do you understand?"

Nevertheless Mirbeau's genuine passion against what he perceives as a wrong makes it easier to overlook any stylistic drawbacks. At any rate it is possible to argue that Mirbeau was the most successful of his contemporaries as he was banned for being obscene. He had embarrassed the establishment.

But while many of these charges are true, Mirbeau is also capable of subtle writing and of witty caricature.

Early on in the novel he describes a crucifix as "painted" and "rotted with damp [it] has only one leg and one arm, but the devout still come and kneel at the foot of the cross". And in the passage with Reverend Père Pamphile and the monastery of Réno, the decay of the building mirrors the decay of the man which in turn becomes an allegory for the decay of the church:

"From the height of a turret which dominated the monastery, he surveyed the spectacle of this destruction and savoured the great, painful joy of it. All around, trees lay, pell-mell, hideously mutilated, some on their side, twisted and bleeding from huge wounds, others trunk uppermost, groaning, leaning on their crushed branches, as if on stumps. One alone stood upright at the entrance to the garden, a stunted cherry-tree, eaten away by disease, astonished to be so alone on this earth, bereft of its hardy offspring, on land completely levelled."

Precisely why Mirbeau could throw his poisoned darts so accurately is because he knew his enemy intimately. This is apparent in his parodic descriptions of the priests themselves. They are venal ("A soul is born and that means ten francs") or stupid, receive legacies from old women, they are puffy, repugnant, heavy, vulgar, carnivorous and egotistical. In the passage where Jules finally cracks there are beautiful vignettes about the priests at dinner which are reminiscent of a Hieronymous Bosch painting.

"The two priests near him, who were telling each other filthy scatological jokes in low voices, containing their laughs, dribbling sauce, all that he saw, all that he heard, set him beside himself," echoes St Jerome's letter on the decline of the priesthood and Jules' reaction is reminiscent of Jesus' reaction to the money lenders in the Gospel of John – and both of these passages will have been familiar to Mirbeau.

The reader is left deliberately slightly confused whether Jules is a good or a bad person. Jules is both an antagonist and a victim. Perhaps it is best summed up by contemporary and friend, Stephane Mallarmé, who admired Abbé Jules very much and praised Mirbeau's "bitter and tender prescience".

Octave Mirbeau
1848 Born February 16, in Trévières (Calvados)
1859 Sent for schooling by Jesuits in Vannes
1870 Joined the army
1885 Conversion to anarchism. Stopped writing for the pro-monarchist newspaper *Le Gaulois* and started writing for radical paper *La France*
1886 Published *Letters From My Cottage* and *Le Calvaire*
1888 Published *Abbé Jules*
1890 Published *Sebastien Roch*
1894 Dreyfus affair
1898 Published *Torture Garden*
1900 Published *Diary of a Chambermaid*
1917 Died February 16

PART ONE

Chapter One

Apart from the days when my father had carried out a difficult operation, a major confinement, and later at table explained the most exciting stages in technical terms, often in Latin, my parents hardly ever spoke to one another. Not that there was any ill-feeling; on the contrary, they loved one another very much, got on well, the best in the world, in all aspects and one could not imagine a more united household; but accustomed to having the same thoughts, and experiencing the same reactions and being unromantic by nature, they had nothing to say to one another. They had nothing to say to me either, finding me either too old to be amused with nursery rhymes or too young for them to bore me with serious discussions. Furthermore, they were steeped in the idea that a well-brought up child should only open his mouth to eat, recite lessons and say his prayers. If ever I occasionally happened to rebel against this family system of upbringing, my father would intervene strictly and enforce my silence by means of this definitive argument:

"What is the matter with you? Do Trappist monks speak? Well, do they?"

Apart from this, if they were not always as cheerful and affectionate as I might have wished, I felt they loved me as best they could.

For them to feel they had permission to unseal their lips, notable events were necessary, aside from professional escapades and day-to-day occurrences, events such as the sacking of an employee, a deer stalked and killed in Monsieur de Blandé's wood, the death of a neighbour, the unexpected news of a wedding. The probable pregnancies of rich clients were also useful as themes for brief exchanges which could be summarised as follows:

"Just as long as I am not mistaken!" my father would say. "As long as she really is pregnant!"

"Ah! that will be a wonderful confinement!" affirmed my

mother. "Four of those a month, I would not ask for more, we could buy ourselves a piano."

And my father tutted.

"Four a month! My word! You are a little too greedy my darling! And in any case that blessed woman still worries me. Her pelvis is so narrow."

Without knowing exactly which mysterious part of the body was indicated by that word 'pelvis', by the age of nine, I knew the exact gauge and childbearing properties of the pelvises of all the women in Viantais. Nevertheless, this did not prevent my father, despite his scientific observations and listings of uteruses, placentas and umbilical cords, from assuring me that babies were found under cabbage leaves. Neither was I ignorant of the exact nature of a cancer, a tumour and a phlegmon; my forlorn spirit had gradually been swamped with horrible images of wounds, a state of mind which I concealed as if shameful; the sorrow of the sickbed had passed over me, chilling the confident smile of my earliest childhood. And when of an evening I saw my father take his bag and spread out on the table the small, fearsome instruments of glittering steel and watched him blow into his probes, wipe his scalpels, polish in the lamp flame the slim blades of his lancets, my prettiest dreams, of bluebirds or wondrous fairies, would be transformed into a surgical nightmare, where pus flowed, severed members piled up and hideously bloodied bandages and dressings lay tangled. Occasionally, he spent the evening cleaning his forceps, which he often forgot in the hood of his gig. He shined the rusty arms with a yellow powder, polished the spoons, oiled the central pin. When the instrument was gleaming, he liked to manoeuvre it, pretending to introduce it delicately into imaginary cavities. Then he would wrap it up again in its green serge sheath and say:

"I don't like using that I must say. I'm always worried there's going to be an accident. They're so fragile, these blessed organs. . ."

"Doubtless," my mother would reply, "But you are forgetting that in those cases you can charge double."

Whilst all this taught me things that children do not usually know, it did not keep me entertained. In my idle existence, nothing was more painful to me than mealtimes, when time dragged so. I would have preferred to escape somewhere, caper about on the stairs, in the corridor, in the kitchen, stay with old Victoire who at the risk of incurring my mother's reproaches, allowed me to potter amongst her saucepans, play with the taps of the oven, wind up the spit, and sometimes told me extraordinary tales of bandits which filled me with a delicious terror. But obedience obliged me to sit rigid with boredom on my chair, the seat of which was too low and was raised by two volumes, two coverless and ancient copies of the *Lives of the Saints*, and I was not allowed to leave the table until my mother stood up, thus giving the sign I could go. In the summer I contrived not to be too bored. The drowsy flight of flies, the droning of wasps above plates of fruit, the butterflies and insects attracted by the fresh scent of newly watered flowers, and swooping down on the tablecloth, were sufficient distraction. Also, through the open window, I liked to gaze at the garden, the distant valley, and even further away, the hills of St Jacques, violet and misty, beyond which the sun was setting. Alas, in winter there were no more flies, no more wasps, no more butterflies, no more sky, no more anything . . . nothing but that gloomy room and my parents, each absorbed in unknown thoughts from which I always felt excluded.

It had rained all day, I recall, and that evening, a particularly sad winter evening, my parents had not uttered a word. They seemed more morose than ever. My father folded his table napkin carefully into a heart-shape, as was his habit every evening when the meal was finished, and suddenly he asked:

"What can he have been up to in Paris? It's inconceivable."

With sharp little movements, he flicked off the crumbs of bread that had fallen into the folds of his waistcoat and trousers, drew his chair up to the hearth where the embers were dying, and, his body bent slightly towards the fire, his elbows on his knees, he warmed his hands, rubbing them together occasionally and cracking the joints. Victoire came to clear away, moving around the table, the sleeves of her dress rolled up to her elbows. When she had gone, my father repeated in an even more questioning tone: "What can he have been up to in Paris? For six years, with no news, ever? A priest! It's certainly odd. I would dearly like to know."

I realised they were talking about my uncle, the Abbé Jules. That morning, my father had received a letter from him, announcing his imminent return. The letter was brief and contained no explanation. There was no trace of any emotion, any affection, any attempt at an excuse for such a long period of neglect. He was coming back to Viantais and was content to inform his brother of the fact in a letter much like the circulars that suppliers send to their customers. My father had even pointed out that the handwriting was particularly careless.

For the third time he exclaimed:

"What can he have been up to in Paris?"

My mother, seated very stiff and upright at the table, her arms folded, her expression vague, nodded. She looked strict, nun-like, an impression accentuated by her black serge dress which was plain and completely without ornament, without any whiteness of linen at the neck or wrists.

"Peculiar as he is," she said, "we can be sure it is not a very edifying tale!" And after a brief silence, she added drily:

"He could well have stayed in Paris. I expect no good to come of his return."

My father agreed.

"Doubtless, doubtless," he said, "with a character like his, life will not be easy, not all the time. No indeed. Nevertheless . . ."

He thought for a moment, then spoke again:

"Nevertheless, there is some advantage, my dear, in the Abbé being nearby, there is some considerable advantage."

My mother replied sharply, with a twitch of her shoulders:

"Some advantage! You really believe that do you? First of

all, he cares as little for his family as he does for saying mass. Has he ever just once sent a little gift for the child, his godson? When you cared for him through the worst of his illness, spending entire nights at his bedside, neglecting your own patients, did he even thank you? You said: 'He'll give us a nice present.' Where is it, this nice present of his? And the rabbits, the woodcocks, the fat trout and all the good things he stuffed himself with! The sacrifices we made for him! He acted, in fact, as if everything was his due."

"Yes, yes of course," broke in my father, "we did our best . . ."

"Oh no! We were idiots. He is a bad brother, a bad priest and a hopeless person. If he comes back to Viantais, it's because he has no more money, he has squandered everything and we will have to look after him. Well, that was all we needed now!"

"Come come my dear, you exaggerate. If he comes back, Lord, it will be because he has never been capable of staying in one place for long. He's a rascal! He's leaving Paris just like he left the bishop's service where he could have achieved anything, like he left his Randonnai parish, where he was living such a peaceful life and was receiving so many donations. He needs change, novelty. He's not happy anywhere. As for his fortune, ha! I don't agree with you at all. He was pretty mean, the Abbé, pretty miserly. Don't you remember?"

"Being miserly, my dear, does not in any way prevent someone from wasting their money on foolish schemes. Who knows what silly notions go through the mind of the likes of him? In fact, you're forgetting that before leaving for Paris, the Abbé sold his farm, his two meadows and the Faudière wood. Why? And where is all the money now?"

"True, true," said my father, suddenly lost in thought.

"Not to mention that he is not liked round here, that he will harm your chances of any public office and even affect your standing with your patients. The Bernard family for instance, that you have been so careful to hold on to. I would not be at all surprised if they left you. Lord, that really is a possibility. And you try to find another family who are ill so often and pay so well."

My father leaned back in his chair, twisted his lip and scratched the back of his neck.

"Yes, yes," he said, over and again, "You're right. That is a possibility."

My mother's voice took on a conspiratorial note.

"Listen, I have never wanted to tell you this so as not to upset you, but I was always afraid I was going to hear something terrible. Think of Verger, who killed the archbishop, Verger was a priest too, mad, fanatical, like the Abbé Jules."

My father turned round swiftly, fear in his eyes. All of a sudden his face was an abyss of horror. Shuddering, he stammered:

"Verger! Why do you mention him? Verger! My God!"

"Yes. Well. I've often thought of it. I never opened your newspaper without my heart in my mouth. Who knows? Apart from anything else, all your family are somewhat . . . unusual."

The conversation ceased and a profound silence descended upon us once more.

Outside the wind whistled, shaking the trees and the rain had started to rattle on the window-panes again. My father, his face stricken, watched the fire die. My mother, pensive, pale from the strain of having said so much, looked into the middle distance as usual. As for me, in that dining room half-bathed in shadow, in that room without furniture, with bare walls, the windows dark with the night-sky, I felt completely alone, abandoned, miserable. From the ceiling, the walls, from the very eyes of my parents, a chill fell on me, which enveloped me like an icy cloak, penetrating my bones, gripping my heart. I felt like crying. I compared our gloomy, monastic home with that of the Servières, friends that we dined with every Thursday. How I envied the soft, intimate warmth of that house, the caress of its carpets, the walls hung with comforting drapes and family portraits in oval frames, the old souvenirs religiously preserved, all those attractive trifles scattered about, which were each a smile, the constant pleasure contained in a glance, the revelation of a cherished habit. Why was my mother not like Madame Servière, cheerful, lively, lovely, dressed in beautiful fabrics with lace and flowers on her bodice and perfume in the blonde twists and coils of her hair? She was so charming, Madame Servière. Everything about her moved me so much that I liked to sit on chairs she had just vacated, respiring the air she had breathed and embracing the places where her body had rested. Why did I not feel the same about my own mother? Why was I not like Maxime and Jeanne, children of my own age, who could chat, run, play in corners, be happy and who had huge gilded books, whose pictures their father explained, amid admiring comments and laughter?

Stifling yawns, I twisted and turned without ever finding a comfortable position atop the execrable *Lives of the Saints* which served me as a seat. To keep my ears and my eyes occupied, I listened to Victoire behind the door, scraping her clogs on the kitchen flagstones, moving crockery about and I contemplated the circle of yellow light which trembled on the ceiling above the lamp.

That evening, my father forgot to note down in his diary the home visits and treatment he had given the sick during the day. I noticed also that he did not read his paper, two actions which he normally performed with pitiless regularity.

To entertain myself a little, I decided to think about my uncle the Abbé, whose return had occasioned a conversation between my parents of such unaccustomed length and vivacity. I was very small when he left the area: barely three, nevertheless I was surprised that I could place him in my memories only very vaguely; since that time, not a day had gone past without someone threatening me with my uncle as if he were a kind of bogeyman, a terrible ogre that carries off naughty children. They had told me how one day I was playing in his garden in Randonnai and fell right into a bed of tulips and that my uncle in a fury whipped me ferociously with a strap. And when they needed to depict the physical or moral ugliness of anyone, my parents never failed to use this comparison: "Ugly as Abbé Jules, dirty as Abbé Jules, greedy as Abbé Jules, violent as Abbé Jules, deceitful as Abbé Jules." If I cried, my mother would shame me by shouting: "Oh just look at him, he's just like Abbé Jules!" If I was disobedient: "Carry on like that, carry on, boy, you'll end up just like Abbé Jules." Abbé Jules! That is to say, every kind of fault, vice, crime and hideousness, every mystery. Often, the priest, Sortais, came to see us and each time he would ask:

"Well then, still no news of Abbé Jules?"

"Alas, no, Father."

The priest would then cross his stubby, plump hands over his fat stomach and shake his head tragically.

"Who would have thought such things possible? Still, just yesterday I said a Mass for him."

"Perhaps he's dead, Father."

"Oh, if he were dead my good lady, we would know."

"Perhaps that would be for the best, Father."

"Perhaps, my dear lady, but God's mercy is so great. One never knows. Nevertheless, it is very sad for the clergy, very sad . . . very, very sad."

"And for his family too, come along, Father."

"And for the region. And in every respect, every respect. Very sad in every respect."

And the priest took a pinch of snuff with a loud sniff.

I remember also stories about the Abbé's youth which my father had told me on days when he was in a good mood, half scandalised, half thrilled. He began them in a severe tone of voice, promising to derive some home truths from them, then he gradually allowed himself to be overtaken by the sinister gaiety of these farces and he finished his tale in peals of laughter, slapping his thigh. Among many, one made a vivid impression on me. Sometimes, when I saw my father's face relax a little, I would ask:

"Papa, tell me about Uncle Jules and my Aunt Athalie."

"Have you been good then? Have you done your lessons for today?"

"Yes of course, papa. Oh, please, tell me the story."

And my father would narrate:

"When she was very small, poor Aunt Athalie – who is no longer with us – alas, was very greedy; so greedy that you could not leave any sweetmeat in her reach or she would devour it. In the servants' pantry, she snaffled the leftovers, she went in the cupboards and opened up pots of jam and stuck her fingers inside, in the garden she bit the apples still on the trees and the gardener was in despair thinking that dormice and other pests were causing these ravages. He doubled the number of traps and spent entire nights lying in wait and your aunt made fun of him: 'Well now, François, and how are the dormice?' 'Don't talk to me about them Missy, them're sorcerers, so they are. I'll 'ave 'em, you mark my words.' It was your aunt that he got though. She was severely punished, because gluttony and disobedience are serious sins. Although she was mischievous – a real little devil – Athalie was not well. She coughed a great deal and everyone feared for her chest. To cure her condition, your grandmother used to make her drink a spoonful of codliver oil every morning. It is not nice, codliver oil and, as I told you, your aunt had a taste for nice things. To convince her to take it, it was the very devil. However, after a few months, she looked well on this regime, her colour had come back and she coughed less. But it didn't prevent her dying later of a pulmonary phthisis. She had cavities in her lungs. When you have cavities, you see, there's nothing to be done; you're going to die sooner or later. And children who are naughty always get cavities . . ."

In order, doubtless, to give my imagination time to absorb these prophetic words, my father tended to stop for a moment at this point in his story. He would look at me sternly, blow his nose at length and while a tiny shudder shook my body at the thought that I too, like my Aunt Athalie, might well have cavities, he continued in a jovial tone:

"One morning, your Uncle Jules – he was ten then – came into his sister's room in his nightshirt. In one hand he held the bottle of codliver oil, in the other a paper bag full of chocolates which he had discovered somewhere or other at the back of a drawer. The poor mite was sleeping. He woke her roughly. 'Right, drink up your spoonful!' he told her. At first your aunt refused. 'Drink up and I'll give you a chocolate.' He had opened the bag, shook the sweets, took handfuls which he showed her, smacking his lips. 'They're good, they're really good . . . and there are some vanilla cream ones. Come on, drink up.' Athalie drank, pulling horrible faces. 'Take another now,' said Jules 'and I will give you two chocolates, you understand, two lovely chocolates.' She drank a second spoonful. 'Look, have a third and you will have three chocolates.' She took a third spoonful. She took four, then six, than ten, then fifteen, she drank the whole bottle. Well, then your uncle was beside himself with joy. He danced about in the room, waving the empty bottle, shouting: 'What a joke! Ha, ha, ha! What a great joke! You will be ill and you will be throwing up for two days! This is such fun!' Your Aunt Athalie was crying, she could feel her stomach churning. She was ill, in fact, very ill, and almost died. For eight days she had a fever and vomited and she kept to her bed for two weeks. Your uncle was whipped. They locked him in a dark cupboard but it was impossible to wring one word of repentance from him. On the contrary, he kept on repeating: 'She was sick, she was sick! This is such fun!'"

And my father burst out laughing and concluded:

"What a confounded child, Jules, eh?"

These details, incessantly repeated, ought to have imprinted the features of my uncle for ever on my fearful child's mind. But no! I retained only a confused, wavering image of him which my fevered imagination twisted pitifully in a thousand different versions, fed by my family's tales. My uncle, the Abbé! When I whispered these words to myself, I saw before me a ghostly face, bristling, split with a grimace, grotesque and terrible and I did not know whether to be afraid or laugh at it. My uncle the Abbé! I forced myself to evoke his true features, I called to my aid all the serious events of my life, from which memory that face might emerge, radiant and real. It was in vain. Of the person of my uncle, as vague as an old smudged pastel drawing, all I could retrieve was a long bony body slumped into a winged armchair, his legs crossed under his cassock, skinny, withered legs, with sharp ankles, ending in enormous feet, square at the ends and shod in green slippers. Around him were books. On a grey wall, in a bright room, a picture depicting red-bearded characters, bent over a skull. Then a voice, whose unpleasant tone still rings in my ears, the breathy voice of someone with pneumonia, always grumbling, irritable and critical. "Wretch!" here and "Wretch!" there and that was all.

I was not desperate to see him again, understanding instinctively that he would not bring me additional affection or amusement, certain too that I could expect nothing from a bad godfather who even at my baptism had refused to pay for the sugared almonds or buy a gift for my mother and never gave me presents at New Year – not even oranges. I had heard it said too that he did not like me, that he did not like anyone and he did not respect the Lord and was always in a temper. And my heart missed a beat at the idea that he might beat me with his strap as he had done in the past. However, I could not restrain a certain curiosity which was sharpened by my father's exclamation: "What can he have been up to in Paris for six years?" This question contained an impenetrable mystery for me. It made me see the Abbé Jules in a dark and teeming distance, surrounded by vague shapes, surrendering to forbidden practices whose purpose I longed to know. Why had he gone? Why did no one know anything about his life there? Why was he coming back? What would I think of him? His bony body, his withered legs, his green slippers, the bottle of codliver oil, the tulips, the strap all danced in my head in a wild sarabande. On the brink of meeting this troubling uncle again I felt the same compelling fear I experienced on fair days standing on the threshold of the animal cages and the acrobat's booths. Was I suddenly going to be faced with a miraculous person, someone incomprehensible, endowed with diabolic powers, a thousand times more terrifying than the clown in a red wig who swallowed swords and flaming tow, more dangerous than the negro, cannibal devourer of children who showed his white teeth laughing like a hungry ogre? All the supernatural which my fevered brain was capable of imagining I associated with the person of the Abbé Jules who, by turns minuscule and gigantic, camouflaged himself like an insect amid the blades of grass and suddenly filled the sky, taller, more massive, than a mountain. I did not wish to reflect any longer on the possible consequences of the installation of the Abbé Jules in Viantais, for terror was gradually taking me over, and my uncle was now starting to appear to me with a hooked nose, eyes of burning ember and two sharpened horns which his forehead levelled at me ferociously.

The lamp was smoking. An acrid smell of burning oil filled the room. But, extraordinary phenomenon, no one took any notice. My parents were silent. My mother, motionless, her eyes vague, face stern, went on dreaming. My father prodded the fire furiously, crushing the coals in the tongs, rummaged in the ash which fluttered onto the hearth in grey-white flakes. The wind died down. The trees snored gently, the rain drip-dripped monotonously onto the earth. Suddenly, in the silence, the bell at the gate tinkled.

"It must be Monsieur and Madame Robin," said my mother. "Let's go on up."

She stood up and took the lamp, turning down the wick. We followed her, I, happy to stretch my legs, my father repeating under his breath:

"What can he have got up to in Paris?"

Chapter Two

The houses in Viantais are built on the slopes of a little hill on either side of the road to Mortagne which emerges from the forest a mile away through a narrow gap in the trees. They are clean, cheerful houses, mainly constructed of brick, with high roofs and windows gaily adorned in summer with pots of flowers and climbing plants. Some aspire to gardens, symmetrically arranged in flowerbeds and the walls which enclose them are covered with lattices and framed with vines. Alleys with sudden views over the fields run off a single main street, which towards the centre of the town, broadens into a huge square in the centre of which is a fountain. Then the road continues to descend right to the valley and the main road, crossing the river over a bridge of pink granite, and continues its peaceful way through the fields, the crops and the woods. High up over the town and linked to it by a huge avenue of elms – a rendezvous for children playing hop-scotch – the church stands, old, hunched, coiffed with a pointed bell-tower like a cotton bonnet. On the right, the schools and our house; on the left, the presbytery, separated from the cemetery by a collapsed wall with large gaps here and there through which one can see the crumbling crosses and the mouldering tombs. At the centre of the avenue of elms there stands a crucifix, whose painted wooden Christ, rotted by damp, has only one leg and one arm, but the devout still come and kneel at the foot of the cross and mutter prayers while reciting their rosary.

At that time Viantais had two thousand five hundred inhabitants and was home to no more than twenty fairly well-off households. People frequented each other very little, even within the family since almost every family was divided by ferocious and petty snobberies or troubled by problems concerned with inheritance. Our own socialising was limited to the Servière family, whose luxurious lifestyle embarrassed and worried my parents and made them wary. We also saw the priest Sortais, a fine and charitable old fellow but slightly undesirable since his excessively open temperament constantly led him to commit the most crass social blunders. Finally, we mixed with the Robin family who had immediately become close friends. Very occasionally we received a visit from cousin Debray, a former captain in the army, an arrant eccentric who squandered his time and his pension on stuffing weasels and polecats in comic and pretentious poses, but he was not really welcome because he was unable to open his mouth without swearing and "smelled of dead animals", according to my mother. The Robin family, from the moment of their arrival – they had only been living locally for four years – had formed a close bond with us. At first sight we recognised each other as members of the same race. Since there existed between the Robins and my family no conflict of interest or ambition and they had the same instincts, the same tastes and a similar lack of understanding of life, a firm friendship was forged. Moreover, it was a friendship restricted to the facile observance of cordial selfishness, which would certainly not have survived the shock of the merest demand for sacrifice or devotion.

Monsieur Robin, formerly a lawyer in Bayeux, had sold his practice and been elected magistrate in Viantais thanks to the protection of a senator. He spoke of this senator ceaselessly, in any context and with great enthusiasm. He was about fifty years old, vain, pompous and stupid – irredeemably so. Physically, he resembled a monkey, owing to his upper lip, a broad expanse of skin which was domed and ill-shaven and which created an abnormal distance between his flat nose and a mouth which went from ear to ear. As for the rest of him, he was short, fat, with a yellow complexion framed with a greying beard, and had a pot-belly and hairy hands. Conforming to the habits of a city dweller who has trailed round countless clerks' offices and courts, files under his arm, he never appeared without a top-hat, black cashmere coat, white cravat and clogs, the only concession he made to local mores. Without the historical reasons being clear, he was said to be of an almost savage incorruptibility – an ancient Roman – and yet the day before his hearings, one did see a procession of farmers going into his house with baskets crammed with poultry and game which they carried away empty after some legal discussion, doubtless. Even his political adversaries acknowledged his independence and dignity, though he always showed prejudice towards them and condemned them to the maximum penalties if they had the misfortune to appear in the dock before him. No professor of law could have been better versed in common law than he and he could recite the *Code Civil* from memory, in its entirety, article by article, in the right order. Or at least, he liked to boast of this tour de force, and though very prudent, suggested to the world in general extravagant wagers which no one had so far dared to take him up on, which afforded him a reputation as a phenomenal legal expert both in the county and beyond. Similarly, he was said to know all the decisions of the Court of Appeal. He knew everything. But he had a curious speech impediment. He pronounced the letters B as D and P as T. So there were sometimes very comic combinations of words which were amazing to hear. One day, he said to Father Provost, who was having problems understanding an explanation:

"My dear Father Trovost, you are daffled, are you not? Daffled!"

To which the poor fellow replied, red-faced:

"What d'you mean, Judge, Sir? Is that an insult?"

Nevertheless, it did not harm his established status as a formidable magistrate and accomplished man of the world. He even had the honour of a nickname amongst his discontented litigants: he was known as Judge Daffle."

Sometimes, Monsieur Robin came to collect me to accompany him on one of his walks. We would take the road. Suddenly, he would stop, breathe deeply for a moment, and, his torso tilted backwards, his face turned three-quarters on, waving his arms in domineering gestures, he would practise moments of eloquence for the future.

"And gentlemen," he declaimed, "what can we say of this young man, drought up in the Christian way of life by a tious family, and whom the dase lusts for tleasure and amdition have led to the drink of infamy? Yes, gentlemen."

He would grow animated, invoked Justice, called on the Law, took God as his witness. His arms flailed against the sky, incoherent and rapid, like the sails of a windmill.

"Yes, gentlemen, modern society, whose very dasis . . ."

And while he spoke, his voice swelling, the birds fled with tiny cries; terrified magpies took to the highest branches of the trees. In the distance, dogs barked.

"Then weet, by Jove, weet!" M. Robin yelled at me and finally, out of breath, he would collapse onto the roadside and stayed there ten minutes, dabbing his forehead in a kind of legal ecstasy, in which he saw Berryer smiling at him.

As we walked back home, he gave me advice:

"You will work hard on your law or your medicine; later, you'll go to Taris . . . And then, well! Rememder, my doy, that you must be thrifty. Thrift, you see, it all doils down to thrift . . . when there's thrift, all the other virtues follow."

For the hundredth time, he quoted the example of a young man in Bayeux, whose father, a very rich industrialist, gave him an allowance of two thousand francs a month to live in Paris. The young man denied himself everything, ate and dressed like a pauper, never went out, spent a bare hundred francs a month and with his savings, amassed in a woollen sock, bought shares in the railways and government bonds.

"Dehaviour of that kind is sudlime," he said, patting my cheek, "sudlime. Thrift, my doy. With thrift, not only is a tenny a tenny, dut it's two, as my wife says, who knows everything. And anyway . . ."

Sticking his hat on his head, at a rakish angle, and tracing fantastic twirls in the air with his cane, he concluded roguishly,

"And anyway, it doesn't stot you enjoying yourself, dy Jove. Doys will de doys."

He called this teaching me about Life and preparing me for the struggles ahead.

A skinny, angular, very elongated body, red face with

peeling skin here and there, short turned-up nose with wide-spaced nostrils, hair of greenish blonde, flattened into narrow bands on bruised temples: such was Madame Eustoquie Robin, she who 'knew everything'. It would be impossible for a woman to be less attractive. Her natural ugliness was rendered more complex by all the ridiculous mannerisms which she appeared to take pleasure in adopting in order to underline it. When she spoke, she had a way of detaching each syllable by way of a grating whistle between two breaths, which was as nerve-shattering as the sound of a fingernail scraping on glass. At every word, she gave a pinched smile, little wriggles and nods, a whole range of gauche gestures and pretentious poses which made her body jerk like a broken dummy. Obsessed by a desire that everyone should be ever concerned about her, she constantly complained about some indisposition, a headache, a stomach ache, a pain in her chest, and she sighed and panted and sometimes finally asked permission to undo her corset.

"Oh!" she would gasp. "It's not that it's too tight. On the contrary, but every evening, at this time, I swell up, I swell up to twice my size. It's very worrying. What do you think it could be, Monsieur Dervelle?"

"A touch of dyspepsia, doubtless," declared my father. "Are all your functions in good order. Are you regular?"

And Madame lowered her eyes and simpered:

"Good Lord ... ah! Yes ... More or less, I suppose ... Goodness, doctors' questions do lack poetry, is that not so, dear lady? Really, I would not like to be a doctor. They must see all manner of things. And besides, I have a horror of sick people ... they are like animals."

I loathed her, having had occasion to suffer her spite. Madame Robin had two sons: one, Robert, was twenty-three, a soldier in Africa, was never spoken of and never came to Viantais; the other, Georges, was two years younger than me, a poor, sickly, malformed creature, rarely introduced to people by his mother who was ashamed of his crumpled face, his skinny, twisted legs and the weakness of that body of a late-born, untimely child. My face, which passed for handsome and my robust good-health gave me a superiority over the pitiful runt that could have led me to love him tenderly. He was, besides, sweet and good-natured and so resigned. I would have liked him as my regular playmate, happy to protect him and use my strength to counteract his debility. He desired this too, I could tell from his imploring expression, which conveyed to me the soaring of his repressed and doleful soul, his eyes as of a prisoner, greedy for sun and freedom, his longing gaze, which through closed windows desperately seized on the flight of birds, so as to rise, carried on their wings, to light and the infinite. But Madame Robin constantly placed her jealous shadow between us, her tall, unyielding shadow like a stone wall. She kept us apart, not allowing us to be seen side by side since I made her son's ugliness stand out all the more. Stung both in her pride as a mother and her self-respect as a woman, she resented anyone who was young, handsome and vital. She particularly resented me for my pink cheeks, my solid limbs, the pure, warm blood that flowed beneath my skin. It was as if I had stolen all this from her son and she demanded recompense from me for her disappointment and heartache. Sometimes she stamped on my feet, so hard that the pain made me cry and she apologised immediately for her clumsiness, with a thousand hypocritical endearments. When she had me alone, she slapped me, kicked me and punched me. Often, she would take me into a corner and traitorously pinch my arm till she drew blood, saying in honeyed tones: "Oh, the darling! Isn't he sweet!" while her lips, tight and dry with hatred, bore a hideous grimace of a smile. One Sunday while out walking, we were on a very high embankment and she gave me a slight push with her elbow so that I rolled right down to the bottom of the slope and had to be rescued, my wrist sprained, my face torn by thorns, my body covered in bruises. I did not complain to my parents, deterred by the fear of even crueller persecutions and anyway, since Madame Robin never spoke of me except in admiring and affectionate terms, my mother thought she liked me and was therefore all the more fond of her.

"Come along, Albert dear, be nice to Madame Robin. She is so good to you."

This exhortation, repeated every other second, enraged me and outraged my sense of justice. But what could I do? No one would have believed me. If I had spoken out I would probably have been punished.

Every day except Thursdays, the Robins came and spent the evening with us. My mother and Madame Robin busied themselves with needlework and chatted about household affairs, lamenting the rising cost of meat.

"And bread should not be taxed! Is it not a scandal? And is it not astonishing to see Madame Chaumier, the baker's wife, wearing shawls of a quality that we cannot afford? With all the money we have!" That word, 'money', rang on their lips with an insistence which irritated and embarrassed me as much as some obscenity.

As for Monsieur Robin and my father, they played piquet, very serious and thoughtful, preparing in a hostile silence formidable tricks and astonishing *quatre-vingt-dix*. Sometimes they talked about politics, shuddered over bloody recollections of 1848, went into ecstasy over the merits of Monsieur de la Guéronnière and compared Jules Favre to Marat.

"He came to Dayeux once," said Monsieur Robin, "I saw him. Ah, my friend, what a terrifying face he has! He is tositively frightening. But, honestly, we must de fair, he steaks well. In any case, you know, what he says is tre-arranged!"

On Sundays, a game of cards was organised with Father Sortais; and though the stakes were represented by mere beans, Madame Robin proved to be grimly ferocious in the matter of winnings and wherever there was the slightest doubt demanded reference be made to the written rules. As a man used to the obscurities of legal exegesis, Monsieur Robin was responsible for explaining the game, commenting on it, discussing and judging it.

"Dridge," he affirmed, taking up the august stance of an assizes judge, "dridge is not at all like law . . . However, clearly, there are tarallels, similarities and I would go so far as to say analogies."

33

Eventually, he always sorted out the problem in his wife's favour.

On the pretext that they had found nowhere suitable into which they could move their furniture, which they had left in Bayeux in the care of an aunt, the Robins provisionally occupied the first floor of a house rented to them by the Misses Lejars. These were two old maids, rich and devout, fat and ludicrous, both dressed alike, both adorned with a monstrous goitre – one of Viantais' curiosities. The flat was small and wretched, containing the minimum of furniture. The Robins had no servants and never entertained.

"How can we?" said Madame Robin by way of excuse. "How can we force our friends to come to such a hovel? But when we have a house and when we have our furniture! Ah, well then . . ."

Her hesitation, glances and the nodding of the head which accompanied them seemed to conceal promises of unimaginable parties, extraordinary meals, undreamed of throughout the county. In that "when we have our furniture", uttered in a mysterious and protesting tone, there was a spurt of multicoloured light, a dazzling flash of silverware, crystal and china. In it you saw the red flame of fine wines glowing, ornate rooms floated by, scented structures of biscuits and nougat arise, bunches of gilded fruit sway and it made the people of Viantais say:

"Oh, the Robins! It would seem that no one knows how to entertain like they do. You'll see when they have their furniture."

They were consulted on questions of etiquette, on what was 'done' and what was 'not done', on the symbolic order of the dessert, a serious and engrossing study. Each time they accepted a dinner invitation at our house, Monsieur Robin would exclaim:

"Oh, we owe you so many dinners! It must de more than a hundred. It's shameful. Dut when we get our furniture . . ."

Then everyone would talk about this famous furniture, for which the houses in Viantais were either too large or too small, too dark or too bright, too sunny or too damp. Madame Robin told of the splendours of her bedroom, decorated in blue reps; her salon in yellow damask. She sang of her linen, embroidered in red; her glassware embossed with gold filigree; her coffee service, made of china and which was never used as it was too fragile and which graced the glass cabinet of her mahogany sideboard. Monsieur Robin for his part waxed lyrical on the magnificence of his liqueur cellar, which contained a "stecial section for cigars", and his desk, "a dureau in scultted oak with secret comtartments."

"Anyway," he repeated, "you'll see it all when we have our furniture."

The truth was that the Robins, confident of the senator's promises, were awaiting a promotion soon and did not want to pay removal expenses twice over. They waited twelve years in the house of the Misses Lajar and throughout those twelve years they never ceased to excuse themselves at every new invitation.

"Oh, we owe you so many dinners! It's really shameful! But when we have our furniture . . ."

My mother had not been mistaken. It was the Robins ringing at the gate. They came in, he puffing and panting, his face buried in a thrice-wrapped black and white checked muffler. She simpered beneath a little red woollen hat adorned with a large black velvet ribbon.

"What awful weather my friends!" exclaimed Monsieur Robin, snorting like an old horse, "What weather! And the daromoter is still falling."

Madame Robin pouted and assumed an affectionate and concerned expression:

"We were just saying, my husband and I, at dinner, let's hope that poor Dr Dervelle isn't obliged to go out in weather like this to visit any of the sick. Poor doctor! What a difficult profession . . . it's so dark tonight!"

"Indeed, indeed," my father declared, "weather like this is not very encouraging. But what can you do? If it is necessary, it is necessary. And not always sure of being paid, there's the rub. And it's the poor that are always the most demanding."

"Naturally!" retorted Monsieur Robin. "They're never dothered adout other teotle's extenditure!" And he laughed.

My mother helped Madame Robin take off her hat and coat.

"And little George?" she asked. "You haven't brought him again?"

"In weather like this, dear lady! And in any case he's a little unwell, he's coughing a great deal. Just imagine, I haven't even brought my needlework with me, this terrible weather makes me feel so weary, so weary. My limbs ache all over and my head . . . !'

Spotting me, she advanced on me, her hands stretched out.

"The little darling! I hadn't noticed him! So handsome still and so well-behaved! Give me a kiss, sweetheart!"

She offered me her lips to kiss, those horrible pallid lips, which were more repugnant to me than the maw of a wild beast.

Everyone settled around the table by the fire and my father said gravely:

"My friends, I have some important news for you."

The Robins looked up, very interested and immediately gripped.

"Well . . . er . . . Abbé Jules is coming back to Viantais."

The magistrate trembled on his chair, his mouth opened, disproportionately far and he sat for a few seconds gaping with astonishment. He cried out:

"Addé Jules did you say?"

"He wrote to us this morning," continued my father. "Oh, just a few lines. And we're expecting him any day now. As for what his intentions may be, he has told us nothing."

"Dut is he coming dack for good? Or is it merely a little tassing visit?"

"For good. At least that's what we understand from his letter. Naturally there's not a word about what he can have been up to in Paris, not a word. Is he still a priest at least?"

And my father appeared to be searching the magistrate's

eyes for an opinion, some advice, for all his doubts had gripped him again, and I am sure that at that moment the vision came to him of the Abbé Jules, wearing the long beard of a layman, hanging down over the long jacket of a defrocked priest.

"Well, well, well," said Monsieur Robin, "so we're going to meet him at last, this famous Addé!"

"So we'll have an extra mass on Sundays," declared Madame Robin with relish. "Well, that's not a bad thing. Since Monsieur Desriches, the vicar, was made chaplain of Blandé, the service has really not been satisfactory."

Turning to my mother, she asked:

"Has the priest here been informed? What does he say? What does he think?"

"Ah," sighed my mother, "the priest is delighted. But he is delighted about everything, as you know. He never sees evil anywhere and yet he must know the Abbé well, he must. Not to mention all the problems they'll have getting on together. That's going to be a fine thing."

"But in what capacity will the Abbé settle here?"

"We don't know. As a non-beneficed priest, no doubt."

She added, in a voice which betrayed the distilled bitterness of all her grievances:

"Non-beneficed priest! A man who could have been bishop, if he wanted, and do so much good for his family. We could have pushed Albert into an ecclesiastical career. Instead of which, what is to become of us?"

Madame Robin twisted about on her chair, flexing her meagre chest. Her mouth tightened in a sour little moue.

"What can you do, dear lady?" she sympathised. "What's done is done. The important thing for you is that he's coming back. You must be overjoyed at his return."

My mother gave a little shrug.

"In one sense, yes, in another, no. You don't know him."

"I know just one thing," replied Madame Robin gravely, "that he's a priest. In any case, it's always preferable to have a relative near one. You can take care of him, keep an eye on him, you know what he's doing . . . and one is always in time to do something about it if things don't go as one would have hoped..."

"I do realise that," said my mother, "it is indeed an advantage."

"If someone's far away, you can expect anything, that is, you can expect nothing. There's no lack of schemers these days. But anyway, listen, let's not prejudge the case. Perhaps he's changed, Monsieur l'Abbé. What if he comes back with a fortune?"

Light dawned briefly in my mother's eyes then quickly died away. Shaking her head sadly, she sighed.

"One might well have hoped that for him, but Abbé Jules is not that sort of man. If he has changed, he has changed for the worse, there, that's my opinion. And we may well have to keep him into the bargain. Paris is so big, so tempting. Some peculiar things happen there, there are such nasty people there."

"Luxury!" exclaimed Monsieur Robin. "In Taris it's luxury that leads to terdition. They can't think what more to invent to make teotle stend money. Imagine, in the senator's house, in the hallway, there are two dronze negroes, three times life size, carrying gilded torches. It's incredidle! In the evening they light up. I've seen it myself."

"Yes," hazarded my father, "one evening at the theatre, someone pointed out George Sand to me. Well, she was dressed as a man! I think Jules must have dressed as a man too, I bet he didn't wear out too many soutanes. But going back to George Sand, you could tell it was a woman easily. You could tell too easily actually."

"How vile!" said Madame Robin in disgust and turned her head away and waved her hand as if chasing away a bothersome fly.

My father was about to embark on a detailed and ribald description, but my mother stopped him, indicating me with a brief glance, for, unless the subject was medical, they were very strict in their choice of words in front of me.

The conversation continued on the subject of Abbé Jules and my father had to recount his life story, from his childhood to his departure for Paris. I was very sleepy that evening despite the excitement of such important events and the unbearable presence of Madame Robin, and so I have not retained much of this account. I can just about recall the scandalised exclamations of our friends which punctuated the riper episodes.

"Lord, is it possible? A priest!"

I also remember there was much talk of lady called Boulmère, who had died in childbirth a few days earlier, and I can still see my father explaining the problem.

"You see ... look ... the uterus, or the womb, if you like, is like a balloon. The bit that's inflated is at the top, isn't it? Well, it's heavy ..."

Then they got back to Abbé Jules. It was two-thirty by the time the Robins left.

"Think carefully, my dear lady," said the horrible Madame Robin as she put her hat back on. "Don't rush anything. One never knows what might happen. And if you need us, don't be embarrassed. You are so dear to me ... and your little Albert ..."

My father and Monsieur Robin were chatting.

"Women, terhaps?" suggested the judge.

"No, no," replied my father, "there must have been something else. What can he have been up to in Paris?"

Chapter Three

Before continuing my personal reminiscences, I would like to go back into Abbé Jules' past and paint a picture of that strange figure, based on my own memories and the thorough and determined research I carried out among people who knew him in the various places he lived.

My grandmother was undoubtedly the best-loved and most respected woman in Viantais. I can say, without exaggeration, that she was venerated as a kind of saint. She showed an infinite kindness towards everyone. Her charity to the poor was inexhaustible. The daughter of country folk, she had kept faithfully to traditional peasant dress even though her marriage had given her some standing amongst the bourgeoisie of the area. But she had a modest nature, a rare delicacy of feeling and rare common sense. She was perhaps a little too devout. I can see her now, seated in her enormous armchair with its beige cushions, tiny, shrunken, wrinkled under her broad white linen bonnet which gave her aged skin delicate waxen tones. She knitted and knitted ceaselessly, stockings, waistcoats, skirts for the less fortunate. How industrious and nimble she was, despite being bent with age, her fingers knotted with arthritis. Every morning I used to go and visit her – or rather the maid took me to her – and before kissing her I would look on the mantelpiece where I would find a little wooden dog and under his tail, every time, I would discover a five centime piece. She would pretend to be astonished, would laugh and exclaim, shaking her knitting pins:

"No, really! Has that little dog done his business again and left his ten sou coin? What a funny little dog he is!"

Though she carried sorrow deep in her heart, the result of a lifetime's suffering, she constantly had a charming smile on her lips which aroused confidence and made people adore her. But that smile hid many tears, the tears of a child, of a woman and of a mother. Naturally gentle and more sensitive than country girls usually are, she had spent an almost painful childhood, constantly wounded by the roughness of other people and the crudity of their habits. It was not that she despised the environment in which she had been born nor that she dreamt of living in more elevated circles, but she would have liked more goodness around her, more restraint, more gentleness. Then she had married. My grandfather, whom I never knew, was apparently a very violent man, a despot, a womaniser and a drunk. He ill-treated her, as he ill-treated everyone, without logic or pity. A horse breeder, obliged by his job to attend distant fairs and live for most of the time in inns along with shady dealers, it was there, doubtless, that he acquired his deplorable habits. He died after a kick in the stomach from a horse at the Chassans fair, and my grandmother, still young, was left a widow with three children, my father, my Aunt Athalie, who died at eighteen from a chest disease, and my Uncle Jules.

No-one had ever known a child like Jules; surly, irksome and cruel, the only pleasure he took was in playing nasty tricks. His brother and sister suffered a great deal at his hands and his mother was in despair, for it was hopeless to beg or punish him, since reprimands and entreaties only stimulated his unmasterable nature.

"He's exactly like his father," the poor woman would say, in tears.

And in fact, she noticed, terrified, in her son, the same mannerisms and the same look in his eyes that her husband had when he returned home after a long absence, bawling, cursing, stinking of cheap wine and stable dung.

He was sent off to boarding school very early and there Jules fought with his fellow pupils, told on them and rebelled against his teachers. But he was very intelligent and actually hard-working and always came top of the class. That was how he avoided being expelled twenty times over. Once he was back home, his baser nature, fed by a freer, lazier lifestyle, took over again. He caused a scandal in the neighbourhood by his dissolute behaviour, constantly in taverns and guilty of numerous thefts from houses. No-one could say the slightest thing to him without him flying into a fury and threatening to smash everything. He had such terrible rages that everyone trembled before him and even he, once the crisis was past, would be ill for hours, his head splitting, terribly pale, like an epileptic laid low by his sickness. When his mother asked him what career he was planning to pursue, he would not answer, whistled a tune and turned his back. She tried to place him in a solicitor's office in Mortagne, but after three days he ran away after soiling a considerable quantity of legal-stamped paper with obscene drawings. At the same time, he was gripped by a real passion for reading. He read everything: novels, poetry, science books, philosophy, revolutionary pamphlets lent him by the pharmacist, an elderly, excitable and demented republican, who thought of nothing but the guillotine and the universal good. Both worked towards an undefined cataclysm and prodigious overturnings of the social order. Jules amused himself by expressing terrifying opinions in front of mother tearing from the unfortunate widow cries of pain:

"My God! Can this really be my son?"

One day she was seriously considering having him put away or sent to a reformatory, and Jules declared he wanted to be a priest. She let out a cry, raised her eyes to the heavens, covered her face with her hands, as if she had heard some vile blasphemy.

"Holy Mary! A priest! You! A rogue like you! It's an offence to God to say such things."

"I want to be a priest," repeated Jules firmly, "And that's that."

He dug his heels in, flew into a rage, ranted, threatened.

"I want to be a priest, for Christ's sake! A priest, damn it!"

And his mother fainted, saying:

"I have given birth to the Antichrist. God forgive me."

The local priest was consulted and he saw in this strange vocation so strangely expressed nothing but heaven's sudden grace, a miracle. He was overwhelmed with joy.

"It is a miracle, a great miracle. In my sermon on Sunday I am going to let the whole parish know. What a miracle!"

Madame Dervelle was sobbing.

"But he was cursing, Father, he was cursing like a heathen."

"So he was cursing, he was cursing. Of course he was cursing. That was the evil spirit leaving, my dear lady. Jules wants to be a priest. Ah! We must thank the good Lord. You know, for me this is one of the most dazzling triumphs of our faith. It reminds me of Saint Augustine. Yes, your son is to be a second Saint Augustine. What an honour for you, for the parish and for the Church. Ah! This is a great miracle."

"Father, Father," groaned my grandmother, wretched and tearful, "Father, are you sure you're not mistaken?"

"There now, pull yourself together my dear lady, there now, I am not mistaken, come along. It is a great miracle. Tomorrow I will say a mass giving thanks. Now, let's see, don't cry any more, pull yourself together."

Two months later, Jules entered the seminary in S.

What had prompted him to take this determined and unforeseen route? Had he discerned in the rôle of priest a plan to make his future existence independent and easy compared to other careers? Perhaps he had been driven by his taste for excess and sacrilegious bravado. Maybe he was not as perverted as he liked to seem. Could it have been that the deplorable ideas he liked to parade so blatantly had only a superficial reality, like a mask, and deep in his heart he still carried the imperishable seed of a Christian upbringing?

No-one ever knew, for Jules remained an indecipherable enigma all his life.

However, the years he spent in the seminary did mark a new phase in his life, when he made energetic efforts towards good and struggled ardently against his own character. Whether it was ambition to achieve some high ecclesiastical office, or repentance or reflection, he worked furiously at taming his rebellious nature, attempting to break it down with harsh discipline, erase it with humility, not by prayer at all, or the passive observance of pious practices, as the weak do, but by some kind of muscular strengthening of his will, a kind of physical tensing of all his intellectual faculties. Unfortunately, despite his courage, he had violent reversions to wickedness, surges of bad instincts which were so sudden and ferocious that in a moment they were able to overthrow all his defences which he had built up so slowly and with such difficulty by himself against his own self. Then he had to start all over again. This persistent battle between spirit and body, this moral and emotional spasm that he inflicted upon himself, prevented Jules from shaping himself according to his environment, from acquiring what could be called the house manner. Quite on the contrary, his huge gangling carcass emphasised all the more his rough edges, his hypocritical sallies, and he never mastered the unctuous, oily gestures, that sour gentleness, those poisonous caresses, that tortuous flexibility, that whispering silence of the sacristy and confessional.

He did possess a prodigious memory and rapid understanding and so he was soon noticed by his teachers and was even a source of worry for them. The daring of his ideas, his penchant for aggressive discussion of dogma, his tendency to mix elements of science and forbidden philosophy with the barbaric inflexibility of theological doctrine, the flame of passionate eloquence with which he set alight his most abstract compositions and above all his indomitable repugnance for the performance of the sacred rites, which the seminarists were made to rehearse like actors rehearse a play, all this, much more than the involuntary discrepancies in his behaviour, moved his superior to feel he ought to point out the danger to the bishop. The bishop, a gentle, indulgent old man, decided after some thought that it was merely the exuberance of youth, and that the austerities of the rule and the numbing effects of routine would soon have the better of him and, remarkably for such a scrupulous man, he became fond of Jules and took an interest in his future precisely because he was not like other seminarists. On several occasions, he had him taken out and brought to his table. Far from being intimidated by the bold manner of his protégé, he felt all the more drawn towards his enquiring intelligence and his gruff determination which he felt "changed him a little" in the way he interpreted the world about him. One day, the vicar-general expressed doubts as to the seriousness of Jules' vocation and said, his head bowed over his joined hands:

"His soul seethes, Monseigneur, it seethes most vilely. I fear it may not resist infidelity and sin." The bishop replied:

"We will soothe it, Monsieur l'Abbé, we will soothe it. And you will see, that lad will go far, very far. He will bring honour to the Church."

Then, after a silence, in a voice full of regret, he added:

"What a pity that he is so ugly, so poorly formed."

Jules did not like his fellow students at all and avoided their conversation and games as far as he could. In lessons or out walking, he distanced himself from all groups, an outsider, striding fiercely, kicking large stones, shaking tree branches, apparently constantly drawn towards acts of destruction. Among the most fervent and intolerant of his fellows, he had detected the odour of suspect friendships, happened upon bizarre communications, and he often entertained himself by pursuing them with cynical pleasantries and indecent suggestions, keeping them in constant terror of denunciation and public shame, exposed before their masters. He disdained the pink, chubby-cheeked youngsters, with their slave mentality and ignorant souls, who learnt the faith like one might learn cobbling and concealed beneath their submissive, devout exteriors the crude bigotry and base appetites of the stubborn peasant. Their inherently suspicious nature bolstered by a completely new strain of hatred for the semi-bourgeoisie and for one who was neither of their physical stock nor their social class, they hated him. They feared him too, thanks to the 'scandalous' protection offered him by the bishop and because of his terrible rages and cruel mockery and they saw in him, aghast, the apostle of future heresies, an iconoclast, a sworn enemy, a 'Lamennais'. For Lamennais, on the rare occasions when they allowed themselves a moment's free thinking, represented for them the latest incarnation of the devil. Jules completed his religious studies without too many mishaps and when he came out of the seminary entered the bishop's household as the Monseigneur's secretary. On that day, Madame Dervelle forgot the anguish of the past and tasted all the delights of maternal pride. She went to see the priest, her soul stirred by a happiness so sweet, that she felt as though hymn-singing angels were bearing her towards the light of Paradise.

"Well, my dear lady," exclaimed the good priest, squeezing his beloved parishioner's hands warmly. "Well now, what did I tell you? Is this a miracle or is it not? Is this not a miracle, praise God?"

She could not find words grand enough, noble enough to express her gratitude. Her throat constricted by emotion, faint with joy, she could only stammer,

"Oh, Father, Father!"

"Now, now! Will you just believe me one more time, Madame Saint Doubting Thomas? It is not over yet you know. Your son will be bishop, the dear child. Bishop, you hear me? As sure as two and two make four."

Bishop! So they were talking about that now? She saw him beneath vertiginous cupolas, resplendent in gold, wearing the three-tiered crown, ruling over the souls of kings of the land, prostrate at his feet.

In accordance with a touching custom, it was in the church in Viantais that the Abbé Jules celebrated his first mass, surrounded by an unusual amount of ceremony and by all the population of the village who had known him as a child. Something happened on this occasion that was so memorable that people still talk of it there and will talk of it for a long time to come. The young priest climbed into the pulpit and there, in front of everyone, he confessed his sins and omissions. As the very first words fell from his lips, the crowd of the faithful were stupefied and amazed.

"My very dear brothers," came the dull, faltering voice, "I am a great sinner. Though my life has barely commenced, already I feel my soul is weighed down with crimes, more heavy with iniquity than the souls of sinful, aged men or a conquering army. It is before your eyes that I have lived this sinful life, grown up in doubt, rebellion and vice. So it is before your eyes, you people who were the sad witnesses to my years of shame, that I wish to strike my breast. Public scandal demands public humiliation. That is good and just and Christian. It does not suffice for the penitent to dwell in the mute shadows of conscience. Listen to me: I have denied God and blasphemed his holy name. I have sinned against the sufferings of Christ and outraged the radiant, nine-fold immaculate womb of the Virgin Mary. I have despised my mother, the blessed creature that gave me life, and I have hated men, my brothers in pain. I have lied, stolen, kicked aside the sick and the poor, Heaven's sad chosen people. My mind dreaming of criminal acts, my flesh burning with monstrous desires, without remorse, without hesitation, I have come to the Holy Table and given the sweet body of the Saviour the soiled bed of a sacrilegious soul. Finally, I have coveted my neighbour's wife, debauched the souls of young girls, and in the open fields, under God's infinite eye, like a filthy goat, I have fornicated . . ."

He uttered this last word in a loud, vibrant voice and a long murmuring was heard in the church which soon drowned the sounds of chairs shifting in embarrassment and the 'ahem, ahem' of shocked coughing, echoing from one end of the nave to the other. The priest was shaken to the depths of his stall as if by the force of an electric charge, and inexplicably, miraculously, the organ let out a cry of distress, which crossed the vault of the church and died in the choir-stalls, above the heads of the deacons and the consternated choristers.

"I have fornicated!" boomed the Abbé Jules again with all his might.

His voice thundered. He beat his breast furiously and the sleeves of his surplice flapped about him like great panicky wings.

Then, one by one, he went over his past faults, setting them out with pitiless severity, emptied his heart of all his perverse thoughts, all the secret shame that tainted him.

Faced with the spectacle of this man, who, like self-mortifying pilgrims of old, flogged himself, tore at himself, spread apart with his fingers his streaming wounds, scattered with hideous, self-inflicted blows shreds of his flesh and drops of his blood, the faithful, at first astonished and embarrassed by the violence of his words and the Biblical crudity of his admissions, then felt a peculiar malaise overwhelming them. Anguish tightened their throats, an unfamiliar pain twisted their stomachs. They experienced a novel, heart-stopping sensation, the sensation which grips a person watching a trapeze artist somersaulting over the void. Something like the shock of returning from the dizzy brink of death. Two women, looking very pale, supporting themselves with difficulty on the backs of the pews, left the church, almost fainting. Another blocked her ears and cried out:

"That's enough, enough!"

And from every other gasping chest the same cry rose towards the pulpit, awesome, full of pain:

"Yes, yes! Enough, enough!"

He stopped. He was out of breath. He wiped his forehead from which sweat was pouring freely, he pushed up the too slack sleeves of his surplice, and then, a miracle ... A ray of sunshine, coming through the rose window facing the pulpit, crossed the nave and lit up the face of the preacher in a strange rainbow glimmer. Everyone looked up simultaneously towards the light of annunciation and believed they were witnessing the transfiguration of a saint. But a cloud came over the sun and the aura disappeared.

Now the Abbé had calmed down. He continued his sermon, slowly pondering his words. Formerly bitter and vengeful, his voice had become sweet and suppliant. Suppressed tears made it tremble slightly and gave it an ineffable tenderness. His hands joined, his eyes fixed on the vault where dying wisps of incense still floated, he begged forgiveness of men, the saints, the Virgin, of God, in a kind of intoxicated delirium. He even invoked the pity of the environment.

"And you too, virginal and fertile Nature, whose rutting

seasons are beloved of God and who reclothes in glorious life the released bodies of the just, you who so many times I have soiled, you who I have profaned, forgive me. Forgive me and reward me with pain, for pain is good for a man who has sinned. When I am hungry, be miserly with your bread and your fruits, when I am thirsty, refuse my lips your pure spring water, when I am cold, keep from my chilled limbs your sun, your shelters and your refuges. Tear the soles of my feet on the thorns of your pathways and make my knees bleed on the sharp edges of your rocks. Oh Nature, be the implacable and motherly scourge of this idle, shameless and rebellious body, and hew in the heaviest, hardest wood you have in your forests, the cross of redemption, beneath whose burden, bent low, I will walk towards eternal brightness."

An inexpressible emotion filled the eyes of the faithful, twisted their faces, oppressed their hearts. The priest made a strenuous effort, pulling hideous faces in an attempt to keep from shouting out. His cheeks puffy, his tonsure purple, he twisted and turned in his stall in agitation. In their pews, the churchwardens, unnaturally serious, held their hands over their mouth and chin. The sound of still stifled sobs mingled all over the church, echoing from one nave to the other. The Abbé Jules finished his sermon thus, on a note of ardent prayer:

"My very dear brothers and you too my beloved sisters, if you have any pity for one who admits his sin and repents, when the angelus, ringing from the bell tower prostrates you in the evening on consecrated earth or at the foot of your family crucifix, oh I beg of you, add my name to the names of your dear departed whom you mourn, and to the names of the poor wretches who have erred that you wish to lead back to God. And may the sad and comforting song of your united prayers bear to the One who judges and pardons the love regained of an unworthy son who swears to adore His holy name and to glorify unto his death His indestructible Church."

When he came down from the pulpit, the sobs, hitherto held in check, broke out, filling the church with an extraordinary confused mixture of human noises, some muted, others sharp, still others like the clucking, braying or whinnying of animals let loose. As the Abbé walked by, heads bowed, eyes moistened with tears, as at the passage of a saint. Enthusiasm welled up and addled brains. A mother flung herself before the young priest, begging him to bless her child which she held out to him, a grimacing parcel in her outstretched arms. He pushed her away gently.

"I am not worthy, my sister," he said.

A few jostled forward to touch the holy folds of his surplice and the beadle and the verger that preceded him, terrified, swaying on their legs like drunks, shouted out without respect for the holy place:

"Make way! Make way now, confounded women!"

Suddenly the organ's sonorous tones swelled and overlaid the noise of the crowd with a triumphantly cheerful piece. The mass resumed.

There was a grand dinner in the presbytery to which had been invited all the priests and notable persons of the region. Before going into the dining room, the good priest Sortais still deeply moved, went up to the Abbé.

"My child, my dear child!" he exclaimed. "How wonderful that was! What a great and magnificent and sublime example you have given! How wonderful that was! See, see, I cried, I'm still crying, look. Ah, how wonderful that was!"

He wanted to take his hands, draw him to his breast.

"I am happy, very happy," he kept saying.

But Jules disengaged himself. He had assumed his nasty look again, that harsh, sarcastic glare, and it instantly froze the old man's warm effusions.

"Good, good," he said. "You're very welcome." And he burst out laughing, turned his back and went off cackling.

Later my grandmother said that during the ceremony, which ought to have given her more pleasure than any other person, it was impossible for her to join in the general emotion. As Jules became more and more eloquent in his repentance, by one of those strange intuitions which the soul experiences without understanding what is happening, she felt a chill come over her and take her heart in a painful grip. And though she was crying, it was from fear and an indefinable sorrow. Oddly, despite her efforts to put to flight the harrowing images of the past, she saw her son once more, not as he was at that moment with his face lit up by faith, but as he looked the day he came to her with his terrifying demonic laugh, when he announced his desire to enter the seminary. And beyond the words of humility and contrition which caused so many joyful tears to flow around her, she could still hear her son vomiting the impious words:

"I want to be a priest, God damn it! A priest, damn it."

It was not all over, as the priest had foretold.

In the bishop's palace, Jules very soon achieved a kind of bizarre omnipotence. As it was necessary to refer to him before approaching the bishop and as the bishop in his turn never approached his subordinates except through his personal secretary, Jules took advantage of this situation in order to terrorise the petty vicars and petty priestlings, who were mainly former fellow students of his from the seminary. He amused himself by upsetting all their plans, dashing their poor ambitions, surrounding them with persecutions that were so ingenious and so refined that several of them, at the end of their tether, left the diocese or gave up the cloth.

"So much the better, so much the better," said the Abbé, "that's one piece of vermin the less."

He succeeded in exercising an implacable tyranny on those around him which was not without a certain sinister gaiety and which often did not even spare his protector, the old prelate. Without deploying the tiniest ruse associated with ecclesiastical diplomacy, by the mere fact of his effrontery, he had, if not made the vicar-general completely fall out with the bishop, at least destroyed his influence totally and limited his authority. Not only did the vicar-general not count any more and was no longer consulted about anything, but the Monsignor had withdrawn from him a few of his most valuable powers, in favour of Jules. Serious and unexpected events resulted from this which, as will be seen later, eventually shook the Catholic world and threw all the chancelleries in Europe into confusion for a few months.

The bishop was a very tolerant man, very accommodating in all things, of a wise and discreet liberalism which enabled him to live in peace with civil authority and with Rome. He liked flowers and Latin poets and when he was not in his garden grafting his rose bushes or repotting his geraniums, he worked in his library where he translated Virgil into outmoded verse. He hated noise and anything which resembled a battle or conflict and possessed a rare skill for managing cliques and coteries, and he avoided taking the initiative whatever the issue involved as assiduously as he avoided any evil action. In his sermons, pastoral letters and pronouncements, he carefully eschewed prickly subjects and limited himself to ambiguous banalities and the basic recommendations of the catechism. One might search in vain for anything that could be considered an opinion; his entire intelligence was devoted to not expressing one. Thus the drafting of his letters, which the vicar-general who possessed an inextinguishable supply of meaningless and florid words, usually collaborated in, was an enormous business. It was tackled three months in advance. Every day the bishop copied and recopied them over and again, cutting out paragraphs, correcting a phrase, pausing at each word, which he would discuss, then soften, always thinking he had discovered a hidden meaning, susceptible to malicious interpretations. Every other minute he would say:

"Let's go through that again, Monsieur l'Abbé, let's go through that again. And I do beg you, let's try not to compromise ourselves. We are the soul's missionaries of peace. Our duty is to conciliate, appease . . . let's not forget that, Monsieur l'Abbé."

"Of course, Monsignor, however, perhaps this year we could . . ."

"No, no, Monsieur l'Abbé! Not this year and not ever. Did not our Lord Jesus Christ say "Do not stand in judgement". Let's go through that again."

At night, in his dreams, he saw the sentences of his pastoral letters, steel-helmeted, bristling with terrible weapons, ranged in battle and hurling themselves on him with savage yells. He would awaken suddenly, sweat on his brow and stay awake for long hours, very unhappy, tormented by the fear that a badly placed comma might lead to a gloss on the meaning, disputes, incalculable disasters. Gradually his head began to spin; in the darkness, the terrors born of shadows and fears born of silence slipped into his tormented soul. Trembling, he relit his lamp, went down in his nightshirt to his library and came back up with the proofs of his letter which he would reread till dawn, pausing only to address fervent prayers to God.

He brought the same doubts and the same exaggerated weaknesses to the administration of the diocese which in the end he abandoned to everyone's whims.

"Matters are not going well," he would groan. "I do know that, but what can I do? I am nothing, I can do nothing, I am helpless."

If he had dared, the intimate and almost painful excuse which he would have given for his conduct would have been as follows.

He had inherited a small legacy from a devout lady, a friend of his mother. This legacy dated from the beginning of his ecclesiastical career. The natural heirs, furious at having been dispossessed, spoke of improper solicitation and shameful manoeuvrings and spread the libel in the local newspapers. Eventually, they contested the will. At the hearing, the lawyer representing the frustrated family hurled the most false of accusations and the most dramatic calumnies at the young priest's character. He made the chamber shudder when he described his opponent as "one of those shady men who insinuate themselves into the beds of old women in order to steal their money, the words of love on their lips." Despite the vividness of this language, the family lost the case and in a verdict which vindicated his good character, the legatee was given sole possession of the contested fortune.

However, this misadventure had left him with a sort of terror which the years, his successes, his rapid elevation to the episcopate, made still worse. Originally a timid person, his personality had degenerated into the most contemptible weakness. In order to atone for wrongs which he had not actually committed, he thought his kindness had to extend as far as deceit, indulgence to complicity, modesty to the point of total disregard of the self. He imagined that he detected reproach in every glance, disdain in every gesture, a painful allusion to his former troubles in every word. In order to mollify these illusory accusers, he forced his life to become one long act of humility, a constant supplication. The older he became, the more he regretted not having disdainfully kicked away the cursed money which in any case he did not profit by and which he only used for good works of an often dubious usefulness. He was haunted by remorse, as if he really had committed some dishonourable, base action. Thus, when he sighed, discouraged:

"I am nothing, I can do nothing, I am helpless," he was responding to the secret revolt of his conscience, rather than complaining of a genuine lack of authority. This strange mania became so powerful that he could no longer utter or write certain words, such as "fortune, inheritance, lawyer, old woman" fearing that he would reawaken cruel memories and give rise to unfortunate comments.

Abbé Jules' room looked out onto a narrow terrace over the street two floors up. From this terrace one could see a part of the town which went down towards the valley and beyond the town, a broad expanse of countryside, where crops and meadows alternated with woodland. Sometimes, in the evening, the Abbé would lean his elbows on the iron railings of the terrace and stay there for a long while, watching the horizon disappear behind the mists, following with his gaze the fading metamorphoses of the heavens. His huge, lean, bony form, black in the dusk recalled images of ghosts and infernal apparitions. The inhabitants of the town fully expected to see the figure bent above them suddenly unfold immense membranous wings and glide above the roofs like a giant bat. The room, whose sole window glowed till very late at night and its terrace, higher than a citadel rampart, had become places of mystery and terror and walkers hurried fearfully by. The fact was that since that figure had started prowling around up there, the bishop's palace, normally so calm, so walled in silence was in complete disarray. An abnormal state of agitation rumbled behind the thick walls of grey stone which gave the episcopal residence the sombre, deathly aspect of an ancient, abandoned castle. A wind blew from there, laden with bitterness and anger, which passed over the whole diocese and savagely rocked the poor village presbyteries where peace no longer dwelled. Everywhere, denunciation reigned supreme. Everyone felt threatened, spied upon, betrayed; terrified priests flitted past one another all day long, through the creaking doors of the palace, one also encountered, along the paths and the hedgerows, the trembling, furtive shapes of clerics, suspicious black silhouettes like hunted beasts. Most amazing of all, the caretaker himself, the caretaker, known for his ingratiating manner and honeyed obsequiousness, the caretaker who advised visitors as piously as he might have served mass, this caretaker had assumed the aggressive mien of a guard dog and bared his teeth.

"Tsk, tsk," he would mutter, grumpy and surly. "You want to see the Abbé? Well he's busy. Ask his assistant. I'm supposed to be the caretaker aren't I. Or not? Eh? What? Tsk, tsk."

People had even noticed that his black velvet skullcap, which he now perched over one ear, was remarkably crumpled and threatening and that when he walked, his long, filthy coat billowed out in a hostile way.

Among clerics, from the humblest sacristan to the most glorious verger, from the most insignificant parish priest to the most firmly ensconced dean, none made any approach except with the most extreme circumspection and people's unease was such that it could have been the Terror all over again. Choirboys no longer drank the altar wine and, on the way back from interments, the bearers no longer fell down drunk into the ditches alongside the road, the cross between their legs. Very old priests were transferred, which caused a real public outcry and there were unexplained summary dismissals, attempts on ancient customs, which were perceived as sacrileges. The priest of Viantais, whose age, virtues and bonds of friendship linking him to the Dervelle family should have protected him more than anyone else was not spared. In a sour and impertinent letter, he was ordered to send away his niece, an eighteen-year-old orphan, a hunchback and a halfwit, whom he had in charity taken into his home, and whose "presence under his roof, at his table, was a constant outrage to proper behaviour and a bad example to young priests". He was also obliged, after a formal injunction, to cease visiting the Sisters of Christian Education and limit his relations with the convent to the briefest execution of the duties of his ministry. This was a terrible blow for this excellent man. To be suspected of such things at his age! Who on earth could have imagined such a thing! For several weeks he was stunned by it and, so to speak, rendered stupid. He could not resign himself to believing that it was true, he persuaded himself that he had misunderstood the letter or that he had dreamed it up. He kept taking the letter again and studying every word and at every word his venerable, open face went puce with shame and he cried out, raising his short little arms to the heavens:

"At my age! At my age! Ah!"

Then he would make the sign of the cross and in a fervent tone add:

"My Lord and God, I offer thee this chalice of bitterness to thee who knowest how chaste my soul is!"

He did not think for moment of accusing the Abbé Jules. On the contrary. In the infinite naiveté of his heart, he felt there was no better course than to write him a long letter, an absurd, touching letter, beseeching him to intercede on his behalf with His Eminence. Naturally the letter went unanswered.

The Abbé's power went from strength to fearsome strength. He had to contend with a few attempts at resistance. Some secret gatherings met, instigated by the archbishop of Mortagne, a fat, sensual, vengeful man, who was furious to see his influence over the bishop slipping away. Rumours were spread regarding the morality of the personal secretary, his orthodoxy was called into question, his sermon in Viantais recalled, the unsuitable words he had used, his invocation to Nature, which was the abominable act of a pantheist, a pagan, a savage, a worshipper of vegetables and white rabbits. In his turn, he was spied upon and set about with treachery. But the Abbé's nerve, which never failed in the face of the most outrageous attacks, soon got the better of the intrigues and the intriguers. The ecclesiastic's ruses, his subtle and twisted acts of hatred, failed piteously when faced with the huge and brutal imagination of the supreme hoaxer. One evening when there was an important gathering at the bishop's palace, he went up to the archbishop, who had carefully not addressed one word to him and drew him into the archway of a window.

"Why are you looking at me like that?" he asked him. "How can it be that you look at me like that?"

"But I am not looking at you like anything, my dear Abbé," replied the fat priest, assuming a derisive tone. "I am not looking at you at all."

"Well, you have made a mistake," declared Jules, "you have made a mistake, I can assure you . . . because . . . because . . . I could . . . I ought to . . . you yourself will agree . . . I ought to for the honour of the Church, for my own conscience, for my own satisfaction . . . Ha, ha, ha! That surprised you, didn't it? You are not looking at me like that anymore . . . you're looking at me, if I can so describe it . . . you're simply looking at me . . . ?"

The archbishop shrugged his shoulder and said faltering:

"I'm looking at you, not looking at you . . . And so ? What is all this nonsense?"

"This nonsense? You will soon see," continued Jules. "I have proof, my dear Father, proof. It is in a drawer, hidden away safely, and every day I study it. Your behaviour is odious, ridiculous and even unbelievable, though not rare. Ha, ha!"

"Come along now, this joke has gone far enough," said the priest with dignity.

However, his face expressed his embarrassment. He had gone very pale. Jules looked straight into his eyes.

"Joke," he repeated. "You astonish me, my dear Father. No, to tell the truth, you shock me. Stealing from the Church fabric fund, debauching little boys, are you really saying that that, logically, is what one might call, in proper terms, a joke? Huh? What do you think of that, priest?"

The other man was disturbed to the extent that for a moment he appeared faint. Trembling, livid, a cold sweat on his brow, he clutched the window-catch to prevent himself falling. He was gasping for breath, suffocating. With a violent and all too visible effort of will, he tried to regain his self-possession and his mouth gaped as with little jerky movements he retied his bands, which he had undone unconsciously.

"I . . . you . . . Monseigneur will appreciate . . . I might say . . . And even were I to . . . yes, were I to . . . I will have you driven out, like, like, like . . . It is an outrage, an outrage, an outr . . ."

He could not finish, his words stuck in his throat. In his huge terrified eyes was a mixture of anger, confusion, hatred and terror, a look so irresistibly comic that Jules burst out laughing. He then patted him on the shoulder familiarly.

"Relax, calm down, Father," he said, still laughing. "Your filthy habits are not my concern, though, in all fairness, I must hold onto the proof. Am I making myself clear? Your habits are not my concern, but they do interest me, that's all. Merely that, Father, so you can calm down."

With a sharp swift movement like the snap of his fingers, he tucked in the corner of a band which was sticking up beyond the neckline of the priest's soutane.

"Only," he continued, "I do hope that you are going to leave me in peace, you and your hangers-on, just leave me alone, understood?

And he turned on his heel, still laughing, whilst the archbishop, appalled and silent, wiped his brow and struggled to conceal his dismay.

The Abbé celebrated his triumph by redoubling his persecutions with an impudent joy. When he had taken some provocative measure, he was careful to make an appearance in public and, an insolent smile on his lips, defiance in his eyes, strode through the streets with unseemly speed. When he accompanied the bishop round the various parishes for the confirmations, his provocative manner and the humble submissiveness of the prelate, caused a stir everywhere.

"Did you see how he had the bishop in his pocket?" said the perplexed priests among themselves. "He certainly has the upper-hand, the jumped-up scoundrel."

"And the bishop! You'd have thought he was worth more than that, to let himself be led by the nose by a pagan, a heretic!"

"All the same, it would be best to keep on his side. The vicar-general, the Mortagne parish priest, what good are they to us? And what's more, it would seem that he has them well under his thumb, that wretch . . ."

"That's so! I must say, with all the tales, one hardly warms to him."

Like all timid people who are dazzled by the appearance of strength and who, by the eternal attraction of opposites, are fatally drawn to violent personalities and daring temperaments, the poor bishop had let himself be seduced by Jules' determined and masterful manner without discerning the element of cynical effrontery concealed behind it. And then immediately, Jules had dominated him by fear. Once he realised what inevitable battles and what dangerous responsibilities he would be drawn into by this reckless man, it was already too late to react against the first unconsidered instinct of sympathy towards him. Jules had him in his grasp in every respect, his authority, his conscience, his mind, his repose, and he could never even think of escaping from those rough hands which constantly made him aware of their heavy weight. As he submitted to this new tyranny, he had nothing left but to marvel at the ease with which he had let it be imposed, despite the superior at the seminary, despite the vicar-general and perhaps also, if he really thought about it, despite himself – and it seemed inexplicable to him but above all regrettable.

"For once I acted of my own free will," he often said to himself, "I still don't know why or how, and it must be admitted that my inspiration was ill-advised, very ill-advised. I was definitely not born to be a leader, I can't manage other people or myself. Oh dear, was there ever a sorrier figure?"

Right from the first day that he took office, Abbé Jules had set himself apart from his master. Objects, animals, people: he overturned the lot, thrust everything aside. If the bishop dared to make some timid observation to him, he soon repented: Jules froze him with a look; the Abbé's mouth ever open to utter imprecations terrified him; and he resolved to let himself be led by this one man from now on, just as docilely as he had let himself be led by everyone up till now. In the long run, he found his own situation improved like this, for he feared no-one any longer, apart from the Abbé and he hoped that the latter would be willing to defend him and so protect himself. Then he reckoned to benefit from the fear which the new secretary inspired in his entourage. In any case, he would have preferred to brave the diocese, the Church and God rather than displease Jules. He spoke to him like a small child, respectful, guiltily. He seemed to say to him, his eyes disarming and imploring, "I cannot prevent you doing things which distress me. Do them, but at least spare me, protect me, be strong for both of us." Every morning, he gave his secretary the mail unopened – as Jules wished it – and in the evening he signed the correspondence and documents without being so indiscreet as to read any of it.

"I must have confidence in you, my dear child!" he would sigh, handing it all back to him.

"What is that supposed to mean?" Jules would reply harshly. "Do you perhaps think I would make you sign love letters? Or banker's drafts?"

"Now, now," the prelate would say soothingly, turning the conversation round, and then apparently sympathetic would murmur:

"What a lot of paperwork! Good Lord, what a lot of paperwork! You must be completely overwhelmed. Nothing important, I imagine? Nothing new?"

"Nothing," replied Jules. "The usual."

"Good, good. And that business . . . how is that going? That business with the Curé Legay, I think it was, where has that got to?"

"Who mentioned that to you? The vicar-general, for sure. Has he been complaining to you, burdening you with his usual lies? You conspire with my enemies and yours against me? You have a fine diocese here, a delightful diocese. Oh yes, you can boast of a fine diocese."

"My dear Abbé, I beg you, do not get angry. Lord! I asked you that without attaching the slightest importance to it, not the least idea of blame, a simple request for information, I can assure you, curiosity, natural curiosity."

And Jules snorted as he turned away:

"Natural! You call it natural do you? The business is at the point it ought to be, that's all."

Then the bishop pondered with a martyr's eye his ivory crucifix, where the tortured body hung on a cross of scarlet plush and he groaned:

"A dog! I am less than a wretched dog. The way he speaks to me, my God!"

Jules was a strange and disconcerting character. What kind of man exactly was he? What was he seeking? What did he want? His early years had revealed a man of action, an ambitious and skilled politician, despite his acts of bravado, his excessive teasing, his pointless acts of persecution. A glance had sufficed for him to recognise the moral state of the diocese, the relaxation of discipline, the vanity, plotting, unrestrained appetites, all the fault of the weakness of a leader who had voluntarily abdicated his authority; all of a sudden, without giving this small world the time to gather its wits, he had pounced upon it, had forced individuals into submission, put others in their place, taken for himself alone the power which had been anarchically disseminated in the hands of a multitude of schemers. Though his methods were bizarre, it is true, he had in fact succeeded in recalling lazy and indolent priests to a dignity more in keeping with their nature. But what drove him to act was not the ardour of a faith that tolerates no weakness, the grandeur of an aim dimly glimpsed nor calculation based on some personal interest, but the gross and perverse need to amuse himself by terrorising other people. Even when he knew he was achieving good and useful ends, he always found the means of fulfilling this baser instinct with a piquant stew of wickedness. There was a gap between his basic ideas, which were often strong and just, and their realisation, which he leapt over with a grotesque caper, like a clown. His most serious projects turned into bitter farces, his most refined ideas had some cruel joke to crown them. Even his actual emotions, his bursts of enthusiasm, the generous and spontaneous blooms of his soul, were soon distorted into an insulting grimace, withered in the slavering of rage. Furthermore, despite his brilliant intellectual qualities, he was nothing. Despite his incessant activity, he was seeking nothing in particular. With an energy that was almost ferocious, he desired nothing. His eloquence, his passion, his creative abilities, his sensitivity, whatever awakened in him grand dreams and lofty aspirations, were all so much lost energy. All was consumed in the sterile fever of caprice, in the delirium of his fantasies as a déclassé. A person in conflict with his own self, a parody of his own personality, he lived in a perpetual imbalance of spirit and heart.

Sometimes, faced with the poor bishop, so sad and so good, looking at him with his gentle childlike eyes – a child who fears being beaten – he felt enormous pity for him. He felt remorse for not treating him more gently, for not loving him, for meanly profiting from the old man's touching weakness. In a flash he would pass from harsh words to an act of exalted contrition, from hatred to tenderness. He glimpsed a thousand possibilities for sacrifice and devotion. Such was his love in those short instants, that he would have liked his dear bishop to go blind, be paralysed or leprous, to have no other solace, nothing, so that he alone could guide him, support him, tend his wounds, console him. And, all of a sudden, he would throw himself at the prelate's feet, kiss his hands:

"I am vermin," he would mumble again and again.

"Oh no, no! Do not say that, my dear child."

"Yes, yes, I am vermin, filthy vermin, rotting vermin. Even less than that. I am . . . oh, whatever is most disgusting in creation. I do not deserve the dwelling-place of a beggar. Why do you not drive me away? Why do you not crush me? Drive me out I beg you, drive me out, like a rat, shamefully, for tomorrow, this evening, Monseigneur, I will probably start to hate you again and make you suffer. The spirit of evil is in me. It impels me to do hateful things. Drive me away, I am vermin."

For the bishop these moments when Jules suffered such excesses of repentance were delicious. He softened, forgot every wrong, each time imagined the start of a new life, a life of peace, concord and love about to be born.

"Drive you away, my child? For a little over-zealousness? For a few hot-headed acts, which are perfectly excusable at your age? You are hasty, which is tantamount to saying that you are young. Come now, that is no great crime. I am an old man, I have my obsessions, my whims, and it is not always agreeable to live with old people, I am well aware of that! But in the past I have known great sorrows, great pain and I would be so happy if someone loved me just a little . . ."

He gave in to emotion and his voice faltered.

"Often I must seem worried, distant, rather strange, is that not so? Yes, but it is because I fear I am not loved, not loved by anyone and above all not loved by you, my dear child. And that hurts me. Besides, why should anyone love me? I am old, pathetic, I can never think of the right thing to say to comfort those around me. I sense that I am an embarrassment, that I dampen the mood, I, a person who so wishes happiness for everyone!"

"You are a saint," Jules would cry, whose frenzy manifested itself in a succession of incoherent and peculiar gestures and expressions.

"No!" the bishop would defend himself, a little alarmed.

"No, I am not a saint, never say that I am a saint. I am nothing. Let us pray, my child, let us pray for you, for me, for all sinners. Come along, just a Pater Noster."

Making the sign of the cross, then joining their hands, they both murmured in low voices the words of the prayer:

"Pater noster, qui es in coelis . . ."

Once back in his room, the Abbé would soon regret his excess of emotion. He would be furious with himself for having let himself be drawn into such an inexplicable and ridiculous softening of heart. Dashing aside chairs, scattering the papers on his desk in fury, he groused:

"I must be mad! What possessed me to say all those stupid things to the old man? What do I care whether he is loved, not loved, whether he cries or sings for joy? His suffering, I know all about his suffering. Ha, ha, ha! It was all to do with him scrounging from the will!"

He would not be able to calm down until he had persuaded himself that it was "all a joke" and then he would start thinking up new tricks.

One evening, having been more irritable and tense all day than ever, he went out. He sometimes took long walks alone after dinner. He would go to the highest vantage points, where the air is sharper and the horizon more distant, he would go deep into the countryside and come back late, his soutane filthy and his limbs aching with a delicious fatigue. Still scented with the night air, he would stretch out on his bed, half-undressed, revelling in feeling calmer, more at peace, better. His nocturnal forays had at first been judged imprudent, then unsuitable for a priest who ought to be confined to his home after the last notes of the Angelus. People talked about it, knowing and disapproving. Nobody could accept that it might be for the simple pleasure of enjoying the fields in the moonlight that the Abbé wandered so in the quiet hours when everyone else was sleeping. It seemed too much like a criminal adventure, a forbidden rendezvous. There must undoubtedly be a woman waiting for him somewhere under the obscene protection of darkness, and if this woman was perhaps the wife of some impious fellow, a Republican maybe, what pleasure there would be in catching him with her and adding to the sin of impurity, revealed *in flagrante*, the element of betrayal, a pact made with the enemies of the Church! In the hope of uncovering a scandal which would have rid the diocese of its tyrant, he had been followed, watched, spied upon. But nobody had been able to discover anything untoward. There was no sign of a woman and no hint of a plot anywhere. The Abbé would walk, hurrying, it is true, as if he had some goal, but he just walked, feverishly, furiously and that was all. If the grass was crushed where he had passed, it was merely because of the broad, steel-tipped soles of his boots, which rapped on the ground, and struck sparks off the pebbles. At first people were severely disillusioned by this fresh disappointment but soon had to get used to idea that the Abbé's mysterious walks were one of the many inexplicable peculiarities of his life.

That evening, as usual, he headed for the higher land beyond the town, and after a mile or so, left the main road and took a path which climbs through fields and fallow land and leads to the forest of Blanche-Lande which, in the distance, crouched before him, a mass of dark clumps in the setting sun. Night came, perfumed and superb, still glimmering with rosy light over the hills, the paths, the furrows, whilst the darkness, also clothed in a slowly unfurling pink mist, gradually crept along the hollows of the valleys.

Dazzled, charmed, he walked fast, inhaling with delight the freshness diffusing through the night air, and he looked at the sky, shot through with gold, a splash of flame at the horizon, and above his head the sky, still one calm steel blue, a dark blue where the stars were soon to appear. Suddenly, he collided with an obstacle blocking the whole width of the path. His eyes and mind had been quite lost in space and so he had not noticed it. It was a wheelbarrow loaded with freshly-cut clover. A young country-girl was seated on one of the arms of the wheelbarrow and was wiping the sweat off her forehead. Balanced on the heap of grass, a scythe gleamed like a crescent moon fallen from the firmament. At first the girl seemed frightened by the sudden appearance of this phantom, so black, so large, darkening and extending the gloom. But when she realised it was a priest, she calmed down and in any case the Abbé spoke to her gently:

"Don't be afraid my child, I'm not the devil."

He leaned against the heap of grass and looked at the girl.

She was a fine healthy young thing, with solid limbs and generous hips. The half-light encompassing the scene lent mystery to her veiled eyes, her darkened face in which very white teeth shone. She wore a tight bonnet of blue calico from which strands of black hair escaped and clung to her forehead. Her bare feet and calves could be seen beneath short rough-spun skirts, whose thick pleats accentuated the powerful curve of her hips. Her upper body was protected only by a blouse of a loosely-woven, coarse-stitched fabric, which fluttered and revealed through a broad tear, the rosy nudity of a strong, supple torso and two enormous breasts, more splendid than those of a marble goddess. And this girl gave off a pungent, intoxicating scent, the smell of wild creatures, of musk and stables, of wild flowers and flesh honed by work and sun.

The Abbé was stunned by her.

As he breathed in the crude scent, he felt a surge of violent, biting desire. A flame leapt in his veins. He shuddered. His nostrils quivering, like a stallion sniffing the scent of females on the wind, he uttered a sigh very like a whinny. Take her, turn her over onto the path, lie her down on the grass she had just cut, he thought. Greedily knead that naked flesh and, sprawled over her, make her struggle as he trapped her with his arms, cry out as he bit her with eager mouth, that was what he wanted. But urgent and imperious as the temptation was, he simply did not dare. A vague sense of unease mingled with almost unconscious shame, held him back. And then he did not know what to say to this girl, how to approach her; he sought a word, a gesture, a means, and he found none. His restless fingers clutched at the grass. He tore out fistfuls which he mechanically carried to his mouth and chewed on bestially. Then, in order to break a too long silence which troubled him and to give himself courage, he asked in a trembling, tortured voice:

"What is your name?"

"I am called Mathurine," replied the girl after a moment's hesitation.

The Abbé cast a long, wild glare about him, scanning the countryside. The shadows were thickening, the fields were deserted, no silhouette of man or animal appeared against the skyline. He felt reassured.

"And where do you live?" he enquired in a slightly firmer voice.

The girl pointed, about three hundred yards from where they were, on the left, a mass of shadows, in the midst of which houses could be made out vaguely amongst the trees.

"Over there," she said.

The Abbé listened; not a sound reached them, not a single sound except the slow, constant whisper of night-fall.

In his thoughts he undressed Mathurine, pictured her shameless, totally naked, and already he could see in his mind's eye as he imagined raising the crude coverings that veiled her, the beautiful burning blossom of her sex offer itself, lascivious, unbridled, to the curiosity and transports of his lust. His brain was in crisis.

"And your lovers? Do you have lovers? Tell me. What do they do to you? Do you sleep with your father, with your brother? Tell. What do they do to you? Have you ever dreamt of the touch of a ram or a bull? I'll be your ram, your bull. Do you want me to sit close to you and hear your confession? Together we will insult the good Lord. Would you like that? Answer me."

The girl did not reply. She could not grasp a thing amid these mad ramblings, these words which devastated the silence. But terrified by the deranged expression on the priest's face, she tried to get up.

"No!" he commanded. "No! Don't get up. Don't go. Stay. You're beautiful. The scent of your skin intoxicates me. It's dark. Nobody can hear us. Why are you afraid? Answer me."

The girl would not reply.

He thought:

"She is going to resist, call out perhaps. I could give her a few coins and she'll keep quiet. But will she keep quiet?"

He touched the pocket of his soutane and reassured himself that he had not forgotten his purse.

"If necessary, I'll give her more," he promised himself, "I'll give her more, I'll give her everything ... Or else, I could stuff some hay into her mouth ..."

"Come here!" he said.

The girl did not move.

"Come here, I said!" repeated the Abbé.

He was gasping, his voice hoarse. A curious fury of passion made his arms move forwards, twisted his hands, precipitated his whole flesh towards some absurd and fatal crime. The scythe gleamed on the grass next to him. He thought of seizing it and striking. What was left of reason was swallowed up in a kind of vertigo. He could not tell what madness controlled him, which instinct he was obeying, murder or love. A few clouds, with strange and changing shapes, floated in the sky, reddened by the glorious glimmerings of the sunset and to him they looked like monstrous sexual organs seeking one another, coupling and bloodily tearing each other apart. For the third time he ordered, hissing through his lips, menacing:

"I said, come here!"

The girl did not move. Stupefied, her eyes full of terror, she stared at this huge man, this hideous priest, this black devil before her.

Suddenly, like a beast pouncing on its prey, he hurled himself on her. Risking strangling her, he locked his arm round her throat, and with the hand that was still free, he grasped her breasts and furiously kneaded, pinched and pounded them in a savage, fearsome embrace. Once, he felt beneath his fingers a scapular, crosses, holy medals which the unfortunate girl wore against her skin, hanging from a steel chain and he experienced a terrible joy, a sacrilegious joy in twisting and breaking them, pressing them into this female flesh and making them part of the profane caresses with which he tormented her. At the same time he spat out terrifying, filthy words, meaningless words, blasphemies, interspersed with hiccups and gasps.

"Don't say anything. Come here, nearer, more naked . . . I'll pay you. Yes! I . . . Listen! Quiet. On the grass, there . . . Kill you on the grass . . . suffocate you . . . Shut your mouth!"

But the girl had managed to get up. With a sudden twist of her back she detached herself from him. She struck out with her fist and drove the Abbé off. He staggered back several paces and stumbling, nearly fell over backwards.

"Great brute!" she said simply, adjusting her blouse which had become entirely unstitched and knotting her torn skirts on her hip. "What's got into you, huh? Leave me be, filthy dirty priest."

She hitched herself up again to her wheelbarrow and slowly set off, turning round from time to time to see whether the priest was following her. He stood motionless as if turned to stone. His soutane unbuttoned, head bare, arms hanging by his side, he had not thought to pick up his hat which during their brief struggle had rolled onto the ground. He watched, though without seeing, the outline of the girl which sank into the shadows and finally drowned, blending in with the dark colours of the earth, and, without hearing, he listened to the sound of the wheelbarrow dancing over the ruts in the path, tapping out a far-off drumbeat as it grew distant. Then there was silence all around him and it was dark, a disquieting night, profound and moonless, a night which entered his soul, and, under the pale light of the western sky, with the encroaching mystery of its shadows, reflected for him the grimacing, vengeful images of his own remorse and fears. Suddenly filled with an immense self-disgust, the Abbé joined his hands as if to pray, sank onto the ground in a great gesture of exhaustion and for a very long time he wept.

For more than an hour he stayed there, motionless, no thoughts, his head heavy, his limbs aching, his mind confused, so completely drained that he could not remember clearly what had happened. Of that moment of madness, that second of crime, he had retained only the sensation of vague and painful disgust, the devastation of his physical and moral self. He was as if in a feverish sleep where things happen one after the other, incoherent, ironic and painful. Despite himself, the impure obsession with the woman returned, linked with his shame and, with an involuntary shudder of his muscles, bones trembling to the marrow, he could see it all again, in himself, around himself, even in the density of the shadows, in the wandering symbolism of the skies where the clouds evoked impossible nakedness, impossible entanglements, a multitude of onanic, twisted shapes like grotesquely enlarged prints from an obscene book which he had owned when he was a student. And beneath this polluted sky, the forest, displaying its confused, vast, distant masses, extending its terraces, colonnades, stairways, temples, reminded him of some extraordinary architectural monument, some dark Sodom constructed in honour of eternal and triumphant Debauchery. Fatigue overcame him. He felt an irresistible desire to sleep, experienced a kind of narcotic luxury at letting himself slip into vague oblivion, the void. He did not attempt to tear himself from this drowsiness which he preferred to the brutal alertness of reason. Ah! If only he could have sunk forever to the depths of that blackness, never to climb out again! And, stretching himself out on the ground now damp with dew, like a vagabond, he fell into a deep sleep.

When the Abbé returned to the town, it must have been very late. All was sleeping. No light glimmered between the closed shutters of the houses and the street-lamps on top of their gloomy gibbets had long since been extinguished. Near an inn, beneath a market stall trailer, a dog growled. Though his limbs were stiff from the damp, he hastened his step and reached the little hidden door to the garden, whose key he always carried with him and quickly went up to his room. He was eager to find himself once more between protective walls, surrounded by familiar objects, far from that terrifying sky and those accursed horizons. Moreover, his legs were trembling and all strength had left his body. He sat down on the bed and gave a sigh of relief. But soon the darkness seemed terrible to him, peopled with the same images and spectres as out there. He lit the lamp then decided to look at himself in the mirror and was terrified by what it revealed: a shattered expression, blades of grass in his hair, a muddy soutane, stinking, matted with filth. Vainly he searched for his bands which he had doubtless lost on the path in his tussle with the girl.

"Abject lump of flesh!" he cried out. "Uncontrolled filth! Swine! Swine! Swine!"

He wished he could hit himself, torture himself, dreamed of hair shirts, torments, the lashes whose whistling steel tips send spattering the blood of saints and the flesh of martyrs. He spoke aloud:

"What foulness is here in me? Did my mother feed me excrement along with my milk?"

Clawing at his own throat, he yelled:

"Will I never be able to conquer you, vile carcass!"

Then he struck his breast hard.

"Will I never be able to control you, noisome, festering creature!"

He thought again about his missing bands.

"And what about your bands, miserable wretch? Someone will find them and will say; 'Ah, there's where he wallowed in the filth.' Well so much the better, let people run along the streets shouting, 'He wallowed in the filth there!' At least my shame will be complete and maybe people will chase me away with sticks like they do with coupling dogs."

He felt such disgust at his past life, his present life and such fear about his life to come that he opened the window, leaned over the sill of his terrace and measured the void beneath him.

"No," he said, pulling back. "Perhaps there is a God!"

Despite his confusion he could not help smiling at the idea: the suicide of a priest; it seemed strange and comic to him. That relaxed him a little. Feeling calmer, he allowed his thoughts to stray. As ideas flooded into his mind, he promised himself harsh expiations, going on extravagant new pilgrimages, barefoot, a cord round his neck, devoting himself to absurd vocations. Yes, he would go all over the world, preaching to adulterers and prostitutes, preaching continence to the debauched. But first, he wanted to beg pardon of his mother, of the good priest Sortais, of the vicar-general, the archbishop, of all those he had persecuted. Then, at the end of a road planted with calvaries, sown with crowns of thorn and bramble, he glimpsed, as a refuge of light, a Trappist monastery, the peace of its long silent corridors, the work in the fields, the brief, peaceful sleep on bare boards, the interminable nights of prayer and the little treeless cemetery with its white crosses in such brotherly proximity to one another and the huge pond where the reeds sang and where once as a marauding urchin he had fished for roach under the monks' noses. These visions, these plans and these memories filtered sweetness into his soul and the Abbé softened. And as he softened he found he was the most unhappy of men. What most distressed him was that he was totally alone in the infinite distress of his soul. He wished he had someone there, near him, someone like Francis of Assisi and that this person would speak to him gently, tenderly, in a saintly voice using sublime and consolatory words which would open the way to paradise. He thought of his bishop, and his bishop seemed to him a kind of providence, a marvellous being whose hands can bestow blessings. He was moved as he called to mind his sad face and his martyr's stance. Why should he not go and throw himself at his feet? He would confess all to him. He would recount his whole life to him with such heartrending accents of repentance that he would make him weep. And the bishop would speak to him, rock him, send him to sleep. In that moment, the Abbé Jules rediscovered the innocence, faith and strength of resolution of a small child. He believed in good, in universal charity. He took his smallest lamp and went down the stairs, radiant, knocked at the bishop's door, full of eagerness. The bishop was doubtless sleeping and had not heard him. He did not answer. So the Abbé flung the door open, forcing the lock and went into the room.

"Who's there?" shouted the bishop.

Woken with a start and dazzled by the sudden invasion of light, he had half sat up, the sheets about him, his mouth agape, his skull a dishevelled mass of grey strands pointing in all directions, his eyes between their sleep-swollen lids glinting with terror. He braced his arms against the wooden bedhead, to buttress his unsteady trembling body.

"Who's there?" he said again.

The Abbé crossed the room, placed the lamp on a table and threw himself down at the foot of the bed.

"Do not be afraid, Monseigneur," he said humbly. "It is I, your unworthy son. If I dare to cross that threshold and disturb your sleep, it is because I am in so much pain. It is because I must speak to you, tell you everything, everything! It is suffocating me. I cannot wait any longer. I cannot bear it any more."

The old man rubbed his eyes. He glimpsed in horror this black thing, on its knees beside him, making noises and gesturing.

"Tonight," the Abbé said, the words tumbling out of his mouth in a confused tangle, "just a moment ago, down there, I met a girl, sitting on a wheelbarrow. She was resting. And then, what happened in me I just don't know. I was mad. I flung myself on her. Something was making me drunk, drove me. Did I rape her? Did I kill her? I can't remember any more. I don't know what I wanted from her, no, I don't. Sex maybe, blood perhaps. Yes, if I'd had a knife I would have stabbed her. She was young, strong, she fought back. And I dirtied my hands on her impure flesh. I am a great sinner, a criminal. I am . . . look at my face, my clothes. Do I not horrify you? Look at me . . ."

"What?" interrupted the priest who had not grasped a word of this strange recitation. "What? Is that you my dear Abbé? Oh! you frightened me coming in like that. I was dreaming . . . I thought . . . and then . . . So, it's you? But of course! What time is it?"

"I don't know. And what does the time matter? Why the time? When a starving man asks for bread, when a man in despair seeks consolation, when a dying man begs for a prayer, do you answer 'What time is it?' Is there a time then for human suffering? I am that starving, despairing, dying man. I have come to you. Talk to me."

The bishop's face registered ever greater stupefaction. The poor man made prodigious efforts to understand but could not. Surprised in this intimate state of undress, in that ridiculous posture, he truly lacked dignity and was even grotesquely comic. But Jules did not dream of laughing. He clasped his hands together.

"Ah! Speak to me Monseigneur!"

The bishop rubbed his eyes again, his head lolled and slowly he yawned.

"Speak to you my dear Abbé? Yes, yes, speak to you, is that it? But are you talking sense, hmm? Are you sure? Speak to you? I would like to my child, but say what? And why?"

Jules raised his voice impatiently.

"Speak to me can't you! Say one word of consolation, to comfort me, or punish me, how should I know? A single word, like Jesus in his divine pity found for unfortunate and repentant sinners, do you understand? Eh? Do you understand?"

"Like Jesus?" repeated the bishop through a lengthy yawn. "Like Jesus. Yes, of course."

And he added:

"But this is hardly the moment, I feel . . . Tomorrow perhaps . . . tomorrow morning come back . . . Let me think . . ."

The Abbé Jules stood up. He gave the old man a hostile stare, shrugged his shoulders and without uttering a word took his lamp and went towards the door. Standing very stiffly, he made no reply to the prelate who was saying as he settled under the covers again:

"That's it, tomorrow. Understood? Tomorrow morning you come back to me and ask me again and . . . actually . . . well, sleep well."

Jules closed the door angrily.

"What a savage," he thought as he climbed the stairs again. "So that's what guides souls is it? A thing that sleeps and a cry of distress can't awaken? Could our great saints have been like that? Ah, I'd like to have known them, the Francis of Assisis, the Vincents de Paul and the others and all the celestial mob. Maybe that thing'll be canonised too, who knows? He'll have his statue in niches between two vases of paper flowers. He'll make barren women fertile and they'll come carrying candles and kiss his stone big toe. And they'll set up commemorative feast days in his honour! And build cathedrals in his name. And he'll be paraded in the church calendar ... No, it's too comic. So, in this life, no-one loves anyone, no-one helps anyone, no-one understands anyone. Everyone is alone, completely alone, amid the millions of people around him. When you ask someone for a little of his pity, his charity, his courage, he sleeps. You can cry, hit your head against walls, die, they sleep, they all sleep. And God? What is he doing amid all these sleepers? Is he snoring too in his cloud? Does he reply to all the wretches who stretch out their suppliant hands: 'Let me sleep, scum. Tomorrow ... ?"

By the time he went to bed, all his pious plans, his repentance, his remorse had fled. He was astonished to find his conscience clear, his heart calmed, even cheerful. He amused himself thinking of the bishop's terrified expression and felt very proud of having frightened him. Besides, what evil had he done? Was he not a man after all? Had he not responded to a natural impulse of the senses? What about the other priests who did not deprive themselves of that form of entertainment, for instance that ordure of an archbishop who would end up in court one day and the vicar-general who despite his puritanical manner was always receiving hysterical, devout women in his parlour. Not to speak of the others, who installed concubines in their presbyteries, calling them nieces, cousins, servants. So, he had desired a woman and had wanted to take her? He should have resorted to the conniving darkness of the confessionals where the breath of priests mingles with the breath of penitents, where questions which drain the will and avowals which inflame the senses escape from half-closed lips! He was really too stupid, always exaggerating things, twisting them, getting carried away, losing his head over nothing. And Mathurine appeared in his mind as he had first seen her in the setting sun with her heavy limbs and powerful, wild scent. Not only did he not try to reject the image this time, but he forced himself to retain it, to fix it in his head, to complete it, in some way render it tangible and recreate the exquisite and furious disturbance which had shaken him so bizarrely. He jerked obscenely and with violent thrusts of his body made the bedstead crack and said through a cackle:

"I'll get you sometime, bitch!"

The following day, at the usual time, Abbé Jules, somewhat pale, came into the Monseigneur's office. He was sorting the letters and said to Jules in a very gentle, hesitant, trembling voice:

"Well, I'm all yours my dear child. What did you want to tell me?"

"I?" said the Abbé, looking surprised. "Nothing, Monseigneur."

"You did! You wanted to tell me something, when you came to my room last night."

The Abbé stared at the bishop, affronted.

"I? I came to your room last night? I?"

"Of course. You must remember. Last night?"

The Abbé shook his head and said curtly.

"I did not come to your room last night. You must have dreamt it."

The winter which followed passed without incident and the months went by, monotonous and calm, without the slightest upheaval at the bishop's palace. The Abbé's nerves seemed to have disappeared. At any rate, he made very few appearances outside, neglected his responsibilities and even took little interest in the affairs of the diocese, which he dealt with in a perfunctory manner, as a dull duty. Apart from mealtimes and services, he stayed locked in his room almost all the time, obstinately refusing to attend to anything which was not strictly part of his job. The bishop, who had feared the unexpectedly enthusiastic activities of his secretary, dreaded still more his inaction, since the weight of the administration fell on his shoulders and he felt quite crushed by it.

For fear of angering Jules and engendering scenes, he did not want to approach the vicar-general for help in difficult cases; on the other hand, he was incapable of making any decision at all alone. So he grumbled, panicked when faced with the ever-accumulating files and letters to write, never received any visitors and never did anything:

"I have been disarmed! Totally disarmed!" he tended to say to himself, trying to stifle the inner voice, full of reproach, which rose from the depths of his subconscious. He also started to spend more time confined to the library and, hoping thus to escape from the embarrassment of the present and the responsibilities of the future, he set about retranslating Virgil into octameters, with a passion. For a while, the bishop's palace regained its gloomy aspect, its silence as of an abandoned house but a silence interrupted towards evening by strident noises, a strange brassy cacophony which resounded in the village, showers of wrong notes and squawks, a shambles of refrains of popular songs and plain chant, military airs and psalms, leaping polkas and grave *Te Deums*. It was the Abbé playing the cornet as a means of relaxation after the strange work to which he devoted his days.

For the Abbé had been gripped by an unexpected passion: books. It was an exclusive and tyrannical passion which assumed in him the obsessive nature of a mania and the savagery of rage. He had immediately dreamt of setting up a great library such as no-one had ever seen before. All at once, he wanted to own every rare, curious, useless work, from the earliest huge printed editions to elegant modern editions, arranged by categories in high-ceilinged rooms on shelves superimposed ad infinitum and linked by stairways, railed galleries and movable ladders. As soon as his mass was said in the morning, he poured feverishly over catalogues and checked through bibliophile journals to which he subscribed, wrote letters to Paris bookshops, made out interminable lists of volumes, worked out fabulous and ever-insufficient budgets. And the library made scant progress. At that point it consisted of the contents of three small trunks, which he constantly opened up and then shut again with a groan of impatience, having noted the poverty of his acquisitions. But what was he to do? His church income was small; and paltry too was the monthly allowance he received from his mother. He had converted into cash his meagre personal possessions, deprived himself of even the most necessary items, refusing to replace his tattered and greasy soutanes, his threadbare hats or his shoes which gaped like fish heads. Alas, his resources and his total savings did not add up to large sums. He started to go further and further into debt with each day that passed, buying books on impulse and subscribing to numerous publications which ate up his monthly income in advance. What angered him above all was to see all around him priests being showered with rich gifts, gorged with money by the town's devout. He could not bear to think of the vicar-general for whom pious ladies embroidered stoles, copes, cushions, table linen, to whom delicately, on certain anniversaries, they slipped fat offerings ostensibly for notional poor people and vaguely-defined good works. He alone had never received anything, not even a box of matches, not even a few pence. Wasted as a skeleton and dirty as a beggar, he was obliged to witness in others, hatred in his heart, the blooming of cheeks which sweated idleness and gluttony, the spreading of fortunate bellies, voluptuously tight beneath warm soutanes and new overcoats. Having exhausted the patience of his mother whom he besieged with repeated demands for money on the pretext that life was very luxurious at the bishop's palace, he was obliged to keep face there, having extracted a few meagre sums from the bishop on behalf of supposed charities, he had reached the point of considering the possibility of dishonest expedients, and he devised plans in which the novelettish fused with theft and simony. He visualised the legacies of very rich old women, mysterious and productive love affairs with very beautiful châtelaines. As naturally as could be, he thought of selling his influence and protection, but to whom? Of selling the sacraments, making a market of holy objects, but how? Extending the scope of his dreams, he worked at inventing sophisticated pilgrimages, exhuming miraculous saints, discovering unknown and surely exploitable virtues in the Virgin, but all that had already been done and a long time since! "The Virgin has been fleeced, well and truly fleeced!" he said to himself, thumping his hands on the desk in a gesture of resignation. All these ideas, which seemed simple at first when they initially occurred to him, on reflection became fraught with difficulty and impractical to realise. He rejected them, turning to others which were even more complicated, more extravagant and which came to the same negative conclusion. Thus, in the evenings, full of disgust, irritable, he furiously played the cornet as if he were chopping wood, as if he were picking a fight with someone in the street, so as to relax his nerves and forget for a moment the sorrow in his soul.

One day, alone in the bishop's office, he spotted on the mantel a few gold coins amid the pieces of silver. Instinctively, without any precise intention, he glanced to check that the doors were closed properly and that he was quite alone and no-one could see. Then, tiptoeing, he went up to the chimney-breast. Gold and silver, the coins glimmered there, near, right within his reach, scattered higgledy-piggledy, coins which had just been pulled out of a pocket, negligently. His nostrils flaring, eyes glittering with greed, he counted them several times: eleven golden louis. Delicately, avoiding disturbing the others, he took one louis and as he slipped it into the pocket of his soutane, beneath his handkerchief, he experienced a little frisson at his fingertips and a mild tingling at the roots of his hair. At the same time his heart beat faster but with a regular, pleasant rhythm, which felt like a very gentle form of physical pleasure. He did not wonder whether he was committing a low or shameful act, he did not question himself.

"That will make a round number for him," he said to himself simply, thinking of the bishop. As he considered anew the heap of gold which hardly seemed diminished by this theft, he added jocularly:

"Too round perhaps!" He took a second coin. A third had slipped off, ringing on the marble with a clear metallic sound. The Abbé hesitated, perplexed; should he appropriate that one too? He decided that it might be noticed and put it back regretfully. He promised himself to come back to this room more often at times when he was likely not to meet the Monseigneur and to inspect the furniture with more care than hitherto. Certainly, he did not hope ever to acquire millions like this, but one louis here and two louis there would nevertheless mount up to a respectable sum in the end. Very calm, he stretched out on an armchair and lost himself in vague and innocent thoughts. When the bishop came back, Jules showed no embarrassment and chatted with him most freely and with open affection. He was charming. This affection was not assumed in any way, it was sincere and profound. At that instant, he really felt filial respect for the old prelate and a sense of calm recognition detached from all remorse, the like of which, in his sudden leaps from hatred to tenderness, he had never yet felt up to that point. His heart softened, melted by the delicious warmth of generous sentiments and generous thoughts. The theft had made him a better person. He stayed a long while, happy to be near his bishop, to show him endless kindnesses. He discovered the caressing, tender words which women use with the men they have just deceived, those consoling words which fix confidence in hearts. The bishop tasted a few instants of real joy and when the Abbé had gone he said to himself, his face serene:

"A little hot-tempered sometimes, a bit of a devil, ah! Lord, yes! But fundamentally, he's good."

Jules placed the two stolen coins in a drawer of his desk and, glancing gloomily at the three trunks which contained, converted into volumes, all his savings, his privations, his vices and deceits over several months, he sighed:

"Two louis! How pathetic! I'll need more than that if I want to rival the Bollandistes!"

The following day, when he woke, he had an idea he thought admirable. He got up, dressed hastily, went down to the chapel, hurried through his mass and went out. The air was chill, the rain fell fine but penetrating and a bitter wind chased huge dirty clouds, as if ink-washed, across the sky. However, he did not feel the cold, the rain or the wind.

"This time," he said to himself, walking with a long, rapid step, "this time I will have my library. I will have it or the devil take me. How can I not have thought of it before?" An hour later, out of breath, soaked with sweat and rain, he arrived at the entrance to the Réno abbey.

Two enormous pillars with no capitals, no grille nor gate, led the way into emptiness, an ancient, rutted, former avenue, overgrown, bare of its trees, which had long since been cut down. At the end of the avenue, whose original course through the uncultivated land all around it could no longer be traced, except for a double row of parallel trunks cut almost down to ground level, stood strange, gloomy structures, silhouettes of crumbling walls, sunken roofs, and, braced against the glowering sky, the black carcasses of the frameworks of buildings. All around these ruins a naked, desolate space extended, treeless, without a single plant or any vegetation, save the sad grey-green of burgeoning brambles growing freely, each day devouring still more of that abandoned corner of the earth. As he turned into the avenue, the Abbé met an old woman, carrying a filthy wooden bowl.

"Is the Reverend Father Pamphile in the monastery?" he asked.

"Yes indeed Father!" replied the woman. "'E's there all right . . ."

She pointed to the bowl, marbled with streaks of dried grease, and explained:

"I've just taken 'is soup. "E's by 'is church, shiftin' rocks. 'E's shiftin' some rocks 'e is, by 'eck 'e's shiftin' some rocks, 'e is."

Faced with this bleak expanse, the sulky sky, the distressing misery of the whole scene which, as he walked, he had not yet noticed in his excitable mood, the Abbé suddenly regretted having come. His enthusiasm had waned. He no longer believed his idea could succeed. Why did he want a library? Was he even sure of wanting it and wanting it regardless of all else? In truth he really did not know. Was it not a hoax he was playing on himself, one of the gloomy tricks he invented to disguise the bottomless *ennui* of his existence? He suddenly felt disgust at the mean act committed the day before and fear of what he was about to do.

"Bah!" he said, "Let's see anyway."

The rain intensified. He wanted to hurry but was obliged to go more slowly because of the thorns which caught at the hem of his soutane, clutched at his legs and hampered his steps with their snaky, scratchy, persistent embrace. Obliged to hitch up his skirts like a woman, furious at himself and at the creepers which had spread everywhere, nearly tripping him up at every step, he made his way painfully forward. Finally, grumbling, swearing, shaking his feet, he managed to cross the most difficult part and found a path leading straight between the outcrops of thorns. Soon he was merely a dark shape, moving in the distance, no larger than a crow coasting over the tall grass.

Réno Abbey dated from the thirteenth century. It had been built by Saint John of Matha and Saint Felix of Valois, founders of the Trinitarian Order, otherwise known as Redemptionists, an admirable and powerful order which sent its monks to rescue Christians held captive by the infidel. At first, it was enclosed within a small area, made up of kitchen gardens, a little wood and a few meadows, but the abbey gradually increased its holdings, encompassing fields and forests, ponds and villages and all the land about it as far as the eye could see. In the seventeenth century whose severe and grandiose architectural imprint the ruins left standing still bore it possessed, it is said, ten thousand hectares of forest and fifteen thousand hectares of arable land, not counting the vast waterways of the Andennes, Vaujours and Culoiseau, famous for their fabulous carp and huge mills which ground the wheat gathered from more than ten leagues around. Of the original humble, primitive buildings, enlarged, replaced and embellished from century to century, at that time, there only remained a small fountain, carved with naive sculptures, now half-effaced by time, half-eaten away by moss, beside which legend had it that the sacred deer appeared to John of Matha, bearing between its golden horns the red and blue cross, the distinctive emblem of the order. The Revolution came and the monks of Réno were driven out, their goods appropriated and the abbey demolished. The Revolutionaries committed the abominable crime of destroying the chapel, one of the purest and most exquisite masterpieces of the Renaissance, of which only a few pillars survived and a few expanses of wall, sad, intermittent indications of the position of the original building. The monks let the wind of revolution and imperialism blow through France, then came back in 1817 to their Réno monastery, which had become an astonishing heap of rubble contained within the modest enclosure it had been at its creation. They began by clearing away the ruins and repairing as well as they could the least damaged buildings. Once that was done, they did not know what else to do. La Redemption, at least as regards its original conception, had lost its *raison d'être*. There was no more need to rescue Christians from barbarian pirates; some other role had to be found. Deprived of their land, they could not turn to farming like the Trappists. Having no particular staff of teachers, they could not devote themselves to education like the Jesuits. Two attempts that they made, one to run an orphanage for small boys, the other a school, failed. So in 1823, discouraged, they decided to leave, some emigrating to Spanish monasteries, some taking refuge in Rome with their general. The abbey was abandoned and left, at his request, in the care of one of them, the Reverend Father Pamphile, who retained a stubborn faith in the return of the Order to its ancient traditions and who passed for a great organiser as he was a southerner and very talkative.

As soon as he was alone, the first thing that Père Pamphile did was to sack the gardener, the carter, the poultry man, and sell the two horses, four cows and hens that were left. Then, for the price of six sous, he arranged that a neighbour whose husband used to work on a daily basis for the monastery, should bring him a bowl of soup every morning and a piece of black bread every evening and that her husband would be the server at his mass into the bargain. After which, relieved of the problems of housework, food and administration, he walked amid the mute ruins, grave and deep in thought. For six months, from dawn to dusk, he wandered about like this, ever more absorbed, narrowing each day the scope of his walks until finally he limited himself to the boundaries of the ruined chapel. Oddly, talkative as he normally was, he did not suffer at all from the almost total silence to which he had voluntarily condemned himself and already, his jovial monk's face occasionally bore that expression of grandiose stupefaction, touched with madness, that one sees on the haggard masks of solitary, old people. Living by himself and relying entirely on his own resources, with no intellectual contact, haunted by a single thought, in that dead solitude, in that silence troubled only by the sudden collapse of walls and the dull cracking of insecure beams, a strange idea crystallised in Père Pamphile's brain. After some hesitation, doubts immediately rejected, objections all the more easily refuted since he was alone in discussing them, Père Pamphile convinced himself irrevocably that there were still captives held by the infidel. His imagination fed by legends of the past, having no other notions about human life apart from those acquired in ancient Latin texts, celebrating the miraculous history of his order, he thought that the captives were a necessary and permanent product of nature, and that there are captives, just as there are trees, corn and birds.

"And not only are there captives," he said to himself aloud, in order to give this conviction a definitive authority, "but there are ten times more now that we have stopped redeeming them. That's obvious. And our superiors can't see it! What blindness!" So the extravagant idea grew in his head that he had mission to fulfil, an inevitable and glorious mission: to reconstitute the Trinitarian Order, such as it had been established by the founding saints, John of Matha and Felix of Valois.

"And I will build it up again!" he exclaimed, with the ardent faith of the prophet, describing with his extended arm a gesture which embraced the whole world.

But, owing to a complication of his superstitious nature, which took all things back to the will of God, he was convinced that the Most-High would not give him the strength to accomplish this great work unless first he rebuilt to its former magnificence the chapel destroyed by the impious. He summed up the situation thus in these simple words.

"The chapel first, the Order next. Right, that is good."

When he had to examine the practicalities of his decision, Père Pamphile was at first somewhat disconcerted. He had a moment of stupor, despair. In his crazed meditations, he had never thought about the material difficulties of such an enterprise. Did he imagine then that churches build themselves, and that only a little faith is needed for them to rise from the depths of the earth towards the sun, vibrating to the notes of the organ? Alas! He had imagined nothing, the poor, good man. He saw in his mind the beloved chapel, where each stone spoke of the memory of ancestors, heroes, saints, martyrs. He saw it as it had been described, reproduced in all its parts, in a very old book which he had learnt by heart and which he reread every day. He saw it with the purity of its lines, the proud spires, the beauty of its portal which contained, sculpted in granite, the immortal history of La Redemption. He walked beneath its sonorous vaults, between its tall pillars which stood silhouetted against the marvellous harmony of friezes and architraves. He knelt down on the flagstones of polychrome marble, driven to ecstasy by the angelic pallor of the frescoes and the flaming gold of the altar and the irradiating prism of the stained-glass, and he did not wonder what this vision, which seemed so lovely to him, so simple to behold, represented today in terms of lost art, impossible struggle and unfound millions . . . The first moment of surprise over, Père Pamphile set to work with that blind confidence which the pursuit of the melancholy Ideal gives to all.

First he sold all that could be sold, from the rubble which filled the courtyards to the ornaments of the little chapel which the Fathers had improvised in a former refectory on their return. What need had he of a chapel just for himself?

He could perfectly well go and celebrate mass in the neighbouring parish. He sold the furniture, keeping only a board bed to sleep on, a table, a few devotional texts, a crucifix and a coloured picture of John of Matha. In his passion to sell, he sold the old hinges of the carriage gates which he unscrewed himself, the old locks, the old firebacks, the garden tools, the leaking guttering pipes, he sold the lot. Every time he discovered a piece of iron, a scrap of copper, he was exultant, crying out:

"I'll build it!"

And just as he sold everything, he destroyed everything. He cut down the trees in the avenue, enormous oaks which had offered their venerable shade to twenty generations of monks before him. He cut down the little wood of fir and chestnut which provided the monastery with a kind of rampart of greenery and where the paths, trunks, even each moss, evoked a faithful memory. He chopped down the arbour containing a calvary, whose steps bore an imprint worn away by the knees of those who had come to pray. He cut down the fruit trees in the garden. He cut down the cypresses, guardians of the tombs in the cemetery. And, bare-headed, amid the woodcutters, his white robe hitched up to his waist, he urged them to work and swung his heavy axe with all his strength and buried it in the red heart of the old trees, gasping wildly:

"I'll build it!"

From the height of a turret which dominated the monastery, he surveyed the spectacle of this destruction and savoured the great, painful joy of it. All around, trees lay, pell-mell, hideously mutilated, some on their side, twisted and bleeding from huge wounds, others trunk uppermost, groaning, leaning on their crushed branches, as if on stumps. One alone stood upright at the entrance to the garden, a stunted cherry-tree, eaten away by disease, astonished to be so alone on this earth, bereft of its hardy offspring, on land completely levelled. Driven from their places of shelter, the birds flew about in the sky, terrified, uttering pitiful cries.

But Père Pamphile was already blind to this battlefield

where the fallen giants lay dying. He could see instead his church gradually rising from all those ruins, all those dead, taking form, rising, still rising, borne on the shoulders of an army of workers. He could see himself also, clinging to the sides of the new basilica, climbing from stone to stone and fixing atop the steeple the cross of gold, regained and triumphant.

He divided the trees into two piles, one of which he sold and the other he kept with a view to future construction work. When he had nothing left to sell or destroy he went to the diocesan architect. Solemnly he unfolded his plan for the chapel, explaining one by one and at length the drawings in the book, embroiling himself in incomprehensible detail.

"This is what I want to construct," he said. "All this, you understand. How much do you think it will cost altogether?"

"I have no idea!" replied the architect, horrified. "How should I know?"

"Approximately! Come along, something close . . ."

"I really do not know. Three, four, five million perhaps. It depends."

"Five million," said the monk getting up. "Very well, I shall find the money."

And Père Pamphile went in search of it.

He went from village to village, from farm to farm, from manor house to manor house, door to door, holding out his hand, head bowed, living off the cheap bread which he had made his sole nourishment on his way. In the evening, if he were too far from Réno, he begged shelter in presbyteries, where he was sometimes taken in, but with suspicion. He carried on under the blistering sun, in deathly cold, without ever stopping, without ever resting, preceded by the luminous vision which seemed to lead him and protect him. Unwelcome here, insulted there, pursued in the streets by urchins who made fun of his dirty beard, his white robe patched with black and his black coat patched with white, he tasted every bitterness, endured all the shame of the sorry state of beggarhood; and, however he suffered, he was not discouraged. Awkward and timid at first, he soon grew bolder and with a facility which was extraordinary in one so loyal, naive and totally ignorant of life's shadier side, he learnt the tricks of the trade to the extent that not one of its thousand dodges, which at base are nothing other than disguised abuses of trust, was unfamiliar to him. He knew how to speculate on the vanity and lower nature of men and did not recoil from actor's patter, lies, louche attitudes, spying, cunning set-ups. At first, he reproached himself severely for these affronts to his conscience, in which his dignity as a man and his nature as a priest were forgotten. He ended up by excusing his behaviour on the grounds of the grandeur of the aim and he eventually even found it fed his enthusiasm. Sometimes, after a bad day, counting up a poor yield, dark feelings of revolt rumbled within him. His confused thoughts mingling with stories of pirates, with which his Trinitarian memory was crammed, he caught himself dreaming of bold strikes, grandiose thefts, armed bands at the head of which he would hold nations to ransom. Within a few years, Père Pamphile became an accomplished beggar. In the drunkenness of sacrifice, the irresponsibility of madness, his scruples were eroded more and more, his moral sense disappeared. Whether it was habit or the spirit of renunciation, he hardened himself against outrages and accepted ill-treatment as one of the necessities of his condition. He adopted the servile posture, nervous stance, oblique glance, weak, uncertain and grasping hand of the virtuosos of mendicance.

Stories of his foul adventures were told, which the populace made fun of. But more far-sighted souls might easily have perceived a kind of heroism in him, which was superior in its sublimity of degradation to the conventional false virtue, false courage, false honour with which the cardboard of human pride is fabricated. One morning, Père Pamphile was passing the residence of a former butcher, a vicious criminal, who had become rich by means of the acquisition of numerous national treasures. Drunken, vulgar, hard on the poor, 'le Sieur' Lebreton – for so this character liked to be known – was most notable for his cynical lack of piety and his ferocious hatred of priests. Throughout the county he was loathed and feared. Père Pamphile was familiar with all this. But he had met other people, more terrible than this Lebreton, who had softened at his approach. He had even observed that the most apparently fierce often prove to be the most generous, whether out of pride or on a whim. Risking an insulting refusal – which was in any case as nothing to him – he went through the gate and introduced himself at the château.

"Of all the bloody idiots, what's this filthy friar doing here?" yelled Lebreton. "Well, you've got a nerve dragging your dirty feet into my house. What do you want?"

The poor monk cringed. Drooping his shoulders, almost supplicating, he stammered:

"Good sir Lebreton, I . . . " He was immediately interrupted by an oath.

"No play-acting, huh? What do you want? Is it money you want, huh? Filthy beggar! Wait, I'll bloody well give you money, I will."

The vile creature was about to push him out through the door, when he changed his mind, and conceived the idea of amusing himself at the expense of the monk, so he said in a mocking tone:

"Listen, my old friar, I really want to give you some money, but it's on one condition, that you come and collect it from where I put it . . . and I wager you won't do it."

"I wager I will," said Père Pamphile firmly, gravely.

"Very well, wretch. We shall see. First, do me the honour of going right to the end of the room. Now, go down on all fours like a dog, your dirty muzzle facing this window . . . and wait."

While the monk lugubriously obeyed, Lebreton walked over towards the window, putting the whole length of the room between himself and his victim. He pulled a fistful of gold out of his pocket, placed the money on the floor, dropped his trousers, knelt down and hitched up his shirt with a vulgar gesture:

"I bet you won't do it, coward," he yelled.

Père Pamphile had paled. His neck extended, his back

arched, his eyes dull, fixed on this offensive display of flesh, he hesitated. However, in a voice trembling on the edge of tears, he replied:

"I bet I will."

At this, Lebreton sniggered, took a twenty franc piece and inserted it between his tightened buttocks.

"Right then, come here," he said. "And, wretch, take it not with your hands but with your teeth."

Père Pamphile set off, but his whole body was shaking; his legs gave way, his arms felt weak. He advanced slowly, swaying like a bear.

"Come on, hurry up," grumbled Lebreton who was getting impatient. "I'm catching cold."

Twice he fell, and twice he got up again. Finally, he braced himself for a last effort, pressed his face against the backside of the man and rummaging with his nose between the buttocks which had tightened still more, he snapped up the coin in his teeth.

"Son of a bitch!" shouted Lebreton, turning round and seeing the gold glinting between the monk's lips. "Well now, wretch . . . they've all got to pass that way. Either I peg out or you do. Right, to your place."

Ten times Père Pamphile underwent this horrible torture. Eventually, it was the former butcher who gave in first and put a stop to the performance. He got up, his face very red, groaning:

"That's enough now. Christ, he'll swallow up all my money, will that filthy friar."

Despite his fury at having lost ten good golden louis, he could not disguise his admiration and he prodded the monk's belly.

"You are quite a fellow," he concluded, "but a blackguard all the same. Come on, let's have a drink."

Père Pamphile refused with a mild gesture, said goodbye and left.

A mile away along the road, there was a wayside calvary. He knelt down before it and prayed fervently. Then he continued on his way, his eyes raised to the heavens, dazed eyes which seemed to pursue a smiling and radiant image amid the clouds. In a voice strengthened by faith, he cried:

"I will build it!"

After his journeys, he would go back to the monastery and there he always found new evidence of decay. In his absence, another roof might have fallen in; new cracks would trace strange branching figures on the larger walls; floor joists might have given way. And the thorns, thistles and nettles crammed into the courtyards, covered all openings, blocked the doorways in bristling thickets. The wind ferried wandering seeds and inseminated the stones; enormous vegetable growths emerged from the walls, protruding in dishevelled tufts, widening the cracks, which groaned beneath the impetuous force of the rising sap. Driven from one room to another, from one building to another, by the threat of a broken ceiling or a cloister about to collapse on top of him, Père Pamphile had taken refuge on the first floor of a small wing which he could not reach except by means of a ladder, for the ground floor, which he used as a store-room, had no staircase. He had carried there his board bed, his table, chair, crucifix and portrait of Saint John of Matha. There he continued to eat his bowl of soup, a vile, stinking dishwater of scraps, which dogs would have refused. The wind howled in through the glassless windows, rain dripped through the roof, as riven with holes as a sieve. But the walls were solid and that sufficed. Besides, the priest gave scant attention to such things, absorbed as he was ever more deeply in his obsession: his church.

His church! During these sojourns at the monastery between quests for money, he expended an extraordinary and ruinous amount of effort on the chapel, whose original site, completely consumed by long grass, could not even be seen any more. Before considering making the first pickaxe blow into the foundations, he bought freestone, limestone and cement. The courtyards were full of these materials and had the powdery, white dustiness of a building-site. When carts arrived, he leapt to the horse's head:

"This way, this way! Unload here! Whooah! Ah! what

lovely stone! Ah! what lovely limestone! Ah! the cement! Whooah!"

And he leaned his weight on the levers, raised the winches, emptied the chalk into the trenches he had dug, shifted sacks of cement, yelling with a childish, heartbreaking joy:

"It's happening! It's happening!" And he said to the cart drivers: "Ah, my friends! This is good. You have contributed to the construction of the chapel. You are good people. God will bless you." Of course, the wood rotted away, the stones froze and cracked, the chalk soaked in the rain and dissolved, the cement went hard in its sacks. The few materials that were not damaged disappeared during the night, carried off by marauders. These losses did not put a brake on his courage, nor these misfortunes reduce his confidence. He contented himself by saying gaily: "We'll replace it!" There were also long discussions with architects and building contractors who, recognising immediately Père Pamphile's madness and anxious to exploit it, made the most baroque proposals, incited him to pointless expenditure, set to ferociously, vying with each other to steal most from him. Measuring, calculating, unfurling huge sheets of yellowing paper on which geometric figures were etched, they strode between the blocks of stone or through the brambles, busy, dusty and genial. With expansive gestures, they sketched in the air Babylonian architectural projects, built cathedrals with the tip of a finger. And Père Pamphile, his book in hand, gave historical explanations.

"You see, gentlemen, we are not creating anew, we are reconstructing, it's very different. Look, that is where the main altar was, in sculpted stone, thirty-two figures! A masterpiece! There, the reredos, not as old but very ornate, made of porphyry, a gift from Louis XIV."

"Porphyry!" the contractor would say. "As it happens, I have a batch of it which would just do the job . . . Very good stuff too and cheap!"

"Good, send it along, I'll have it . . . There stood the capitular stalls . . . marvels . . . made of solid oak!"

He accepted everything he was told, regaining, when he

was no longer begging, the ludicrous innocence which made him such a good dupe.

Then he would set off again.

Country by country, he travelled through France, Spain, Italy, Austria, Asia Minor. Wherever he went, he made powerful contacts and gained political influence and worldly protection which he learned how to exploit with incredible skill. One day, he was received at the palace of a Roman cardinal, who entrusted him with a secret mission. On another occasion, he sailed on a steamship with a company of travelling players and organised shows on board and pocketed the receipts. Once, he was captured by brigands who forced him to go with them when they sacked a convent and then released him with his share of the booty. Sometimes roughneck, sometimes fool, sometimes spy, sometimes missionary but always beggar, Père Pamphile spent thirty-five years embodying the type of romantic adventurer, able to metamorphose, ready for all eventualities provided that the pay was good. By dint of adaptability, self-abasement, courage and folly, on the great highways of Europe where he trailed his robe in the dust, he gathered the incredible sum of five hundred thousand francs.

As far as these messy encounters were concerned, these acts of moral decay, committed one after the other, this ever swifter slide into the mire of a shameful way of life, the monk suffered no remorse, no self-disgust, not the slightest hint of any taint. He had only one memory which had hardened into a ferocious hatred, the memory of a Capuchin he had met in Spain who was on the same quest as himself in the same places. Apart from this memory, which set him off in transports of fury against the Capuchins and against all mendicant orders, he spoke of his most repugnant experiences as of something perfectly natural, with a lack of awareness that was pitiful to behold. One sensed, listening to him, that this gentle man would take to crime as prostitutes take to sex, without even realising what he was doing. In this impudent, vagabond life, so perfectly designed to destroy his dream, he had seen nothing, nor understood anything, nor experienced anything except that dream. One fact dominated all, a fact beyond all human conventions: the building of the chapel. For him, there were no longer nations, individuals, justice, duty nor anything at all; there was only the chapel. The original point of departure of his folly, the reconstruction of the Redemption Order, no longer crossed his mind. The pirates, Trinitarians, the captives and Saint John of Matha were so many distant shadows which gradually faded into insignificance. The chapel filled the earth, filled the heavens. The sky was its vaulted ceilings, the mountains its altars, the forests its columns, the oceans its fonts, the sun its monstrum, the wind its organ. During this period of his dream, while he travelled on foreign roads, the abandoned monastery served as a refuge for homeless vagabonds and for lovers; wild cats pursued one another from stone to stone, coupling on the ruins, more ghostly than ever beneath the tragic pallor of the moon.

Now Père Pamphile was seventy-five years old. Despite this great age and although his skinny, sinewy body was bent double, he was still robust and vigorous. The same youthful faith as ever shone in his eyes, despite their drooping eyelids. The same enthusiasm drove his stiffened limbs towards illusory goals. He had the smile of a small child. One year he would be at Réno, working harder than any labourer from morning to night; the next year he would be abroad on his quest for money, never taking a moment's rest. The digging of the foundations of the chapel had at last been started, then abandoned, owing to lack of money. All of the five hundred thousand francs had been spent on architects' plans, preparatory surveys by contractors, on buying materials and tools which were constantly lost or stolen and constantly replaced. But the old man did not despair. When he returned from his long journeys, his pockets full, he kept buying. He conferred again with architects and contractors; and the same rôles, the same farces were enacted. They measured, calculated, unfurled the same yellowing papers, exclaimed over the same projects; Père Pamphile, book in hand, began on the same explanations.

"Excuse me, gentlemen, but we are not actually creating anything here, we are reconstructing. Over here was the site of the main altar . . ."

He had never altered his daily routine; in the morning he was brought his soup and in the evening his piece of bread; then at night, he climbed into his room in the little lodge, now a squalid hovel, the walls covered with filth, the floor carpeted with muck. After a prayer before the crucifix, he stretched out on his wooden bed and while an icy wind lifted his beard, the owls, no longer afraid of him, perched on their beams in the vault of the roof, trained their enormous eyes on him as he slept and covered him with their droppings.

Abbé Jules knew Père Pamphile through his frequent contact with the bishopric and, like everyone, took him for "an old rogue", aware of the base acts he committed. With the facility which all optimists possess of improvising bold and rascally plans without troubling to develop them properly, the Abbé, that morning, when thinking about Père Pamphile, had in the space of a minute, vaguely sketched out an admirable plan of blackmail whose success his recognised authority and the terror he inspired could scarcely fail to ensure. So he had set off in haste for Réno, his ideas still uncertain and confused, but deferring the problem of sorting them out until the moment arrived.

He walked the length of some low-level constructions, so dilapidated that it was impossible to specify the exact nature of them; he crossed two little courtyards where the broken arches of a cloister could still be made out, and where the earth, soaked by rain, scarred by the wheels of carts, was just a sea of mud on the surface of which there floated rubble and debris of all kinds; he passed beneath a porch propped up on rotting beams. Then the Abbé came out in a huge courtyard, enclosed on four sides by constructions which were uneven in height and oddly silhouetted against the sky, some disembowelled and like rock falls, others moss-covered and so smothered in varied and luxuriant vegetation that they looked more like a nook in an untamed forest. At first he could see nothing but a riot of freestone, untreated wood, rough-hewn beams, scattered tools and, above this chaos, the sketched beginnings of some scaffolding and two cranes, silhouetted against the chalky background of the yard, long-necked like skinny beasts; it had the stillness and poignancy of a building site abandoned in mid-function. Then he thought he heard a dull sound, like the noise of a pick against earth. Guided by the sound, he spotted a freshly dug hexagonal shape a few metres from the scaffolding, in a cleared space. He spotted the pick coming out of the earth and going back in, in short, regular blows, without being able to make out the arms which were deploying it. He went towards the scene, losing his footing in the maze of stumps and blocks of stone, skirting lakes of chalk, stepping over tree trunks, and eventually discovered Père Pamphile at the bottom of a trench. His feet in the water, his face streaming and very red, he was fiercely wielding the pick-axe.

"Good day, Father!" said the Abbé.

Père Pamphile looked up and recognised the Abbé.

"Ah, it's you, Abbé," he said, joyful and surprised. "You've come to inspect the works! That's very kind of you. As you can see, things are coming on."

"And what are you doing there, Father, with that pick?"

"I'm digging, Abbé, I'm digging the foundations. But the weather is terrible."

Père Pamphile dropped his pick, wiped his long, mud-spattered beard and pulled his robe, which he had knotted round his waist, back down over his legs.

"Terrible," he repeated. "And it's this water which is foiling me. Give me a hand, so I can climb up. Ah, that's very kind of you to have come. Only, I really can't invite you into my quarters. Just imagine, someone stole my ladder yesterday . . . So, Monseigneur, how are you?"

Still talking, helped by the Abbé, he had left his hole and leapt in one nimble movement out onto the ground. Various politenesses exchanged, the Abbé asked:

"So that's your church is it?"

The old man swelled with pride. Pointing to the hexagonal area, once covered with brambles and now an expanse of turned earth marked out with a thin rope stretched between stakes, he replied:

"All that is my church. Yes, my dear Abbé, all that. And who would have thought that I could rebuild it, huh?"

"Rebuild it?" said Jules, who thought the old Trinitarian was making fun of him. "Listen, you've been building it for forty years and there's nothing there!"

"Nothing?" cried Père Pamphile, indicating in a broad, furious gesture the whole yard littered with materials. "Well, what's all that? And that? What is it then? What I mean is, the most difficult part has been done. Now I only have to build. Shall we take shelter somewhere?"

Jules refused and sat down on a block of granite. Without pressing him further, the monk squatted on a heap of pebbles opposite him. Both stared at one another. The wind blew harder, whipping up the rain which slashed through the sky in slanted, stinging streaks. Now and again, stones broke away from the walls, thudding softly onto the ground and splinters of slate flew through the air.

"Have you funds?" asked the Abbé brusquely.

"I am always in funds," replied Père Pamphile. "In fact, eight days ago I got back from Hungary. It was a good trip. To Esztergom. Oh it was funny! Imagine, I went to the Primate, a very cheerful, jovial man and very generous! He said, "Father, sing me *La Marseillaise* and I'll give you a hundred florins!" Well I sang *La Marseillaise* as if my life depended on it, and every time, the Primate gave me a hundred florins. I sang it twelve times!"

He started to hum:

"*Nous entrerons dans la carrière . . .* "

"So you know *La Marseillaise*, do you?" asked the Abbé, who could not help smiling.

"Well, you know how it is," said the good fellow, shaking his head, resigned, "in our job you need to know something of everything. You so often have to deal with very odd people! For instance, next year I'm going back to the Orient

... That's another story ... There, they couldn't care less about the *Marseillaise*, all they want is for you to tell them how people are dressed, what's the latest fashion in Paris. Well, I just say the first thing that comes into my head and they're quite happy."

The Abbé was not listening any more and thinking hard.

Now that he was faced with an obstacle to overcome, all his ardour, his feverish impatience had returned. He no longer connected the original idea of the library with the success of his enterprise; now he did not associate any project with it; he had no satisfaction of any new passion in view; now he was acting purely for pleasure. Even, in the midst of rapid and contradictory impressions which succeeded one another in his fevered brain and which made him more tense than ever, he was not far from believing that he was an instrument of human justice and divine anger against a man flaunting social laws and outraging the dignity of the church. What had started out as a shameful plot and ignoble piece of blackmail, became transformed into an act of devotion and this in its turn expanded to faith, and ennobled into a mission. Jules decided he should cut short the monk's chatter and come to the point, brutally, instead of getting involved in complicated tricks which might not succeed with a wily old wanderer as Père Pamphile was. The best course was to surprise him, stun him with a crushing blow, hit hard and accurately. He assumed a severe expression and said:

"I am not here to listen to your nonsense, Reverend Father, and I beg you to give me a few minutes of your attention. I have a project, a great project, for which I need a great deal of money. First, I would very much like to calm your conscience. This is not the same as gadding about abroad under the pretext of building a church, no, this concerns something very fine, very grand, very Christian. If I told you what it is, probably you would not understand. I say again, I need money. You have money. Give me some."

"I cannot," replied Père Pamphile simply, whose expression had altered from the careless gaiety of the Bohemian to the dreamy gravitas of the apostle.

The Abbé stood up, moved by sudden anger. He had counted on stupefaction, shock, collapse, some proper reaction in any case. And here was the man keeping calm and saying "I cannot" in a tranquil, inflexible voice, in which one could hear iron resolution. He contained himself and looked at the monk. A few pebbles had slipped away from under him. He settled himself again gently, his legs higher up. Drops of water trembled in his beard.

"You cannot?" the Abbé growled.

"No!"

"Listen carefully. You cannot?"

"No! If you have a project beloved of God, you must do as I have, the roads are open to everyone."

Jules exploded.

"Do you think then that I am a tramp, a cutpurse, a brothel creeper?"

"You are what you are; I am what I am. Why get so angry?"

"Once more, you say you cannot?"

"I cannot."

The Abbé clenched his fists into the void.

"Well, I will forbid you to beg in the diocese, the police will grab you by the scruff of the neck and throw you in jail."

"Oh," said Père Pamphile, shaking his head sadly, "I'm burnt out in the diocese anyway, no-one gives me anything any more. As for prison, unpleasant people have arrested me many times and I have slept in prison often. Actually it's better than a damp hedgerow."

"Well then I'll write to Rome. I'll have you driven out of here. I'll denounce you to your superior, to the Pope. I'll say what you're really like, all you've done, your filthy adventures, your crimes. I'll denounce you, do you hear, you old tramp!"

"My superior knows me, the Pope knows me. And then, there is someone even greater who knows me best of all."

His forefinger raised, he pointed to the sky and added:

"God! I am not afraid."

"You should account for all the money you've wasted, that you stole, you should, you should . . ."

The Abbé was boiling with rage. His eyes bulged and rolled as if in an epileptic attack, the whites showing, streaked with purple veins. From his lips curses tumbled and jostled and dribbled, inarticulate words lost in a wheeze, a gurgle of saliva. Finally, he was gripped by a fit of coughing which racked his throat and tore at his chest. Bent double, his face purple, veins standing out fit to burst on his tensed neck, he seemed to be spewing out his life-force, retching hideously.

When the crisis was over, the monk spoke to him, very gently, without shifting from his perch.

"Why cause yourself such pain? And why reproach me? For not giving you the money I have collected, prayed for, suffered for? I simply cannot! Listen, often there were poor people, naked, hungry, pitiful children of God, who begged me on their knees . . . I wept but I refused them. I cannot! That money is not mine. It belongs to Her, to Her, the radiant, sublime Bride of my heart. Nothing can distract me from Her, not even to save someone from death, from hell, no, I could not do it."

The rain sang into the puddles, the wind screeched around the rattling ruins and in the sad, damp air, the spindly, grey silhouette of the scaffolding swayed. The Trinitarian continued:

"You insulted me just now. Well, good God, how many people have done that, not knowing . . . I forgive you. If I have a few coppers so I can eat, a stretch of wall to shelter me, a board to sleep on, a little warm blood in these old veins, a few sturdy muscles on these old bones of mine, I am content. Do you really think I care about money? Listen my dear Abbé, the day my church is built, come back, and whatever you ask I will give you, I swear it , God rest my soul, but until that is done, no, I cannot."

Jules was dumbfounded by the monk. Truly he understood nothing any more. Was this lunatic sincere? Was he mocking him? He could not tell. In any case, he had not foreseen this incredible folly or this audacious irony. He was totally disconcerted by it. What was there then behind this ravaged mask, which he had seen twice transfigured, almost dematerialising in the radiant glow of a mysterious and nameless beauty? Despite the anger he felt rumbling in him, the monk intimidated him. He did not know what he felt: pity, admiration or disdain. From the depths of his being, a voice said, "Kneel down, this is a saint." Another voice said: "No, insult him, he's a bandit." Some obscure instinct warned him that the first voice was right, but he obeyed the other. He stamped his foot and cried:

"Words, just words! Do you take me for an idiot? You know quite well that your church is a trick and you will never build it!"

But Père Pamphile had drawn himself up to his full height, his eyes burning, and was so grand, so beautiful, so terrible, that the Abbé backed away, daunted by a glare whose extraordinary and superhuman clarity he was unable to withstand. It was as if an archangel were walking towards him, the savage God of all this dead solitude. He was about to fall to his knees and beg for grace when the monk gripped him by the shoulders and shook him roughly.

"Man of little faith!" he said, "Bad priest! Do not blaspheme, look and understand! Even if I have to cut those blocks of stone and carry them on my old back myself, if I have to hoist those beams, forge that iron, raise the vaults with these arms, even if I have to do it all alone, yes, all alone, clutch it to my chest, lift it off the earth, and set it up right there, straight, you understand, you poor madman, there, there, I will build it! Now, goodbye."

Père Pamphile took a few steps, stopped at the edge of the hole he had been digging when Jules had found him and, hitching up his robe again, lowered himself back into the trench.

For a few minutes, the Abbé stood ankle-deep in mud, motionless, thoughtful: "That was no bandit," he said to himself, "he is something worse, a poet," while the pick-axe took up its rhythmic movement again, appeared above the ground level and disappeared, excavating the earth.

Prey to a vague unease, he felt like turning back to Père Pamphile, talking to him, humbling himself; but a sort of base pride and the cowardice which is at the heart of all violent natures, prevented him; deeply affected, he left. Once more, he set out through the maze of materials, crossed again the two muddy yards, walked the length of the ruins but now it all seemed full of majesty. Everything around him, in harmony with the state of his soul, beneath its infinite sadness assumed a mysterious physical aspect and moral grandeur which troubled him strangely. A life he did not recognise, and before which he felt so small, so ugly, so miserably petty, so completely unworthy, a life to which he could never aspire, opened out through the crevices in the walls, unsuspected horizons, open spaces blooming with the flowers glimpsed in dreams, beautiful flowers above which flitted souls, the souls of children, old men, poor people, beautiful flowers which rocked tiny dead souls within their perfumed calices. On the way, a host of confused ideas, without any direct connection with what he had seen and heard at Réno, clashed in his head. But they all led obstinately to Père Pamphile, and from Père Pamphile to the miracle of religions based on love which generate such joy in suffering, such wisdom in folly, such grandeur in abasement. They led him too to the painful realisation of his own corruption. He searched in vain through his own life from his earliest memories, finding only baseness and shame, with brief escapades, fugitive aspirations towards good, of which the only result was to render his relapses weightier and more irreparable. No faith, no love, no passion even; furious, bestial instincts, distorted intellectual obsessions and with all that the sensation of an unbridgeable void, huge disgust with life, an immense fear of death. Ah, yes, death! For the Christian education of his childhood, the conditioning of his priesthood, stronger than his doubts and his impieties, made him consider the terrible beyond as an eternity of tortures and terrors.

The Abbé walked slowly, his back bent under the weight of an invisible burden, his eyes turned to the ground, where puddles reflected and emphasised the shifting shapes of the slow-moving clouds. The wind had dropped, the rain was no longer more than a light mizzle gradually dissipating; and, in the sky, lit by a whiter light at the horizon, the torn clouds afforded glimpses here and there through narrow chinks, of a few shreds of sombre blue. Gradually, the countryside, greener now, emerged from blueish mists which were drowning the contours and curves of the land in a cloak of smoky mist. Against the background of the hills, a dull violet colour, livened by the bright splashes of scattered houses, the alders of the flat lands and the poplars pruned into tall shapes, climbed upwards, like narrow, trembling columns of pink smoke. On the brow of the hill, as the town and its three spires came abruptly into view, the Abbé quickened his step. It was a Saturday and the bells were ringing, answering one another, announcing the coming of the holy day. They had their festival voices, their joyous voices, singing of the blessed rest of the worker, and the great bell of the cathedral, dominating the other, feebler voices with its great voice, was bringing the good news to the furthest points of the valley. Listening to them, the sound muffled by distance, so sweet, Jules experienced a delicious emotion, whose nature and cause he would have been incapable of explaining. His tension relaxed, his heart melted in tenderness and, smoothly, painlessly, tears flowed from his eyes. The bells rang and rang and Jules wept and wept. And while he wept and the bells rang, a poor woman passed by. She was gaunt and emaciated, her face the colour of stone, wore filthy rags, was barefoot and pulled a cart, in which two children slept in the straw, pale and shrunken.

"Alms, Monsieur l'Abbé!" she said.

From his purse, the Abbé drew two gold coins and placed them in the poor woman's hand.

"Here," he said, "but these are not from me, but from the bishop. Pray for him. Pray for me. And be happy sometimes."

The bells had fallen silent by the time he crossed the threshold of the bishop's palace; but he could still feel their sweet vibrations in his ears and in his heart. When he was back in his room, he prostrated himself before an image of Christ and, beating his breast, implored:

"My God, have pity on me. Forgive me. Help me."

Hands joined, eyes raised to the picture, he remained in prayer till evening.

Lent was approaching. Jules no longer thought about his library nor Père Pamphile, nor death nor virtue. The feelings experienced on his return from Réno had soon evaporated and, more eccentric and tyrannical than ever, he had taken up the affairs of the diocese once more. His black, tormented shadow could be seen once more roaming on his terrace at dusk; priests who had gradually in the absence of the guard dog begun to dance again, soutanes raised, happy in a freedom they believed permanent, began to tremble again, to watch one another and flee each other's company. Around the little village steeples, terror reigned once more. As for the bishop, he was 'in agony'; not at all because of the clamorous return of his secretary, who rather relieved him of a too heavy burden, but because the date was coming, the fatal deadline for his pastoral letter. Now, he had nothing to say, did not want to say anything, could not say anything. However, it was absolutely necessary to put something out. Where could he find sentences that were insignificant enough, words bland enough for the pages he wrote to equate to blank pages and for everyone to be happy. It was very difficult, now that the press had the mania of picking over everything and giving the simplest words, the flattest phrases, terrible meanings, bold interpretations which they really did not contain.

"This, this," he said to himself after long and painful thought, "this is what I can do, I am going to recommend to the faithful that they behave well that . . . that . . . that . . . they go to Mass, confess, observe the fast strictly, in a word, that they be good Catholics, so that God will protect them from sin, hail, fire, sickness. Then, I will show how through faith . . . no, no . . . I won't show anything . . . one shouldn't show anything. And I will end either with a paraphrase of something or other from the Gospel, or an invocation to the Lord, from whom all things come, who gives us bread, wine etc. etc. and the strength to endure life's pains. That does not seem to me to be too exaggerated. I will not speak of His Holiness, because I'll be reproached for being a Vaticanist, nor of the Emperor, for I'll be accused of being a liberal."

Having started from this premise, he already had a heavily scored script, and had inked more than fifty pages. As he reread his work, every word alerted him to some imagined problem and, one after the other, he tore up the pages he had written. The poor prelate sweated, puffed, sighed, despaired.

One morning, Abbé Jules, very well-disposed and in great humour, asked the bishop:

"Have you thought about your pastoral letter, Monseigneur. It's Lent."

"Of course I've thought about it," replied the old man, his face a mask of dread. "Ah, what a terrible thing!"

"Why so terrible?" asked the Abbé.

"My dear child, terrible because of the responsibilities, the care I have to take. In the situation I find myself, a peaceful situation, of concord, reconciliation, great prudence is necessary, no-one must be ruffled, it's all very delicate . . ."

The Abbé seemed to be taking a lively interest in his bishop's problems.

"Doubtless it is very delicate," he said, "would you care to talk about it a little?"

"I can think of nothing better," mumbled the bishop, who could not conceal great disquiet, "but you are rather hotheaded, my dear Abbé, young people do not see things quite like older people do. They tend to . . . tend to . . . and then . . . while . . . well, there you are . . ."

He nodded his head gravely; his forehead creased; his lips, clamped together, emitted tiny brief, sharp clicks. The Abbé replied in an unctuous tone, bowing respectfully:

"Therefore, Monseigneur, I will not permit myself to offer you any advice, but I would merely like to repeat what is said of you in the Catholic world."

The bishop jumped out of his skin. His eyes were round, appalled.

"People are talking about me in the Catholic world? And what do they say?"

"First, there is complete accord and approval regarding the way you administer the diocese. Your piety, charity and justice are greatly praised . . . only, there are complaints that on certain serious occasions, you do not assert yourself enough. For example, your letters are a little grey, a little vague . . . In short, not what one would expect from your Eminence."

The bishop shifted nervously on his chair.

"What one would expect from my Eminence? What one expects! I can't see everything in terms of blood and fire, you know . . . It's not my rôle . . . I'm not an assassin!"

"But, Monseigneur, no-one's asking anything of the sort," went on the Abbé, making a mild gesture of protest. "People would like greater firmness, a more lofty authority in your public actions, more character, more flame . . . That's quite different."

Growing a little more excited and warming to his own assumed rôle, his deceit and trickery, he went on in an eager tone, to which the emotion of something about which he really did feel strongly added accents of sincerity:

"What people would like would be that, faced with the atheism which is gaining ascendance and setting itself up in official seats of authority, overtly protected and paid for by the government, faced with furious, multiple attacks against the holy Church, people would like someone to raise a voice, a voice at once avenging, consolatory, the cry of revulsion and hope of a great Christian. Times are bad, Monseigneur. On all sides, society is falling apart, religion is foundering, everything is disintegrating and rotting. On high, on the throne, an orgy brazenly and openly takes place, a legal orgy. In the depths, there's a ravenous beast howling, thirsting for blood. Everywhere, the rout, panic, the dizziness of the stampede. Abominable generations are being bred which if they are not kept in order will unbolt the body of Christ from the crucifixes and will transform into banks or else into houses of sin our churches crowned with the redeemer's symbol. You have care of souls. Souls need to be supported in faith, encouraged in mourning, reassured in danger. It is not good to take no interest in their moral destiny. And it is a desertion for which God will call you to account, this speaking of peace and concord when war has been declared, the enemy upon us and hunting us down. That is what is being said in the Catholic world. They also say . . ."

"But for God's sake! I really do not see that!" interrupted the bishop who had listened open-mouthed in astonishment to the Abbé's violent outburst. "Those people must be mad. In all eras there have been good and bad people and it will always be like that. What can I do about it? I'm not the one who created the world. Come on, tell me, did I create the world?"

Jules continued in a harsher and more cutting tone:

"I am not passing judgement Monseigneur, I repeat . . . They say too that it must be very agreeable to live in a palace, be well-fed, well-clothed, nice and warm, grow flowers, compose light verse, receive homage and bless passers-by. They say it is easy to take care to put aside any responsibility which might threaten repose, trouble the digestion or disturb sleep, to close one's eyes so as not to see anything painful or stop the ears so as not to hear voices crying out. But they also say that such behaviour is neither good, honest, nor Christian and that it is very like the betrayal of a leader who on the day of the battle abandons his troops and lets them die without helping them. They also say that a person must have secret reasons for behaving like this. They also say . . ."

"They say, they say, they say! What they say is rubbish!" cried the bishop, who looked very pale and distraught. He got out of his chair, turned his back on the Abbé and strode into his office, clearly upset.

But soon he feared he might have reacted too strongly. He did not want to leave things on that note, with that daring gesture, which might unleash one of the Abbé's terrible furies such as he had so often endured. As soon as he had calmed down, he went to see him again.

"Listen, my dear child, think hard. You spoke to me of the Emperor, now what can the Emperor have to do with a Lenten pastoral letter?

"All the evil we are suffering comes from him; all the impiety, the decay which is killing us, comes from him. In his hypocritical guise as friend of the Church, beneath the insulting protection he pretends to offer us, he is the great agent of destruction, the . . ."

"Tsk, tsk, tsk! What do you know about it?"

"I know!" stated the Abbé, clearly, trenchantly, so as to brook no argument.

So, the prelate, discouraged, dropped back into his armchair. He had offered all the resistance of which he was capable and now he had no strength left. He felt it was not possible for him to go any further. Jules' words also troubled him in his conscience. He accepted the justice of these reproaches, whose exaggerated nature he was unable to discern beneath the sonorous, declamatory, pompous phrases. However, he did not quite give in yet and tried to struggle on.

"My dear child!" he groaned. "You can see what a false situation people are putting me in. The Emperor! But he's the one who gave me . . . ! And then . . . and then . . . I'm going to clarify everything on August 15th!"

"Oh, Monseigneur, Monseigneur," sighed Jules sadly. "The great saints, the great martyrs, the very people you revere, whose sublime stories you reread every day, they did not speak as you do. It was on the sullied steps of thrones that they went to carry the word of truth, in the midst of hostile crowds that they confessed their faith. It was in the face of tyrants that they yelled their excommunications."

The bishop thought: "Those saints of yours were insurgents," but he did not dare express this disrespectful opinion and glanced sideways at the Abbé, who had fallen silent. He was standing, head high, eyes drowning in ecstasy, mouth still trembling with imprecations and looked like a prophet. And in truth, at that precise moment, forgetting the act he had put on for the bishop, he was a prophet. A whole mystical and visionary world stirred in him. Like Isaiah, he would have had himself cut in two, a smile on his lips; he would have walked to martyrdom in a delirium. Now he walked out slowly, leaving the prelate deeply troubled in his heart.

Tireless, Jules went on the attack again. He had preserved his mask of inspiration but it was no longer merely a mask concealing the sniggering of the trickster. Each day he presented new arguments, offered new threats, and the bishop, besieged, tyrannised, tortured by this pitiless executioner, gradually gave in on all points, provided that there was no mention of the Emperor in the pastoral letter. He definitely did not want to mention the Emperor, definitely not. His last ounces of strength were concentrated on this single aim; ceaselessly he repeated:

"That! No! Never! He nominated me! And then there are inflexible rules! I want to stay within the law!"

The poor man could no longer eat nor sleep and lived in constant, terrible anguish. So nervous had he become, that the slightest noise made him jump pitifully. He was prey to waking nightmares. Even as he said his mass or recited his breviary, his imagination painted atrocious scenes of martyrdom, bloodstained circuses, the block ... He was not able even for a minute to drive away these tormenting images and taste a moment's calm repose. He wished he could fall ill and die. As he had given in on the rest, so he eventually gave in regarding the Emperor.

"Very well, so be it. But I beg you, not his name, let's not write Emperor or the Empire nor anything similar. Let's put potentate ... no ... tyrant! No, no, let's put people, yes people, that says it all and includes all too. It could apply to anyone. Anyway, no-one will misunderstand. My God, what is going to happen to us? What about the prefect? And the minister? And the Council of State? What a scandal! We will be put under an edict, Abbé, we will be condemned to some shameful punishment."

Jules replied gravely:

"Jesus was crucified, Monseigneur. Did he complain?"

At last the pastoral letter, one fine Sunday, exploded like a bomb in all the parishes. Some priests, better informed than others, refused to read it out.

There was stupefaction, consternation, indignation. People thought the bishop had gone mad. In that strange ecclesiastical document, drafted completely by Jules in brief, rapid, hissing sentences, there was a pamphleteering tone so sour, attacks so direct against the public powers and beyond all this, such a hate-filled claim for the rights of the Church, such an ardent call to arms in the name of religion that even the strictest among the members of the diocese, feeling that the cause was unpopular and not anxious to defend it, raised their voices like everyone else and demanded justice against the bishop. The uproar was such that the same evening, a group of workers, ruffians and petty bourgeois, brandishing tricolours and singing a patriotic anthem came to protest outside the bishop's palace and broke the windows with stones. The affair soon reached Paris from the provinces, then from Paris all France. Within a few days, Abbé Jules' pastoral had assumed the proportions of a European incident. It had put all the chancelleries into action, turned all eyes towards Rome, which preserved a discreet silence, and unleashed the press. The poor bishop, so fearful of scandal, occupied everyone's attention.

From the moment the extraordinary news broke – for the legal formalities of registering the pastoral letter with the chancellor of the diocese had not yet been fulfilled – the prefect had left for Paris. The minister for religious affairs had sent for the bishop. Between France and the Holy See, there was a feverish exchange of correspondence, explanations, reports, a continuous coming and going of cabinet messengers. And the Council of State solemnly deliberated. In cafés, clubs, salons, everyone discussed the grave question of the day. In the evening one might overhear snippets of conversation between people strolling along the boulevards.

"It could mean war."

"They say that bishop's mad."

"And Rome? What does Rome say?"

Serious and well-informed journals established that the bishop was affiliated to secret societies, explained the mechanics of Catholic Carbonarism of which he was undoubtedly one of the most dangerous ring-leaders, and which threatened freedom of conscience and world peace. Around his name and his acts, the most absurd legends grew up; people desperately delved into his private life; his trial was recalled with a lavish larding of insulting comments; illustrated satirical journals regaled the masses with a horrible caricature of him wearing the sombre cowl of Torquemada. No voice was raised in his favour. He was disowned totally and firmly by the clerical press. And while the poor fellow, stunned, panic-stricken, all alone in a hotel room, felt his spirit bend and collapse under the weight of infinite suffering and irreparable shame, Jules exulted in his triumph. He savoured with total joy the unhoped-for and prodigious success of his trickery and, proud of the row he had unleashed, he brandished the pages of the pastoral letter in the air, just as once he had done with his sister Athalie's bottle of cod-liver oil as a boy; and he danced about and shouted:

"Oh, no, what a joke! Ha! Ha! Ha! What a joke! My God, this is fun!"

At last, after a month's absence, the bishop furtively came back home. Blamed by the ministry, by Rome, he had only managed to preserve his job by the ingenuity of his defence and the touching tone of his repentance. He had even been obliged to write a letter, made public, in which he regretted his mistakes, humbled himself and begged pardon. When he had sent away the vicar-general and the palace staff who had come to welcome him home, he said simply to Jules in a very gentle voice:

"Abbé, in future we must be more careful, much more careful. I have promised."

When he saw the old man so bent, so thin, almost unrecognisable and addressing no reproach to him, his eyes seeming to express the gentle sadness of a prayer, the Abbé felt a violent spasm of the heart. All of a sudden he threw himself at his feet, sobbing:

"Forgive me. It was my fault, Monseigneur! It was me!"

"Come along my dear child," the bishop consoled him,

two large tears rolling down his pale cheek. "Come along, now. It's all over now. Don't cry, it's over."

Six months went by. The pastoral letter was not talked of any more. The palace was peaceful again and Jules seemed reformed. Public opinion grew more and more favourable day by day. He had achieved a real success with his "month of Mary" sermon, in which, using a very charming turn of phrase, mystical love poetry veiled in human tenderness, he had conquered women's hearts. A physical transformation had taken place in him. He took greater care of his person, lost his bohemian habits, wore almost elegant soutanes and silver buckles on the finest of shoes. He began to be received with pleasure in certain of the châteaux of the area. Despite his physiognomy, which was still coarse and his manner, which was still brusque, he could astonish by the variety, the delicate and fresh interest of his conversation, occasionally spiced with some slightly outrageous word or idea, which nevertheless was not offensive, even to the most devout. In the course of much reading he had learnt an enormous amount in the most varied fields; and if this knowledge, rapidly acquired, was not categorised methodically in his mind, he knew how to make clever use of it and introduce it without pedantry into familiar conversation. His ugliness actually disappeared, the awkwardness of his long, angular, gawky body did not shock as much; what before had made him look ridiculous now conferred on him a kind of originality, which was quite pleasant, and usefully distinguished him from the heavy, massive, peasant banality of his colleagues. Later, in the midst of a smallpox epidemic which decimated the population of one of the suburbs, he had proved to be courageous and devoted. Giving freely of his time, offering the consolations of his ministry to the sick poor and burying the dead, he had given the consternated and panic-stricken population a fine example of courage. His relationship with the bishop had become excellent, troubled here and there with small clouds which, however, soon dissipated.

*

Since his unfortunate adventure, the bishop had aged a great deal; his health was more delicate, his faculties became less acute. Though he never spoke of the terrible business, one could tell he still suffered by it, that the scar of it was not healed and still bled. Jules tried to make him forget his bad memories, humouring the old man's gentle obsessions. He even studied geraniums and pelargoniums to be able to discuss their cultivation with him. They argued over Latin poets. The bishop favoured Virgil; Jules preferred Lucretius.

"But Lucretius was an atheist!" cried the bishop.

"And what about your Virgil, who believed in the grotesque gods of Olympus? In that imbecile Jupiter? And Juno?"

"Well at least he believed in something! What do you expect? In his time there were no other gods and then he didn't believe in it all that much; he had already guessed at Christianity."

"But Lucretius saw everything, felt everything, expressed everything about nature and the human soul. And how magnificently! Today he still dominates us. Everything is based on him, our systems and poetry, and the further we go, the more his luminous work assumes greatness and astonishes. Without him, we would still be worshipping Minerva and her helmet and that brute Vulcan. As for Virgil, his lovely verses, lovely rhythms, he stole them from Lucretius."

"Don't say that, my dear child," protested the prelate, "Virgil was the source, the only source, believe me. He is the one we have to go back to always, always.

"If only he had just uttered this cry of pain: *Pacata posse omnia mente tueri!* To be able to contemplate all things with a peaceful soul. Without Lucretius, Monseigneur, we would not have either Pascal nor Victor Hugo."

"Victor Hugo! My dear child, he's a monster!"

After these conversations, the bishop would feel very content. He would say to Jules:

"My dear Abbé, you are all I have. Always love me like this."

"Yes, Monseigneur. I have caused you so much sorrow."

"Not at all, I am just like that, it's my nature. Anyway, you are all I have."

The Abbé was far from being as tranquil as he seemed to be, and though his passion for evil had no definite goal at that time, his lower instincts harassed him ceaselessly, drove him to unfocused relapses and he was obliged to struggle fiercely against them. However, something sustained him which had been lacking up till then: an interest, an ambition. How much time he had wasted on criminal and pointless fantasies, how much energy lost on sterile whims, through which he was surprised he had not jeopardised his whole future. Now he glimpsed a new life which could be brilliant and rewarding. Instead of trailing a greasy soutane eternally in the low tasks of the petty priesthood, he could now raise his sights higher. He knew he was eloquent, and his eloquence pleased because it reached for the emotions rather than the reason. He knew also that despite his physical lack of grace which people forgot in the face of the real, vivacious charm of his intellectual gifts, it was not out of the question for him to aspire to worldly success and interest women in his ambition. He had grasped all this very clearly the day when his preaching had won for him a sympathy that was not entirely unequivocal and instantly transformed his wretched state of pariah into the enviable condition of fashionable priest. But his own nature frightened him; he could feel it rumbling and boiling within himself like a terrible lava and he dreaded its fatal and inevitable eruption. He was so attracted by evil that often even as he reflected with the clearest of sight on the folly of his inappropriate past behaviour, he longed to abandon himself to that same behaviour. An invincible force drew him in its wake and made him dizzy at the edge of the abyss. He realised that one day he would suddenly let himself go over a trifle and slip down into the void.

Now that he had more frequent contact with women, he was a slave to his flesh once more. At first, he avoided the temptation by working determinedly and by keeping strict control over his thoughts. But soon work was not enough. The fixity of his way of life condemned him to defeat. Love only ever presented itself to him in the guise of a complex and damaging act of debauchery. Impure images which he found impossible to drive away, danced before his eyes, tore him from his books and thoughts and plunged him into a series of obscene daydreams during which, involuntarily, he found satisfaction and from which he emerged stunned and full of self-disgust. Prayer too was useless and did not calm him. Kneeling before the crucifix, he would gradually see Christ's body oscillate on the bloody nails, leave the cross, hang forwards then fall into the void and in the place of the disappeared God, Woman, triumphant and completely naked, the eternal prostitute, offered her mouth, her sex, her whole body to shameful kisses. To stifle the monster, he started taking his furious walks across the countryside again. He tried to tame the carnal revolt of his irrepressible sensuality by dint of physical exertion.

All these inner struggles, all these dramas of a soul in distress, Jules, with a strength of will which was not without heroism, suppressed silently within his conscience and no one around him had any inkling. In fact, when his torments were at their strongest, when his temptation was most painful, by a pitiful irony which gives virtue nostalgia for vice and vice nostalgia for virtue, he felt an intense and almost intoxicating joy at using his sermons to sing a hymn to unconsummated lust, to the ineffable sweetness of spiritual love, the untroubled love of an earthly dream for a heavenly dream.

Every year, the bishop's feast day was celebrated by pious acts, literary acts of rejoicing and a helping of chocolate at breakfast in the small and large seminaries. After the solemn sung mass, the pupils came and paid homage to Monseigneur, some in Latin verse, some in French verse, some – the brightest – in Greek verse, and then took part in an academic battle of wits, in which they elucidated an obscure point of religious history or else concentrated on a dogma attacked by philosophers. Marches were played in the intervals between lectures. On this occasion, the prelate gave a dinner to which were invited the principal ecclesiastical authorities, the best pupil from each class and a few lay friends. As usual, Jules had the task of organising the party, which in any case never varied.

That day, he was nervous, more agitated than normal. That morning he had had an argument with the vicar-general over the decoration of the main altar and the man had annoyed him. This led him to observe that since he had adopted his new reserve and after his month of Mary success, the vicar-general seemed more high-handed with him and no longer concealed his hostility. Nevertheless, things went splendidly. The bishop endured conscientiously the deluge of polyglot praise and replied as best he could. At dinner, the Abbé noticed that the vicar-general repeatedly looked at him sideways and sniggered with his neighbour, a fat priest whose too short nose was submerged in the puffiness of his cheeks. "Doubtless that rabble is laughing at me," he thought. The sniggering exasperated him.

Furthermore, everything around him exasperated him. He felt insurmountable disgust at finding himself in this milieu which had never before seemed more repugnant. These heavy, vulgar priests' faces, glimpsed between the row of candelabras and baskets of flowers, the hideous smugness of those bellies, those skinny silhouettes of seminarists already jaundiced with spite, balancing above long bird-like necks candid facial expressions which belied the carnivorous jaws and darting eyes of beasts of prey, which all, for Jules, radiated crude jollity, cynical insouciance, fierce egotism, vile appetites, abject ignorance and lack of intellect. The two priests near him, who were telling each other filthy scatological jokes in low voices, containing their laughs, dribbling sauce, all that he saw, all that he heard, set him beside himself. He felt a fierce desire to get up and fling his cassock at the heads of all these people.

Custom had it that at dessert, the vicar-general, speaking for all the diocese, gave a little speech to the bishop. He was sentimental and pretentious, did not spare the eulogies and knew how to squeeze out a tear at the appropriate points.

When the moment came, he left his chair, dabbed his lips with a handkerchief, cleared his throat three times, as was the custom, and the attentive guests turned their moist gaze on him. He began amid an august silence:

"Monseigneur, on this day, blessed among all days, when the children of the holy Catholic and Apostolic Church of Rome, the children whom you guide with such fatherly care, with such admirable devotion, along the sacred paths of faith, of which Bossuet said . . ."

But he was suddenly interrupted. The Abbé had stood up, leant forward, his body right along the table, and was shaking his fist at the vicar:

"Shut up!" he shouted. "Why are you talking, who gave you the right? In whose name?"

The vicar-general was frozen into the pose he had struck up and the gesture half-begun. The bishop, extremely pale, subsided into his chair. One of the servers had swung round suddenly and knocked over a bottle of wine which smashed onto the floor. Everyone twisted their dangling chins towards the Abbé who, his voice vibrating, repeated:

"Shut up! What can you have to say of religion, of the Church? You are nothing, nothing! You are lies, covetousness, hatred . . . Shut up, you lie!"

Amid a deep silence which not a breath disturbed, in that deathly silence which follows the cataclysm, the Abbé went on:

"You are all lying. For an hour I have been watching you. And, when I see it worn by you, I am ashamed to wear this habit, I, I, the infamous priest, the thief, but who still is worth more than you! I know you, come along, worthless priests, dodgers of social duty, deserters of your country, who are only here because you feel too stupid or too cowardly to be men, to accept the sacrifices of the lives of petty people. And it is to you that souls are entrusted, who must shape them, mould them, you whose hands haven't yet had the stable muck properly wiped off them. Souls! Women's souls, children's souls, entrusted to you who have only ever had care of pigs! And you are the representatives of Christianity, you with your snouts of guzzling beasts, you who understand nothing of his sublime plan for human redemption, nor his great mission of love. It makes me want to laugh and cry at the same time. A soul is born and that means ten francs ... A soul dies and that's another ten francs ... And Christ died, didn't he, just to allow you to make a money box slit in the mystery of his tabernacle and change the chalice into a beggar's bowl. But when I hear you say the name of the Virgin, I feel as if I am witnessing the rape of a young girl by a ram ..."

Dull noises gradually swelled and soon became shouts of anger, furious protestations, indignant vociferation and drowned out his voice. Many had stood up, faces apoplectic and were shaking their napkins aloft, brandishing knives, gesturing angrily. Beyond the growing clamour could be heard the sharp clatter of silverware and crockery; the floor creaked; and on the shaking walls the earthenware plates rang, shaken on their hooks. Jules struggled, foamed, yelled into the din, striking out alternately with his clenched fists.

"Get out all of you! Get back to the manure, to the filth. I want you out of here, out of here!"

Then the bishop, paler than a corpse, motioned that he wished to speak and silence was restored immediately. His lips trembled, drained of blood, his teeth chattered. In a voice so faint that it was barely audible, in a voice painfully halting like that of a dying man, he said:

"Monsieur l'Abbé, I am the one you are driving out. You have ..."

"You?" cried Jules, and his eyes glowed briefly with a bloody madness, "You?"

He made as if to barge against an imaginary person.

"You? You have no right. You have stolen the gospel! A mitre for you? Do you know what you need? Four foot of chain and a ball."

The bishop uttered a cry, opened his mouth and grasping at the air with his chilled hands, fell back into his chair, his head lolling, arms limp, in a dead faint.

★

The following morning at dawn, Jules went out. He had packed his trunk and planned to leave on that very evening. But where could he go? He had no idea. In misfortune, a man looking for consolation turns first towards his father's house. Jules hated his home town; he had no fond memories of it, no sense of the joy of youth. The idea of returning to Viantais was unbearable. He would have to explain, listen to criticism, put up with sad or angry faces, listen to sighs and lamentations. None of that tempted him. He would have liked to hide somewhere, very far away, in a place where no-one knew him. Paris attracted him with its mystery and all the vague hopes of crime or regeneration which it inspires in the anonymous degraded. He had no money at all. And in any case what could he do there? He would have to see, think about it . . . While making a decision, he did not wish to stay in the palace, dreading meeting the Monseigneur or some other witness to his stupid misadventure. Off he went, preoccupied, ill at ease, uncertain, kicking pebbles as he went.

As he found himself on the road to Réno, it occurred to him to spend the day with Père Pamphile. After his last visit, he had been left with a great feeling of remorse and greatly impressed, and several times he had promised himself to revisit that sublime lunatic and reconcile himself with him. A mad idea even crossed his mind. Why not live at Réno himself and sort something out with the old Trinitarian? He would dig holes, move tree trunks, beg. No, it was absurd. Give up the priesthood? What wretchedness. The taint never left the man who had once worn the soutane. Disdain, suspicion, that was what awaited him on all sides. So, he thought. A self-sacrificing post in a distant mission? Would they want him though? A monastery? They would certainly not accept him. He thought again, found nothing and felt lost. And he was afraid. Harried, like a beast pursued by dogs, he walked along, bent low, his ears pricked, death in his soul.

The morning, garbed in limpid azure, smiled in the awakening trees; and scented mists rose from the earth which trembled beneath the kisses of the young sun.

A few steps from the avenue, Jules met an old woman, the same one he met before, carrying the bowl of soup for the monk. As on the other occasion, he asked her:

"Is Père Pamphile at the monastery?"

"Well, it's more than a fortnight since I saw 'im, and that by night, Father Sir," replied the old woman. "One day 'e was there and the next 'e wasn't."

"Ah."

"'E'll 'ave gone off on one of 'is trips 'e will, 'e's that keen!"

This absence was a real disappointment for Jules. He hesitated, wondering whether to continue on his way or turn back.

"Bah!" he said to himself, "spend my day there or elsewhere, it's all the same."

And he set off through the brambles along the avenue.

For a long while he wandered among the ruins. The winter which had just passed had been harsh on poor Réno. The thaws and storms had inflicted new and extensive damage. The Abbé saw again what he had seen before, but everything was a little more decayed, a little more derelict, a little more desolate, and the sight of those roofless buildings, those leaning, shaky walls, all the devastation, death, scattered amid the chaos of successive crumblings and continual fallings of rock, was bitterly sad and poignant for him. He read in the image of it all, destroyed for ever, the picture of his own heart, the symbol of his own life. He saw again the hole that Père Pamphile had dug, today almost completely filled by a landslide; another a little further on was the length of a man, narrow and deep like a grave. And he thought it would be good to lie down there, cover himself in darkness and sleep. The pick was stuck into the earth, next to the hole, the pick, illusory and crude instrument of the monk's dreams. Jules picked it up, weighed it in his hands, looked at it tenderly. The steel was dented, the handle twisted, and yet it seemed to him more resplendent than a conqueror's sword, that miserable pick-axe which had never dug more than the clouds of illusion. He carried on walking for a long while in the midst of that infinite desolation prey to funereal thoughts which eventually crushed his spirit. Everything reminded him of death. He could see it crouched behind every block of stone, lying in wait behind each crack in the walls, deep in the shadows of the window-frames, gaping from chasms; and on the old walls which were still standing, lichen and moss traced death's terrifying skeletal shape. To escape this obsession, he tried to think of the Trinitarian's beard, his eyes and their terrible beauty, when he cried: "I will build it!", so gently naive when he told the story about the *Marseillaise*.

"The *Marseillaise*!" muttered Jules to himself, with pity. "Poor old man."

He regretted he was not there on that so melancholy day. Seated next to him, he would have shared his black bread, listened to his eager projects and it would have done him good. But the old man was wandering on some distant road, doubtless, in pursuit of his chimera.

His head was spinning, his stomach empty and his weary limbs demanded some rest so he sat down on a fallen timber not far from the outhouse where Père Pamphile lived, and he went on thinking. In front of him was a pile of rubble that had recently collapsed, for the fragments of brick scattered all around showed a brighter, stronger red where they were broken. Crushed joists, broken planks, thrust their long, sharp splinters between the rubble-stones, bricks and blocks. At first, Jules gave this debris no more attention than the same very sad look that he accorded to all the debris of this kind with which the yards of the monastery were full; and despite his desire for death, judging the place to be dangerous, he went to look for shelter far from the buildings. But soon he noticed a clog in the rubble. The clog was sticking up in the air, motionless at the end of a round, black, swollen thing, glistening with greenish growths. Around the clog, flies flitted, thousands of flies, whose loud droning filled the Abbé's ears with an organ-like sound, a prolonged, monotonous note. At the same time, his nostrils caught a stink, the sour, musty odour of rotting flesh and dead animals.

"Oh no, Père Pamphile!" he cried.

He leapt up, called out as if anyone could hear him in this gloomy solitude.

"Help! Help! Over here! Help!"

Then he stopped, discouraged. In any case, no one replied to his cry of distress and silence fell.

Once the first horrified surprise was past, the Abbé realised that the help he sought was quite useless. The thing had happened about a fortnight ago, since the time the old monk was last seen and people thought he had gone away, but instead he was dead, killed by his beloved ruins.

Shuddering, he approached the heap of stones, his eyes transfixed by the clog above which the flies buzzed, and whose stiffness froze his heart with an inexpressible fear. It was indeed Père Pamphile. In the gaps in the rubble, Jules had glimpsed folds of white cloth stained with black blood.

"God led me here," he thought. Someone else could well have found him. People connected with the law, the church, body snatchers, would have come to get him.

He spoke aloud:

"Be assured, poor corpse, no one will tear you from the peace of this place you so cherished. You will sleep amid your dream, sweet dreamer; you will sleep in this chapel you wanted to be so impossibly magnificent and which at least you will have been able to make your sepulchre. No one will ever hear of you again, ever, holy corpse!"

Resolute, he rolled up his sleeves, bent over the debris and began to shift it. The flies whirled around him; the odour of decay intensified by the minute, a suffocating stench. But the Abbé did not notice the flies with their deadly sting; he could no longer smell the unclean reek. Not for a second did he interrupt his gloomy duty. Sometimes he tore off strips of decayed flesh which were sticking to fragments of wood, glued to pieces of brick; sometimes he pulled out bits of bloodied cloth, fistfuls of beard and sections of stringy, decomposed muscle. Finally, what had been Père Pamphile appeared; horrible remains where not even the position of the members nor the shape of the skeleton were recognisable any longer, a mass of flesh, bone, fabric muddled up higgledy-piggledy, a sticky mud of yellow pus and blackish blood, a moving mud which millions of maggots swelled with monstrous life. Of the crushed face, between a quarter-section of the skull and the bump of a cheekbone nothing was left intact but the round eye-socket whose liquefied pupil streamed in purulent tears.

Jules stopped, undecided, sweat standing out on his brow.

The hole near the church which he had chosen as Père Pamphile's burial place was about a hundred yards away. He could not carry those soft disintegrating remains in his arms; his courage did not extend as far as hugging to his breast those squalid remnants of a man. He looked for a wheelbarrow, a basket, something to help him transport the corpse to the ditch. Finding nothing, he undid his belt and wrapped it round the body, like the bindings of a mummy. With it supported in this way, he began to drag it along gently, carefully avoiding any too harsh jolts or sudden bumps on the uneven earth. The flies pursued him in their deafening swarm and the clog at the end of the stiffened leg quivered.

The ceremony did not take long. Jules lowered the body into the ditch and filled it right up. When it was done he said:

"I owed you at least that, sweet conqueror of stars, naive weaver of mists. Sleep and dream. Now the dream will have no end, no one can wake you. You are happy."

He took the pick, adorned it with a crown of brambles and drove its handle into the earth in the centre of the grave, like a cross.

Then he slumped to the ground, almost faint.

But a sudden feeling of rebellion soon made him get up again, his lips tight, his eyes hard. And while his gaze roamed from the oblong of earth beneath which Père Pamphile lay, to the site of the church, strewn with brambles and covered with dust, he thought:

"So is that what idealism comes to? Love, sacrifice, suffering, God, all that towards which we stretch out our arms and for which our souls yearn? Is that what it is? A bit of dust, mud, thorns? Is that what they use to stupefy us, from our earliest childhood, to tear us from true life, which is hate and merciless strife, and make us prey to fierce dreams and insatiable love! This wretched monk had a dream and had love! And the love and the dream first degraded him, humiliated him and soiled him with every shame, then killed him vilely. There he is now, a stinking corpse in a pile of mud. On what deformation of nature is it then that all religions, every society, all those lies rest? From what fiction did judges and priests emerge, those two moral monstrosities, the judge who seeks to impose on nature some unreal justice or other, belied by the fatal inevitability of instinct, the priest instead imposing some sort of weird pity, before the eternal law of Murder. Nature has nothing to do with dreaming, it's about living. And life is not about loving, it's about taking. Ideals . . . ideals . . . Those fat pigs I insulted yesterday were right. And I was wrong."

The Abbé shrugged his shoulders.

"Ideals!" he said again, aloud. "Wait, I'll show you some ideals!"

He adjusted his sleeves again, shook out his soutane and whistling an obscene song from his youth, set off, without casting a final look at the little corner of earth where he had just piously buried Père Pamphile.

Jules did not want to return to the town before the end of the day. He imagined that everyone must know of the scandal of the night before and were talking about it and he did not like the idea of presenting himself to the curious gossip-mongers who would undoubtedly follow his progress through the streets. Impatiently awaiting nightfall, he roamed about the paths on the outskirts, went down as far as the river and, vague and a little stunned, stayed for a long while beneath a willow, watching the wheel of a water-mill turning. Hunger, uncertainty, the fear of a very grim future, had driven his thoughts towards less philosophical speculations, more down to earth considerations. First, he put off till the next day, the departure which he had too hastily fixed for that same evening. Whatever might become of him later, he could not leave the bishop's palace without saying goodbye to the bishop, without displaying regret and repentance. But where would he go? Even if his transgression were to be forgotten some day, he foresaw long months, years perhaps, going by with him doing penance, kept well away from any proper position. Moreover, he had decided to refuse any possible exile to some small village parish. The idea of a parish made him think of the vicar-general and he felt hatred gnaw at his heart.

"That wretch is responsible for all that has befallen me," he said to himself. "He provoked me and so I let myself get carried away. Wretch! Wretch!"

At that moment, he wanted nothing more to do with society, religion, idealism or any individual; his only resentment was towards the vicar-general, the cause of his misfortune. And he dreamed of terrible, refined vengeance.

The most varied impressions formed, succeeded one another, colliding from one pole of his sensibility to the other. He thought of his month of Mary sermons, of his flattering reception in society; he recalled the charmed crowd tamed by his eloquence. Then a question posed itself, pregnant with problems:

"No, not in Viantais! But where? Nowhere. I have no friends." Recognising his loneliness, he felt his heart swell with sorrow. He came back to the vicar-general. He cursed him:

"Wretch! The filthy wretch!" Suddenly, a sigh:

"Ah that poor devil of a bishop. Well, he's going to be happy isn't he with a wretch like that." Almost cheerful:

"Isn't it strange how I cannot say anything or do anything without a catastrophe ensuing. It is true though ... I blow into a simple pipe and the trumpets of Jericho sound. I'm sure if I spit into this river, its banks will burst."

From the place where he sat, through a gap between the poplars in the valley, he glimpsed a corner of the town, houses piled one on the other, a jumble of blue shadows and pale splashes striped with russet haze, enveloped in the light mist of the encroaching evening. He sought out the bishop's palace, the terrace which he would no longer pace at dusk.

An enormous clump of alders obscured it. But the cathedral tower dominated the town, its dark, square mass solid in the pale violet sky. This vision of the place he was about to leave, driven away like a bad servant, moved and repelled him at one and the same time. Half tearful, half grumbling, he left his willow tree.

"Viantais! Viantais?" he thought. "I'd die of boredom there. It's impossible. But where else?"

As he climbed towards the town, the light waned and night fell.

Avoiding roads which were too wide or too well-lit, he made his way along the tortuous alleys of a rundown suburb: blackened walls, with abrupt turnings, narrow streets crisscrossed by little streams bearing rubbish, with here and there the reflection of a street lamp in the stagnant water. As he walked, Jules felt more and more anguished, uncertain as to whether he should carry on home or flee. He considered.

"See the bishop once more? There'll be more aggravation." Workmen were coming back home, their clogs resounding heavily on the paving stones; women's skirts brushed past him; gradually the walls showed bright spots of light. Suddenly, a lamp lit upon his left, above a half-open door which had an enormous number eight on its grimy glass; and in the shadows of the doorway, he saw a woman, fat, hair undone, in a white camisole. He slowed down and said to himself:

"What if I went in? If I spent the night there? If tomorrow in full daylight, in front of everyone, I came out of that vile den? If I dug that abyss between my life of yesterday and my life of tomorrow in one action? If . . . " A "psst" came from the doorway and lashed him like the crack of a whip across his back. He shuddered, hunched his shoulders and walked on.

"Monseigneur has been asking for Monsieur l'Abbé all day long," said the porter with a dignified air when Jules set foot in the courtyard of the bishop's palace. "Monseigneur has been waiting for Monsieur l'Abbé in his office. I am requested to inform Monsieur l'Abbé that . . ."

"That's fine," interrupted Jules curtly.

He reached his room, rinsed his face, changed his soutane and went to see the bishop. The latter was indeed waiting for him.

"I feared you had left," he said and, pointing to a chair, "Sit down, Monsieur l'Abbé."

The old priest was neither solemn nor angry; he seemed embarrassed, rather. Having shifted his position several times in his seat, he said gently:

"Monsieur l'Abbé . . . I do not want any scandal in my diocese . . . I really do not want it . . . and I was promised that there would not be any . . . it was promised to me formally . . . For your part . . ."

He folded his arms, resting them on the arms of his chair, shook his head.

"For your part," he continued, "you will understand that you must not, you cannot stay here, after the event . . ."

"Monseigneur!" stuttered Jules, profoundly moved, "that was a moment of madness . . . of . . . of . . . of . . ."

He sought words but could not find them. Faced with this poor old fellow, so weak, so incapable of defending himself, so meanly and so often victimised by him, Jules felt an indefinable sense of numbness, sharp remorse and overwhelming pity. The bishop reminded him of a tiny bird, a tiny wren landed confidently on his shoulder and which he had taken in his hands and slowly throttled. The bishop struggled on:

"We have a vacant parish . . . the parish of Randonnai. It's a good parish. I thought I would set it aside for you as I do not want any scandal. There will be some difficulties perhaps but I will sort it all out. Go back to your mother. I have written and told her that you need rest; and pray, pray a great deal, Monsieur l'Abbé . . . pray as much as you can."

Jules was weak with emotion. He wished he could express what he felt of infinite sweetness and infinite cruelty too. He could not. Something unknowable still paralysed his brain, his heart, his tongue and, suddenly stupid, he kept on stammering:

"Monseigneur . . . It was a moment of madness . . . of . . . of . . . of . . . madness!"

"I too will pray for you, Monsieur l'Abbé," said the bishop, his voice breaking.

He stood up.

"Goodbye. Go back to your room. I have asked for your supper to be served to you in your room."

That evening, in his bed, Jules, who could not sleep, lay deep in thought, considering Père Pamphile and the bishop.

"Are they saints? Are they fools? How can such souls exist? It terrifies me."

Two months later, Jules was nominated parish priest of Randonnai.

He arrived one very gloomy Saturday morning, just in time to bury the village notary. The funeral was magnificent and of the highest class. This cheered the new priest up considerably as he sprinkled holy water around the tomb and thought to himself:

"This is a good start. Let's hope it goes on like this." The church looked a miserable affair to him, sad and gloomy with a low, cramped ceiling and huge pillars supporting arches of a vulgar design.

"A real cave!" he thought. "The good Lord must get really fed up in there." Then he examined the priests who had come from neighbouring parishes to be present at the ceremony and they examined him too with furtive glances slipped slyly from behind their Psalters. He thought as he suppressed a grimace, showering the deceased with incense and prayers:

"So that's what I have to live with. That is going to be fun. Where have I seen all those nasty faces before?" He noticed one man, his hair glossy with pommade, whose plump and very pink face seemed particularly familiar:

"Good God!" he recalled. "I do believe . . . It's the rabbit from the seminary."

In the cemetery, while he intoned Latin verses, he spotted a sheaf of straw near the trench. Breaking off suddenly, he turned to a fat cantor standing behind him, a fellow with the drunkard's pimply complexion and who stank of wine:

"What is that?"

The cantor replied hoarsely:

"It's straw, Father."

"I can see it's straw . . . but what is it doing there?"

"In effect it's for the sake of the relatives . . . We put it in the coffin and it stops the noise of the earth falling onto the lid . . ."

"Take that straw away!" ordered the priest. "I do not want that straw here."

"But all the families like it, Father. It's the custom."

"Well the custom will change. Take that straw away, I told you. And as for you, I would be grateful if from now on you would not get drunk until after the service."

And he started his Latin verses again, without paying any attention to the whispering and murmuring amid the crowd.

The following day, at the first mass, he climbed into the pulpit and spoke to his parishioners as follows:

"My brothers, when I arrived here yesterday, I noticed with sorrow that you have some deplorable habits which I beg you, order you if necessary, to give up, for I warn you that I will not tolerate them. What was the meaning of that straw spread on the coffins? Death is a noble mystery which I would like you to respect above all other mysteries. Is it respectful to surround it with the shameful bedding such as you give your animals? I was told that it was out of regard for the living, to spare them the sound of the clods of earth falling onto the bare planks of the coffin. Cowardly hearts that know not even how to weep and reject the suffering that is God's gift! Well, I request that a greater regard is accorded to the dead. I wish that a stranger present by chance at a service in my parish might not say to himself when he sees straw being brought to the graves:

"So they're grilling a pig there, are they?"

Then he made a broad sign of the cross and mumbled:

"In the name of the Father and of the Son and of the Holy Ghost. Amen," and began to recite the lesson and paraphrase the gospel of the day.

For a long time people in Randonnai spoke of this oratorical début of the new priest which made a profound impression on souls.

The presbytery was situated on the outskirts of the town. Screened against the prying eyes of neighbours by a thick arbour and some tall fir trees, its only outlook was onto the open spaces of the undulating fields. Jules liked its isolation and silence. The house was clean, cheerful, newly painted in white, with green shutters and a little double flight of stairs adorned with extravagantly intertwined fronds of wisteria. The staircase led down into a huge garden with many sandy paths which all met at a centre point with a statue of the Virgin at its heart, in the shade of a laurel. An apple orchard adjoined the garden. There was nothing lacking to make life agreeable, the outbuildings were well-preserved and the yard perfectly set up for the raising of fowl and rabbits. Jules did not have to endure too much familiarity with his curate either. He lived in a little wing of his own among the outbuildings and very discreetly never showed himself except at meals. However, once his daily calls were over, he was bored. Everywhere he went he received a very chilly welcome which he attributed to the business at the bishop's palace, without considering that his first sermon was sufficient to justify the frosty manner of his parishioners. Besides, he was not concerned:

"They can stay in their houses, me in mine. That's what I prefer." That was all.

Far from finding relief in this calm retreat from the world, his nerves became even more stretched, to the point where moral sickness was added to real physical suffering. He could not sleep; restlessness in all his limbs drove him from his bed and he spent entire nights pacing his room, his heart swollen with some black sorrow. His mother was gravely worried.

Madame Dervelle had come to Randonnai to help her

son settle in. She had applied to the management of the presbytery all her skill as thrifty and tactful mistress of the house, taking care with the tiniest details, as well as all her virtue as a tender mother. She had chosen the cook herself, a woman who was neither too old nor too young, and there was a gardener who could handle all other jobs. She had sorted out the day-to-day expenses and managed people and the running of the place with all the competence of an accomplished housekeeper. One evening, after dinner, the table had been cleared and Madame Dervelle was knitting. Jules, his brow furrowed, sat thinking. Since the curate had left, neither had said a word.

"Well, son?"

"Sorry?"

"What are you thinking about?"

"Nothing."

"Are you wiser, calmer now perhaps?"

"Yes, mother."

And Jules stood up, walked around in the room, feverish, nervous, shifting the chairs.

"You say yes," sighed Madame Dervelle, "but in a tone which is hardly reassuring, my poor Jules. And then, you always seem agitated, worried. One can't say a thing to you without straightaway ... whoosh! you're off! Are you sick?"

"No."

"Well, what is the matter?"

"Nothing!"

And suddenly, stopping, he yelled:

"All right, it's true! What do you expect me to do in this godforsaken place peopled with idiots? Is this the right job for me? Frankly, is this a job at all?"

Madame Dervelle rested her knitting on her lap, discouraged.

"What do you mean? You have an excellent living, your presbytery is charming. You could be the happiest of men living here. What more can you ask, for heaven's sake?"

Jules set off walking again, stamping his foot.

"What do I ask? How should I know? Something else. There! I feel that there are things in me ... things ... things that are frustrated and are stifling me and which cannot see the light of day in the absurd existence of a village priest, to which I am eternally condemned. In short, I have a brain and a heart, I have thoughts, aspirations which ask only to be given wings to fly far far away. To fight, sing, conquer new races and bring them to the Christian faith ... I don't know ... but a village priest!"

He uttered a long sigh followed immediately by an angry groan.

"Village priest or gooseherd, it's one and the same. Do you remember fat old Abbé Gibory?"

"Who was so funny?" interrupted my grandmother, thinking to introduce a bit of gaiety into her son's expression. "Ah, I do remember! He used to make us laugh so!"

"Make us laugh!" continued Jules, who was getting angrier. "Just so. A fat pig who did nothing but tell stories about cack. Is that your ideal then? To see priests wallow in their own filth? Well, don't worry, in a few years I'll be like Abbé Gibory, I'll imitate the sound of diarrhoea coming out too and say: *Urghhh! Urghhh! The apricots!*"

"Come along," begged his mother, "calm down, difficult child. Just have a little patience, a little courage and you will be everything you hope for. The bishop is right, you lose your head ..."

"The bishop? Huh! What does he know? Why did he send me here? Anyway, it's your fault that I'm a priest."

The poor woman trembled on her chair and made a gesture of astonished denial.

"My fault?" she groaned. "Oh, my Lord Jesus! What are you saying now? Just remember! Try to remember!"

"Yes, your fault, your fault."

He lost his temper.

"And frankly being a priest disgusts me. I have had enough of wearing this ludicrous dress ... of making stupid faces even more ridiculous than this dress, of living like a slave and a eunuch."

His voice had become dull and veiled, the words wrenched from his throat with violent effort.

"I want ... I want to be Peter the Great ... Jules II ... Robespierre ... Bossuet ... Napoleon ... Lamartine ... I want to take a wife!"

My poor grandmother let out a cry and, helpless against the flood of tears she had been holding back since the start of this scene, she sobbed:

"My God, my God, you have the devil in you!"

"Good!" said Jules harshly. "So you're crying now? I'm going now. Good night."

He went out, slamming the door.

After his mother left, the presbytery seemed very empty. He had become used to seeing her there, so sweet, so thoughtful, so active, constantly on the move around the house to which she brought something of the serenity, purity and peace of her soul. There were moments when it did him good to look upon her white bonnet, white as the wings of a guardian angel and on her little black shawl, touching and modest, beneath which she concealed so much simple courage and such goodness. And now that she was no longer there, there was only the same frozen immobility of his surroundings, the same garden, the same horizon, the same curate with his blondish hair and freckled face, smiling and mute. When he was face to face with his curate, whose silence irritated him but whose conversation he suspected would have irritated him still more, the weight of his loneliness was so heavy that he felt he could not bear it any longer. However, he shut himself away all the more, determined to see no one and restrict his relations with his fellow human-beings to the strict obligations of his ministry. He received no one at his table and refused all invitations, to the despair of the curate, who was used to joyful feasts at which he said not a word but took an enormous silent pleasure. As for meetings, he neglected to attend and found scornful excuses for them not to be held in his house. Once the young curate reproached him for this abstention and Jules replied:

"I pay my dues and I leave you your share of the dinner.

What more do you want? I have neither the taste nor the stomach for those little canonical binges. When I want to indulge some base whim of my own, I do it alone and in private."

Fundamentally, the important thing was that he paid his dues. At one of the dinners it was agreed that he should be left in peace.

"He is so charming!"

"He's a bear with a sore head."

"A bear! A scourge!"

This witticism was so colossally successful that afterwards Jules was referred to in all the presbyteries as 'the scourge'.

His behaviour as a priest was exactly as it had been in the bishop's employ and he lost no time in shaking the parish up from top to bottom. To escape boredom, he amused himself by dismissing the cantors, the beadle, the verger and the sacristan. Right down to the choirboys, he replaced the entire personnel of the church, overturned the church fabric committee by dishonest manipulation of authority and set himself up in open implacable hostility against the mayor and the town council. Soon, hatred of the priest bred a spirit of irreligiousness which blew through this little corner of the land, beforehand so calm and submissive. Something was seen that had never been seen before: a non-church burial. On Sundays at service times, the church was practically empty of worshippers, apart from a few obstinate devout who did not count, being, so to speak, part of the church furniture. The situation reached such a level of intensity that the mayor and the priest met one morning behind the cemetery on a path, fell to quarrelling and fought like servants. An anonymous denunciation sent to the bishop, contained the following:

"Finally, Monseigneur, since the arrival of the priest Dervelle, the number of taverns, which was only eighteen in a population of 1,053 souls has increased in scandalous proportions. There are now forty-six. It is the moral ruin of the parish."

These distractions were not sufficient to fill Jules' days. While continuing to exasperate his parishioners with incessant provocations, he then had whims and caprices to which he abandoned himself with delight and which did not last and were followed by other whims and caprices, quickly abandoned. In turn, he cultivated tulips, learned English, raised pheasants, collected minerals, began a work on religious philosophy which was to regenerate the world: *The Seed of Life*, a very vague and symbolic work in which he spoke of atheist and Babylonian Christs in dream landscapes. His head ablaze, he would make wild gestures, describing grandiose thoughts and settings and suddenly say:

"There, some columns. And Jesus moves amid the crowds. A woman comes towards him, hideous, blind, her feet are claws: 'Who are you? – I am Human Justice.' Jesus pushes her away and says: 'You will make no judgement.' Another woman appears, smiling, with the body and eyes of a child: 'Who are you? – I am Madness.' And Jesus kisses her and says: 'Go in peace, my daughter and multiply . . .'"

The difficulties of the writing process brought him to a halt in the second chapter and he devoted himself to a polemical work: *The Recruitment of the Clergy, or The Reform of Religious Teaching*, of which he wrote only a few pages, as he was lacking certain documents, which led him to his passion for a library again. Then he threw himself into spiritism. In the evenings, seated between the silent, worried curate and the dozing, stupefied gardener, he sat around a table and until midnight called up Solomon, Caligula, Isabella of Bavaria, the terrible kings of Nineveh, the Shulamite and Marie-Antoinette. Then, descending from the heights of magical speculation, one day he turned up in the kitchen. He surveyed the dishes, tasting the sauces, inventing complex dishes, eating with insatiable piggery, with the result that he woke in the night with painful, terrible, exhausting indigestion.

For ten years he lived like this, in a state of siege, breathless, without a moment's respite from others or from himself, ever buffeted from the crudest of lusts to the most unrealisable dream, precipitated from heights haunted only by eagles down to the filthy trough where pigs wallow. This period of his life was a long torture and I am still astonished today that he did not attempt to tear himself from it by suicide. He had said to his mother and often said to himself:

"I sense that there are things in me which are suffocating me and cannot come out."

And I wondered sometimes what man my uncle would have been if this cauldron of lava of thoughts and passions which devoured his whole being had found an outlet for proper development. Perhaps he would have been a great saint, a great artist or a great criminal!

Far from being stupefied by the narcotic of habit, his character became more acerbic day by day. Anger took the form of a real madness of fury in him. It was a distressing spectacle to see this eloquent man reaching the point of not being able to finish a sentence and only able to use swear words, soon drowned in an epileptic babble. His opinion of people would be summed up in this sound, something like a sneeze:

"Allimb'ziles!"

When anyone spoke to him of priests, his eyes seemed to go purple and bloodshot and stand out from his head.

"Imb'ziles! Imb'ziles!"

He neglected himself and became disgustingly dirty. His soutane was squalid and full of holes, the straps on his sabots flapped, he wore an eight-day old beard. As he passed by no one addressed him and children fled squealing at his approach.

Sometimes though, he could be seen walking through the fields as if floating above the ground, raised up by the grandeur of his gestures. He was thinking about his interrupted project, *The Seeds of Life*.

"Here and over there, the Oceans . . . above, the Heavens . . . And Jesus stands amid the motionless waves of the sky and the troubled waves of the seas. He says to Space: 'You will swell the organs where the poet's soul sings.' He says to the Infinite: ' You will dwell in the gaze of women, idiots, the poor and the new-born.'"

This intellectual disorder and moral disorientation was aggravated by a typhoid fever which almost killed him. My father abandoned his clients and sat by Jules' bed and cared for him with admirable devotion. Later he recounted this particular detail. The delirium took a specific form in the Abbé's case, which was so scandalisingly erotic that the nun who was caring for him left. At the height of his fevers, he would utter terrible words and carry out acts of terrifying inappropriateness. His hands had to be tied down. His convalescence was lengthy and further complicated by the irritable temperament of the patient, who never ceased to insult my father.

"'Mb'zile! Get lost. It's you giving me the fever. What do you know? 'Mb'zile."

He only left his bed to attend my grandmother's funeral. She was found dead one morning in her bed, killed by a stroke. Jules wept sincere tears.

"She died of sorrow," he cried. "I am a miserable wretch. She was so good, so saintly, so holy. I killed her!"

With my father and mother he watched over the corpse and wanted to bury her himself.

"You are still weak," said my father. "Rest, you will do yourself harm."

But Jules repeated:

"No, no. I killed her. It was me. Why did you get me well again? Why did she have to die?"

At the cemetery, when the grave was filled and as the crowd dispersed, he fought for the holy-water sprinkler and knelt on the damp earth, beating his breast with extravagant gestures.

"Gentlemen," he groaned, "ladies, I killed her. Forgive me!"

He had to be dragged away in a faint. That evening, he refused to hear anyone speak of my grandmother's will in which she divided her fortune between her two sons.

"Don't anyone say anything to me about that. I do not want any money. I am giving everything to the poor."

But the following day, having thought over the details of the will, he forgot his sorrow and grew angry.

"Oh no! Oh dear no! I do not accept that. I have been robbed. I'll appeal."

Later, he showed a ferocious harshness in the division of the household possessions and threatened to send lawyers round to my father over a tea towel or a saucepan.

Finally, once affairs were in order and he had his inheritance in his grasp, he sold everything he had and left for Paris.

For six years he gave no sign of life. Was he dead or alive? What was he doing? My father tried in vain to gather information. He learned that Jules had left his parish without authorisation and that was all. Whenever Monsieur Bizieux, a Viantais draper went to Paris to buy, my father always begged him to ask around, to look, to search the streets. Who knows? Perhaps by chance . . . ! Monsieur Bizieux would always come back:

"Well I certainly saw plenty of people. That wasn't the problem . . . But no Monsieur l'Abbé."

Once, in the rue Greneta, he had passed someone who looked remarkably like him. But it was not the Abbé. Another time, in a café . . .

"In a café!" said my mother. "That must have been him."

Then my father thought he found a means of getting in touch with him and wrote letters addressed to:

Monseigneur the Archbishop of Paris: to be forwarded to Monsieur l'Abbé Jules Dervelle, parish priest of Randonnai.
Paris

The letters remained unanswered. Days went by, then months and years. Maintaining in spite of everything affection for this bad brother whose life he had saved, my father from time to time, intrigued and sad would ask:

"What can he have been up to in Paris?"

Chapter Four

"Well, he's arriving," cried my father, breathlessly waving a letter as he came into the bedroom where my mother was dressing me. "He is arriving tomorrow on the three o'clock train."

"Tomorrow," said my mother, in a resigned tone. "Very well."

And she added, being a well-organised woman full of foresight:

"Make sure you reserve the large carriage. He is bound to have a great deal of luggage. I will be going to the butcher's."

"That's it! What do you think, sweetheart?"

"What?"

"If we invited the Robins to dine tomorrow with the good priest? Eh? It's quite an occasion . . ."

"As you wish. Which room shall we give him?"

"Indeed, yes! The blue room I think."

My mother pouted in annoyance.

"So there we are. Nothing but the best for him. What else? Shall we warm his bed for him?"

"Come along, come along," said my father soothingly. "We can hardly put him in the boxroom, can we? After all, when all's said and done, he is my brother."

"Ah yes, your brother. He has really acted like a brother to you. Well, this is what you wish and I will say nothing, but God willing you won't regret it."

This happened a week after the evening when the Robins and my family had discussed my uncle Jules at such length. It was a Tuesday as I recall. I awaited the following day with feverish impatience, anxious for something abnormal, enormous, which would break the monotony of our existence. The whole day, my father was even more excitable than usual, almost in a state of joy. My mother was very serious and thoughtful. At dinner, she did not open her lips except to ask with a note of sarcasm in her voice:

"Do you know what he takes for breakfast after his mass, this brother of yours? Do we need to prepare something special for him?"

"Oh I should think not," replied my father boldly. "He'll have what we do, soup."

My mother shook her head doubtfully.

"It's just that in Paris he must have acquired certain habits and we are not millionaires."

I slept very badly that night, prey to painful dreams in which the grimacing face of my uncle appeared and reappeared.

Viantais had no railway station at that time and was served by Coulanges station which was ten miles away on the other side of the town. That was where we were to meet the Abbé. At first, Father Sortais intended to join us, but the weather was cold and the old priest suffered from rheumatism and so preferred to save himself till dinner. The Robins had come over several times, bustling, very agitated, offering their services as if we were being menaced by some danger. They would really have liked to accompany us to Coulanges station, but as they did not know the Abbé that would have seemed strange.

"We cannot," mused Madame Robin, who was very well up on etiquette. "That would be most irregular. Still, you will pass by at four o'clock. We can watch from the window."

"I," announced the magistrate, in the tone of a general giving a rendezvous to his soldiers on the battlefield, "I shall be in the square."

"Right, right. And then this evening, come early."

"Till this evening!"

The large carriage arrived at last before our gateway in a great scrunching of gravel. It was a very old barouche, venerable and falling to pieces, which my father hired from the Three Kings Inn for memorable occasions. I loved it because it only had happy associations for me, outings and parties. Besides, it always seemed to me, as I sat on its grey silk cushions, that my little personality immediately gained in importance and I must be attracting people's admiration, being drawn by two horses on four wheels, like Monsieur Blandé himself. So, it was full of real emotion, combined with a slight swelling of pride, that I seated myself in the antiquated vehicle on the front seat, facing my parents who were seated at the back and were very serious and self-important too. We proceeded through the town in triumph. From their doorways people smiled at me. And I was happy, though struggling to keep up a dignified mien.

"My goodness me, it really is nice in this carriage," said my father as we left the town, and he closed the glass window and covered his and my mother's knees with the old eiderdown which served as a travel rug for us.

The carriage rolled on, its iron-clad wheels resounding, jolting over the stony road, and my parents fell silent, gradually more worried and thoughtful as we approached Coulanges. As for me, my heart was beating faster and faster and through the closed window, dulled by the vapour of our breath, I watched vague shapes, silhouettes of trees and corners of bleak sky go flashing by.

As we cleared the level crossing, my mother, who up till then had not shifted from her corner, suddenly leaned towards the window and wiped the film off with her sleeve and our three gazes simultaneously followed the line of the rails, to beyond the station and were lost in the mysterious, foggy darkness out of which Abbé Jules would soon appear in a belch of smoke. She rearranged her veil, smoothed the crumpled ribbons of her bonnet and adjusted the knot of my tie:

"Now listen to me, my little Albert," she said, "you are going to have to be very good with your uncle and not put on that sulky manner you have so often with strangers. After all, he is your uncle. You will go up to him and kiss him and you will say, now listen hard, you will say, 'My dear godfather, I am very, very pleased that you are back.' That's not difficult now, is it? Repeat your little speech."

In a trembling voice, I repeated:

"My dear godfather, I am . . ."

But an emotion, fear, struck me silent. As soon as I uttered the words, I seemed to see an atrocious, diabolical image rise up before me, the threatening image of my uncle. And I just gaped.

"Come along!" said my father. "Pull yourself together. And wipe off that funereal look. For Heaven's sake! He won't eat you. Am I afraid? Is your mother afraid? Well then!"

Despite my own emotion, I noticed that my father's voice was very slightly different and he was not as unconcerned as he wished to appear.

We were half an hour early. Though the air was icy and cutting, we walked on the station platform, never taking our eyes off the station clock whose hands moved slowly, so very slowly. A train stopped and left again, leaving behind only a poor soldier who wandered around and about us for a while foolishly, then disappeared, dragging one leg.

"Still seventeen minutes to go," sighed my father. "The Abbé is in Bueil at this moment."

The silence of the little station, broken only by the ringing of the telegraph and the sound of the bells on our carriage horses' harness, tinkling from the other side of the barrier as the horses shook their manes, made a fearful impression on me, intensifying my dread. In this silence, things took on a worrying immobility, an animal, almost sinister immobility. The distance towards Paris, disappeared into space, full of menace, like those heavy leaden skies which threaten hail. Lost in my thoughts, I did not hear my mother saying to me:

"Pay attention to what I said. Try to smile. Don't act like a mummy."

With a wavering eye, I traced the unfurling of the rails which crawled on the yellow earth like long snakes.

A few travellers and some country folk emerged from the waiting room. The station master appeared, bustling, some platform staff went by, pushing packages and parcels.

"There's the train!" said my father. "Stand back!"

At that moment I heard the sound of a whistle, at first in the distance, then growing nearer, a whistle that pierced my heart like a knife. The braying of a horn replied. Then there was a thundering sound like a furious beast, the terrifying rumbling of an avalanche tumbling onto us. I thought all this row, the shuddering of the earth and sky, I thought all the gasping, whistling, howling and spitting of flame and vomiting of smoke, I thought all that was my uncle and I shut my eyes. Then for a few seconds I felt myself dragged, tugged in all directions, jostled against all the parcels.

"Stand up straight!" my mother was saying. "Come along Albert, pet, look what you're doing . . ."

All of a sudden I had stopped still. I opened my eyes and before me I saw a long, black, angular creature climbing down backwards out of a carriage, a creature which ended with an enormous foot below, flailing in the void, searching for a secure foothold. All three of us stood behind this thing, at whose side flapped an overnight bag, bound with red and green straps, all three of us stood in a single, military line, anxious and pale. Not one of us moved, immobilised by emotion as we were. The thing turned round and, amid the sharp angles, the dark shadows, beneath the hat were two strange eyes, angry eyes. Between those eyes, a voracious, pointy nose, like that of a dog, quested, and a glare that could not be withstood, fastened on us. This was my uncle.

"Good afternoon! Good afternoon! Good afternoon!" he muttered, giving each of us a brief nod, dry and hard like a click.

My father hastened to kiss him. But the Abbé, holding out his bag in an imperious gesture, cut short his effusions.

"That's fine. Yes, later. Have you transport? Good. Let's go. What are you waiting for?"

"What about your luggage?" my mother asked.

"Do not worry about my luggage. Let's go."

Muttering, he made his way towards the exit. He could not find his ticket and argued with the ticket collector.

"Oh, here it is . . . and try to be civil . . . imbecile."

My father was concerned, my mother shrugged her shoulders, as if to say, "Well now, wasn't I right? He's worse than ever." As for me, in the confusion of this arrival, I had forgotten my little speech.

We got back into the carriage. My mother and my uncle took their seats at the back; my father and I sat in front. I did not dare look up for fear of meeting my uncle's gaze. He sat hunched, the flaps of his overcoat folded around him. My mother offered him a corner of the rug. He examined the back and then the front, seemed amazed, then wrapped himself in it, without uttering a word of thanks. The carriage set off again. My mother's expression had become impassive and hard again. My father was very embarrassed and did not know what to say. However, he plucked up courage:

"Did you have a good journey?" he asked timidly.

"Yes," muttered the Abbé.

There was a painful silence which no one felt inclined to break. The Abbé tried to squint at the countryside through the small window, but condensation fogged the view. He pulled the window down with such a brusque action that it broke and a thousand tiny pieces of glass showered onto us.

"It doesn't matter, really it doesn't matter," declared my father, who doubtless hoped to soften the fearful Jules with his magnanimity.

And he added smiling:

"Apart from anything else, broken glass brings luck."

My uncle did not reply. His body leaning slightly forward, he looked out at the countryside.

From Coulanges to Viantais, the road is charming. For the whole journey, it runs along a valley, a broad expanse of different shades of green, where the Cloche flows, a winding river adorned here and there by old mills on its banks. That day, it had flooded and covered expanses of meadows turning them into strange lakes, where clumps of leafless willows and rows of poplars emerged, lakeside vegetation, reflected in the motionless, sleeping water. Parallel to the valley, and enclosing it like the fencing of an enormous circus, the hills rose, villages clinging to their slopes. Sometimes, between the contours of the lowlands, could be seen very distant horizons, an infinity of land, as insubstantial as clouds. And over all this, the exquisite winter light which covered the trees in a sprinkling of cracked varnish, all the fine tones, all the fuzzy greys which give opaque mass the fluidity of waves and the transparency of sky.

The Abbé seemed absorbed by this contemplation of his surroundings and the expression on his face softened. A little of this soothing light had passed into his eyes. My father took advantage of it to tap him amicably on the knee.

"I say!" he said, finally overcoming the pain caused him by Jules' welcome. "It really is nice to see you again. After so long! More than six years, by Jove! Sometimes I said to myself 'Well, we'll never see each other again!' Ah, we have thought about you often, my poor Jules."

He seemed not to hear and went on looking out. Suddenly he said:

"But it's a beautiful place!"

My uncle had spoken in a less harsh voice, as if touched.

"Very beautiful, very beautiful."

In fact, he was seeing it for the first time, this place where he was born and lived all his youth. Nature does not speak to the child nor to the young man. To understand its infinite beauty, one must view it with ageing eyes, with a soul which has loved and suffered.

Jules repeated:

"Very beautiful, yes. Those houses and that little clock tower . . . isn't that Brolles?"

"Yes!" replied my father, delighted to see his brother relax somewhat. "That's Brolles. So you recognise it? And there, by the little wood?"

"That's Father Flamand's house. Is he still alive?"

"Still, just imagine it. But the poor fellow is blind. Heavens, he's more than eighty now. You'll not go fishing with him any more . . ."

The Abbé was gripped by a fit of coughing and my father fretted:

"You must change places. I fear you have taken cold with that open window."

"No, no, leave me, I'm happy."

Then I examined my uncle at my leisure as he fell to dreaming again. His features settled into my consciousness again, where they had been only a faded pastel sketch. I now remembered I had seen him before. I could now recall all the peculiarities of that strange and ugly face, that twisted body, and the way the flame in those two lively, dreaming eyes, troubled and fierce, enthusiastic and sad, lent an extraordinary and disconcerting life to his features. How he had aged! He was bent as an octogenarian; his narrow, sunken chest drew breath with difficulty and sometimes an asthmatic wheeze escaped from him; wrinkles scythed in all directions over his greenish, thin mask of a face and flaccid flaps of skin hung below his chin. In that ravaged visage, the only aspect which had retained any youth, apart from the eyes, was the nose, a nose of astonishing mobility whose nostrils quivered like a colt's.

"Are you sick? Are you ill?" enquired my father.

"No, why do you ask that? Am I changed?"

"Changed! Changed! That's not the right word. Heavens! It's just the same for me, no one's getting any younger."

"Naturally," agreed my mother, who hitherto had not opened her mouth.

And in a dry voice, she added:

"And Paris is so unhealthy. But never mind, Viantais is nice and peaceful, rather gloomy when one is used to Paris. There not much to do, not like Paris."

She emphasised the word Paris with a dull rancour against the city which had sent him back, ruined, doubtless, and ill, a relative that would have to be cared for and fed, for nothing.

My uncle gave my mother a hostile sidelong look, a look full of hatred, then huddled up in the corner of the carriage and stayed silent beneath the large hat which enveloped his face in a veil of shadow.

We had passed the village of Quatre-Vents. Evening was falling. A dense mist rose from the fields as in a dream, drowning the hills and trees, whose bare summits frayed in the milky atmosphere. When we reached Viantais, a few reddish lights were glowing in the windows of the houses. In the square, I glimpsed a shadow, the shadow of Monsieur Robin, who gesticulated in the fog and greeted the carriage with broad waves of his top hat. I felt deeply moved. Throughout the whole journey my uncle had not once looked at me. However, he did not frighten me, despite his gruff manners and unseemly harshness. A child's obscure instinct told me that he was an unquiet, suffering soul. I am sure that if at that moment he had addressed a gentle word to me, kissed me, if he had just smiled at me as a few moments before he had smiled at nature regained, I would have loved him.

Led by my father, who was carrying his overnight bag, he reached with difficulty the blue room, prepared for him. Climbing the stairs had made him gasp for air. He was also terribly over-excited. From the moment he crossed the threshold of our house – the family home which my grandmother had given us in her will and in which we had lived since her death – the Abbé's whole manner changed. Every object he recognised was a visible source of pain and irritation. Did he regret that the house was not his? Or was it perhaps that the memories of the past which it evoked emphasised for him more harshly the irreparable voids in his life? He rummaged in his room, impatient, ruminating over old rancours in his heart, and paid no attention to his brother's solicitude, who said:

"We put you in there because the room has a very lovely view towards Saint-Jacques. Look, here you have a cupboard, there is your washstand. I have had the whole house renovated. Ah, it is so good to see each other again, isn't it? Do you need hot water?"

"No!" replied the Abbé.

It was a 'no' that was like a slap. But my father went on:

"The bell is there in the alcove. You . . ."

He was soon interrupted:

"Leave me in peace. You annoy me with all your explanations. What about your wife? She annoys me too. Am I here to put up with interrogations, to be spied upon? Don't worry, I won't be troubling you for long . . ."

"Troubling us? You jest? You are not thinking of leaving?"

"Whether I am staying or going is of no consequence to you. I do not like being pestered. So, shut up!"

"Come along Jules, don't lose your temper. I was hoping that you would stay with us for ever!"

"With you?" sneered the Abbé. "What a ridiculous idea! With you?"

He raised his arms to the ceiling, indignant, astonished.

"With you? And what would I do with you, good God? You are out of your mind."

In his turn, my father lost his temper.

"Very well, do what you like. We dine at six. This evening we have the priest and the Robin family, friends of ours."

A priest opening the tabernacle and spotting of a sudden a toad inside the holy chalice could not have been more aghast than my uncle at this news. At first he was overwhelmed. Then his eyes grew huge and fiery. Gradually his face turned red and blotchy and he twitched like an epileptic, then in a hoarse voice, shot through with anger, he stuttered:

"Idiot! Cretin! Imbecile! I arrive and immediately you get your friends together. So I'm some strange beast am I? I'm a spectacle for you and your friends. You said to them, 'Abbé Jules, a crazy fellow, very odd, a sacrilegious priest! You'll see, you'll be able to touch him and see he's not a trick but a living being.' You're hoping to treat yourself to the little pleasure of showing me off like a bear in a zoo, a fairground freak, a five-legged sheep. And you really think that I am going to stay a moment longer in your hovel with an imbecile like you and a pretentious fool like your wife. You really think so? I am going to a hotel, to a hotel you hear, a hotel."

He put his coat back on, shut his bag and muttered:

"I am going to a hotel. Goodnight."

The Abbé walked out in front of my appalled father, went down the stairs and left. The gate could be heard clanging shut behind him.

Dinner was gloomy and silent. Father Sortais did not eat at all, his stomach disturbed by this unbelievable occurrence. From time to time he asked:

"So he just left? Just like that?"

And at my father's nod:

"But that's impossible, impossible!"

Twice, in the silence, the magistrate threw out a few words to summarise his important conclusions:

"Taris, Taris! Of course. Well, there you are . . ."

Madame Robin sat very stiffly, preserving the dignity of a woman offended by the unseemly departure of the Abbé. She regretted having put on her dress of antique silk in his honour, her dress for solemn feasts, having displayed all her jewels, inaugurated a new hairstyle which hid beneath a sheaf of flowers the bald patches on her horrible, scrofulous scalp. She said not a word, her head half turned away, and shook her long gold chain between her thumb and index finger, with the gesture of a guitarist.

Whilst the three men, silent and grave, warmed themselves seated before the fire in the sitting room, forgetting their poured and steaming coffee, Madame Robin drew my mother into the window alcove and speaking very low, her voice solicitous and her gaze complicitous said:

"And you know nothing? Nothing?"

My mother shrugged and said:

"He didn't even have any luggage. A nasty overnight bag! Ah! I knew it, I said as much!"

PART TWO

Chapter One

Two years had gone by. Father Sortais had died from heart failure and his successor, Abbé Blanchard, formerly the vicar of Viantais and who had given me and continued to give me my Latin classes, had taken his place in our household at family dinners and at the Sunday bridge game. Sometimes the bridge was actually accompanied by music, for the new priest had quite a talent for the flute and, being fond of a good time, liked to regale us with a few pieces he had composed himself. On those evenings, my mother offered tea with slices of cake which the priest devoured greedily, giving a throaty laugh and rubbing his stomach:

"What comes from the flute goes back to the drum."

As for the Robin couple, they were still awaiting their furniture in the house of the Misses Lejars, whose goitres were still growing and wobbled beneath their chins like children's bellies. Slowly, ever the same, life went by: silent meals, occasionally leavened by my father's surgical explanations and his comments on Abbé Jules; gloomy evenings with the Robins when the magistrate's wife and my mother darned the same stockings as ever, chatted about the same things, sighed over the same complaints, while Monsieur Robin and my father played the same piquet game. A single notable event had taken place: we no longer dined at the Servière's house on Thursdays. Our relations with them had initially grown cooler thanks to Abbé Jules, who had become a favourite in their house, and then finally had been broken off following a fire in which Monsieur Servière had not behaved as my father, deputy mayor, would have liked. My father had very sharply criticised the measures taken and before the whole population had disclaimed all responsibility. After this there followed a lively exchange of views, from which the two of them emerged on very bad terms, irrevocably so. I missed that house where my soul basked in the perfumed warmth which rose from the carpets and emanated from the hangings. I missed Madame Servière above all, so blonde, with such rosy skin, so soft to kiss and whose glance brought a little dreamy light into my life, devoid of smiles and caresses as it was. Then, a few months went by and I thought no more about it.

After the unforgettable episode of his arrival and instant departure, we had not seen the Abbé again, apart from in the street and he had not spoken to us. Two attempts at reconciliation undertaken by the old priest had met with no success. He had come up against a definite, permanent resolve and had been unable to extract anything from Jules except the words:

"Imbeciles! I've lived all my life with imbeciles! If only they'd leave me alone!"

Reasoning with him, begging him, had no effect so the priest decided to try threats.

"Listen, Monsieur l'Abbé," he had said to him, trying to give his voice a menacing tone, "you wish to settle here as a non-beneficed priest. You can't do it without my consent. Now, I make just one condition. That you make it up with your family."

Jules merely mumbled:

"Imbeciles! If only they'd leave me alone."

"Listen very carefully, Monsieur l'Abbé . . . I do not know your exact circumstances but I suspect them of being irregular . . . Do not push me too far . . . I will complain to the bishop."

"You can complain to the devil for all I care. Get lost. Leave me alone. Imbeciles."

Upon which, the priest died. The new one liked peace and quiet and did not attempt to go into the matter. Besides, the Abbé had visited him immediately after his appointment. Everything had gone very well. They had agreed on the times of services, discussed the petty duties which non-beneficed priests are obliged to fulfil in a parish, without Jules raising the slightest objection. This submissiveness caused some astonishment.

"He was very obliging, very polite!" concluded Father

Blanchard, who had hastened to report his interview to us. "Do you know, he speaks rather well, quite a conversationalist, an orator!"

My father questioned him.

"Did you ask him what he did in Paris for six years? I mean, it would be worth knowing!"

"Yes ... that is to say, I led the conversation in that direction, but at the word 'Paris', the Abbé was immediately on the defensive and then he left."

"So, we still don't know anything?"

"Nothing!"

"Perhaps we will never know," said my father with a great sigh of disappointment.

Suddenly seized with family pride, forgetting all Jules' wrongs against him, he swelled his chest.

"The rogue can certainly talk, can't he. Yes indeed, he's a long way from being a dumb animal."

We suddenly heard two huge pieces of news, one after the other. The Abbé had bought, paying cash, the Capuchin property. Then furniture had arrived and sixty huge trunks full of books. My mother shrugged her shoulders, refusing to believe it.

"It's impossible," she said, "he only had an overnight bag."

However, she had to give in, faced with the evidence. Then she grew indignant.

"He did it to trick us! He was rich! Where did he steal all that money?"

Normally, so calm, so in control of herself, she lost her head, guessing at a series of crimes definitely committed, possible denunciations and, though nervous, she was pricked by the desire for revenge:

"We must be told what he did in Paris," she cried. "We must be told immediately."

One evening, Monsieur Robin came out with this idea:

"Terhats he tlayed the Stock Exchange!"

Meanwhile, the Abbé was settling down at Les Capucins.

This was a property situated about a quarter of a mile from

the town. No one could remember why it was called Les Capucins. No one, not even the notary, who knew a great deal about local history, had ever heard that there was once a Capuchin monastery or any monks living there. In any case, it did not look like a monastery at all; if anything, it resembled a mysterious romantic refuge. It was a small house in the Louis XV style, pretty in design, but old and very dilapidated. It had only a ground floor, with tall, broad windows, like an orangery. A narrow laurel avenue – almost a path – led to it from the main road. Behind the main façade lay a circular, grassed courtyard, bound by low walls along which grew tangled rosebushes, now completely wild, and exuberant shrubs. Beneath the simple and elegant staircase, steps led down to the basement which was almost completely hidden by two enormous clumps of hortensias. Behind the house, vast gardens lay in three terraces, each bordered by a row of holly bushes cut into cone-shapes, and led down to a meadow, set as deep as the dried-up bed of a lake. All around the meadow, high on the brow of the hill, there rose beech trees which closed off the brief horizon of rolling greenery, leaving only one gap, through which, from a viewpoint right in the heart of the house, could be glimpsed a fanlike succession of layers of distant countryside, misty and charming. The gardens, long untended, were thronged with birds no longer fearful of man. Grass and wild flowers thrived, free, untrammelled, drunk with their own scent, covering the flower beds in patterns such as might have been seen in the Garden of Eden and decorating the old walls with exquisite designs, which mingled with the delicate mosaics of the stones and the swaying weave of the vines; each linked to the other by garlands of wild morning glory, the fruit trees no longer stunted by pruning, extended their knotty branches fearlessly, bronze-coloured and full of nesting birds. Peace reigned in this place, a great domain, a paradise, where it seemed the centuries had never dared cross the threshold. So near mankind and yet so far, only the presence of divine nature could be sensed there, eternal youth, the immemorial beauty of things no longer soiled by the human gaze. In one corner of this silence, a sundial marked with its thin trace of shadow the slowed passage of the hours.

For a few days, my parents' thoughts could not leave Les Capucins, not tasting the charm of its austere poetry, but following the Abbé there in their mind's eye. A great passion of curiosity had taken hold of them both. They wanted to know. From morning to night, I heard only exclamations, questions, suppositions. What was he doing? What was he saying? Why was he hiding away? Ah, there must be some extraordinary goings-on at Les Capucins. Could he not have taken a house in the centre of town like everyone else, unless he had unmentionable intentions? With that tendency that honest provincial women have to attribute worrying semblances of sin to simple habits which are not familiar to them; with that facility of inflation which they have for the physical representation of vice, my mother certainly associated the idea of Jules with the idea of monstrous, confused debauchery. In her passion of emotion, she even forgot herself enough to say in my presence:

"If he had brought back some fancy woman from Paris, it wouldn't surprise me."

My father, for his part, had been very struck by the story of the assassin Verger and his Orsini bombs and imagined the Abbé working away at murky intrigues and concocting infernal machines amid powders and explosives.

The Abbé used to say mass at seven in the morning. Three little rings of the bell; a few murmurings, the blessing sketched out; a few genuflections, the gesture of drinking; a few murmurings again and it was over. When the devout arrived, late and out of breath, the celebrant was already leaving the altar and had reached the sacristy, swinging the chalice beneath its embroidered cover, the chalice emptied of the blood of a God. And then he would go back to Les Capucins.

In the vague hope of finding something out and perhaps also in an unexpressed desire for reconciliation, my mother started attending his mass regularly.

"It's more convenient for the shopping because of the time," she said.

She took communion often. The Abbé placed the white disc of the host on her tongue rapidly, with a brisk motion of his thumb and appeared not to see her. She thought of taking him as her confessor but soon gave the idea up.

"Thank you but no," she decided. "So that he can go round telling everyone my sins."

That was when I was charged with an important mission. Apart from the days when he went visiting the Servières, my uncle was rarely seen in the town. But, every afternoon, he took an hour-long walk along the road with his prayerbook under his arm, though he never opened it.

"Listen," my mother said to me one morning. "Just because we have argued with your uncle, there is no reason for you, his godson, not to get on with him. Listen carefully to what I am going to say to you. It is very important. Every day your uncle takes a walk between Les Capucins and the crossroads at Trois-Fétus between one and two o'clock, doesn't he?"

"Yes, mother."

"Well, every day, you will go for a walk too between Les Capucins and the crossroads at Trois-Fétus between one and two o'clock . . ."

"Yes, mother."

"Naturally, you will meet your uncle . . ."

"Yes mother."

"Above all, don't be afraid."

"No, mother."

"You will greet him. Listen carefully, child. If he answers, ask after his health. If he addresses you, converse with him. I think you should be very polite, very affectionate, very respectful. Show me how you will do it."

We had to rehearse the probable scene between my uncle and myself. My mother took the rôle of the Abbé.

"There!" she said approvingly. "That's not bad. Try to be polite this afternoon."

The walk did not displease me at all, all the more so in that it coincided with my Latin lesson. However, I would have preferred my uncle not to be on the route. The idea of approaching him terrified me. Also, I felt a kind of shame in playing this comedy; and a painful emotion had insinuated itself into my heart, a kind of diminution of respect and love towards my mother. During our conversation, I had seen in her eyes that harsh, greedy expression, that cold, metallic look which upset me when she discussed money with Madame Robin.

Trembling a little, I followed the road, looking straight ahead of me. The sun was beating down on the road, which gleamed white, a creamy white, and the trees, whose dusty greenery had been bleached by the summer, made narrow, lacy, blue shadows along the borders, riddled with drops of light. On each side, between the hedges, the fields stretched out, russet and yellow. I walked slowly, stunned by fear and the heat falling from the sky where a lone cloud wandered, lost in the immense blue like a fat pink bird. The road curved suddenly, disappeared, reappeared. As I advanced, the shadows lengthened, thinned, describing the muzzles of strange beasts. All of a sudden, I glimpsed the terrible soutane, black against the dazzling white, with a little shadow following it, wriggling at its feet, like a little dog. I stopped short, my uncle carried on, taking short steps, bent, his shoulders hunched, his limbs stiff. His soutane, which seemed so black to me, gleamed in the sun like a breastplate. As he did not look round, I started walking again. He turned off onto the verge, bent over the bank of the hedge, picked a piece of grass, then another, which he examined carefully. I took advantage of this moment to hasten my step and when I was opposite him but separated by the whole width of the road, I walked faster still but called out a greeting. My uncle raised his head and looked at me a moment then dropped his eyes onto a magnifying glass he was holding in his hand and continued to examine his blade of grass.

The following day, I was no luckier. The day after that, I came face to face with him seated on a milestone. He was waiting for me.

"Come here, little one," he said, in an almost gentle voice.

I approached, all emotion. He looked at me for a few seconds with pity – or at least so it seemed to me.

"Your parents have sent you, haven't they? Don't lie."

As he spoke, he wagged his index finger at me threateningly.

"Uncle," I stammered. "My mother . . ."

"Don't you know why she has sent you, your mother?"

"No, uncle," I replied, my heart in my mouth and close to tears.

"I know why. She's an honest woman, your mother, and your father is an honest man. Well, all the same, they're pathetic specimens, petty, like all honest people. Do they teach you that at school? Do they teach you the catechism at school? Do you go to school?"

"The priest gives me my lessons," I sobbed.

"The priest," my uncle went on. "He's an honest man too. You'll be an honest man, my poor child." And, tapping me on the cheek, he added:

"What a pity. Now, off you go."

My mother was very vexed at this outcome. Her hatred of the Abbé grew and she held me fully responsible for my lack of success and hurled reproaches at me.

"You didn't go about it the right way. You are good for nothing. We'll never make anything of you!"

She was no less dogged in her desire to know.

Just as she had made use of me, she made use of Victoire, our cook, urging her to ferret about and spy daily on the tradespeople who supplied my uncle, but this never achieved anything but a few insignificant discoveries. On her orders and according to her instructions, Victoire laid siege to Madeleine, the Abbé's elderly servant. Both dallied at the market, at the butcher's, at the grocer's, chatting, asking each other questions, exclaiming. Following the conversations of these two gossips, new, interesting and mysterious discoveries were made which sharpened without satisfying the insatiable curiosity of my parents.

Thus we learned how when the Abbé was settling in he

proved to be of evil temper, hustling everyone, insulting the workmen, indulging in such frenzies that no one wanted to work for him any more. Since then, he had calmed down considerably, did not lose his temper any more, never complained. He seemed rather sad. Besides, Madeleine hardly ever saw him apart from mealtimes and in the morning when he came back from mass and walked in his garden, which he had left uncultivated in its charming natural chaos. In the house, the Abbé had only furnished three rooms – and those very simply – the bedroom, the dining room and the library. It was in this library that he stayed all day, almost till midnight, the hour when he went to bed. Sometimes he wrote; most often he read. He read from enormous books, with red-blocked pages, so large, so heavy, that he had trouble in carrying them alone. Over the door of his library, he had written in large letters: NO ENTRY. And no one, so far, had crossed the threshold. He had set out the library himself, without the help of any workman; he alone, every Saturday, dusted and swept it. When he went out, he was always careful to double-lock it and kept the key on him. And it was terrifying to watch him through the keyhole! Ah! He had so many books, big, medium, tiny, in all shapes and colours, books which, from the wainscot to the cornices, garnished the four walls, were piled up on the mantelpiece, on the tables and even covered the floor. It was equally firmly forbidden to enter another room which was always kept locked, whose door faced the library door, on the other side of the corridor. However, this room only contained a trunk and a chair. The Abbé shut himself in there about once a week, for hours! What was going on? No one knew a thing, but things which were not at all natural must be going on in there, for often the maid had heard her master walking about furiously, stamping his feet, letting out wild cries. One day, drawn by the row and thinking that the Abbé was arguing with thieves, she went and listened at the door and had clearly grasped the words: "Pig! Pig! Abject pig! Filth!" Who was he speaking to like that? Certainly, he was alone in the room with his trunk and his chair! When he came out, he looked a fright; his hair all over the place, his eyes terrible and brooding, his face shocked, pale as a sheet and gasping, gasping for air! Then he threw himself on his bed in his room and fell asleep. It was definitely that trunk, the cause of all these carryings-on. Madeleine had actually seen it. She had seen the chair too. The chair was made of cherry wood with a wicker seat, like all chairs; the trunk was of painted wood and was very old, with thick leather straps round a domed lid, like all trunks ... But this did not prevent Madeleine from being afraid and sometimes wondering whether she ought perhaps to let the police know.

Victoire, trembling with terror, her cook's imagination haunted by the supernatural and tales of the fantastic, interrupted the tale to ask my mother:

"Madame, what d'you think might be in that there trunk? Might it be the devil? Might it be beasts that haven't existed since our Lord Jesus Christ? In fact, Madame, as I stand here talking to you now, when I was a little girl, one day, my father was in a wood and he saw a beast ... Ah, but such a strange beast! It had a long muzzle, long as a spindle, a tail like a feather duster and legs, heavens, legs like coal scoops. My father didn't move and the beast went off. But if my father had moved, the beast would've eaten him! Well, me, I think it's a beast like that, in that trunk."

"Come along, come along," said my mother, laughing with her pinched lips. "You're talking nonsense, Victoire."

"Nonsense! My dear Madame!" exclaimed the maid, scandalised by her mistress's scepticism. "No, no one can convince me that there's not some devilry going on at Les Capucins. In fact, the other day, the doorbell, a large doorbell, fell on Madeleine's head! Well, Madame, Madeleine's head was fine, but the door bell doesn't ring any more. There! That's the kind of thing going on round at your brother-in-law's place!"

At heart, Victoire judged all these phenomena just and normal and was not at all surprised by them, knowing as she did from her friend that in all the house there was not one single holy object. You could search in vain for a crucifix, an image of the Virgin, a holy water stoup, a medal, a piece of boxwood. And the Abbé had never been seen saying grace after meals, nor making the sign of the cross, ever.

The story of the trunk grew more exaggerated, travelled across the region from one house to the next, taxing everyone's brains formidably. Even the most incredulous, the tavern wits who completely repudiated the supernatural in everyday life, felt some unease about the matter. People no longer used the road in front of the narrow laurel avenue which led to Les Capucins without being assailed by frightening thoughts and occasionally terrifying visions. What if, all of a sudden, the Abbé released into the countryside the monstrous beast, that horrific unknown which rumbled deep in the trunk! Immediately, the trees round seemed to take on unusual shapes and the fields rose up in threatening undulations and the birds on the branches had the cynical sidelong glance of the hunchback and wooed passers-by with strange, infernal songs. The library too took on demonic proportions and characteristics in the imagination of the locals, terrified by the two maids' tales. People imagined my uncle dressed as a sorcerer casting spells, while his books, taking on demoniacal life, crept like rats, hooted like owls and leapt like toads, around him.

In our house, nothing was ever clothed in this magical, poetic aspect. Nevertheless, the trunk was a diversion. Clearly there was some mystery there, since there really was a trunk. But what was it? What did that trunk contain? Concerning this trunk, they did indulge in extravagant comments, pathetic suppositions which contained no common sense at all. The library, however, really did excite their curiosity, but in another sense.

"It must be worth a lot, a library like that," speculated my mother.

And my father, taking on a knowing air, bid even higher.

"A library like that? One can't say how much it's worth, twenty thousand francs maybe.

Then my mother would sigh:

"If only he would just leave it to his godson."

But soon normal life, which had been disturbed by all these events returned to its usual routine. It was obvious that my mother was thinking about Les Capucins and that she was dreaming up plans in her head; nevertheless, she did not speak of the Abbé as often any more. She had secret discussions with Victoire, long conversations which no longer crossed the threshold of the kitchen. As for my father, he ended up consoling himself for his quarrel with his brother by saying almost cheerfully:

"Bah! It's always been like that with Jules. It might as well continue. Thank God we're not here desperate for his money!"

Furthermore, two important confinements, of which there was much talk at table, came along to distract him from his family problems and brought to the house a little of that special joy which I knew so well. Every afternoon, I went to the presbytery in melancholy mood, my books under my arm. During the lesson, Father Blanchard sometimes asked:

"Have you not met your uncle since . . . ? What a peculiar fellow though."

And since his clumsy gaiety, proper to the fat, bon viveur priest judged me sad, he decided to teach me the flute at the same time as the *De viris*.

"It's a lovely instrument," he said, "and it will cheer you up!"

It was also doubtless to cheer me up that on Thursdays, when I had been good, my father took me with him in his carriage. I accompanied him on his rounds of the sick. We travelled together without exchanging a word, both buffeted on the ruts of the pitted roads as if in a boat rising on the swell of the sea. In the villages, in front of the houses where poor wretches groaned, we would get out of the carriage; my father attached the horse's rein to the bars on the window and while he went into the sorry homes, I stayed on the doorstep and through the shadows glimpsed smoky, miserable rooms, glimpsed pained, yellowed faces, raised chins, clenched teeth and staring eyes, the dark eyes of people who are going to die. My heart full, terrified by these images of death, I thought about the Servière children whose existence was made up only of consoling and cheerful sights, with parents whose gentleness was like a light, surrounded by beauty which taught them happiness; and I thought too of my uncle, who had said to me in that sad, gentle way:

"What a pity!"

The Abbé appeared in public less than ever and spent even more time in his library. It seemed that his health was poor, he coughed a lot and often suffered from blackouts. He now only said mass on one out of three days. On the occasion of the translation to Viantais of some relics of Saint Rémy, patron saint of the parish – a celebration which drew three bishops and more than a hundred clerics to the town – my uncle had refused to appear in the procession, a gesture which was angrily held against him, even though he gave his ill-health as an excuse. But people felt there were other reasons and amongst them a barely concealed repugnance for everything which was part of the duties of religion and its observance. He was also seen walking out on the road less often; his garden had become his favourite place for walking; on fine sunny days he liked to sit in the grass under an acacia and stayed there watching the merry flight of the jays and following with his gaze across the sky the ascension of the great sparrow hawks. Was this the sleepy calm of solitude, the melancholy and apathy of a man who feels he has been beaten finally? But, from what Madeleine said, the character of her master was undergoing great changes. His fits of anger were less and less frequent; he went into ecstasies of tenderness before plants and insects; and the birds, to which he threw crumbs and corn sometimes followed him, whirling around him. As he was scarcely ever seen in public, now people grew accustomed to thinking of Les Capucins without too much fear, though the library and the trunk sometimes haunted the conversation of good people in the evenings before bedtime.

The incidents which I have just recounted had reinforced our friendship with the magistrate and his wife and forged an even more intimate bond. My mother believed doubtless that she had found serious moral support in them and – who knew – in the event of a court case in the future, a serious practical support. Madame Robin for her part was naturally pleased to play her rôle as confidante in a comedy where no suffering was required of her and which, instead, rewarded her spitefulness with a succession of unforeseen and startling complications. She could not forgive my uncle, either, for refusing to attend a dinner for which she had dressed up flirtatiously. Two years on, she still felt sharp and bitter rancour on account of this slight. So the two ladies saw one another more often than ever. My mother went to see her friend on the slightest pretext; and, for her part, Madame Robin needed only the flimsiest excuse to hasten to see us, her demeanour self-important and mysterious. Both strongly felt the need to consult one another over the merest trifle, quite apart from the small and large episodes, of which Les Capucins was an inexhaustible source.

One day as we passed by the house of the Misses Lejars:

"Just a moment," said my mother, "I must ask Madame Robin something."

The Misses Lejars lived on the ground floor. The first and only other floor was occupied by the Robins. Raising my eyes towards that dwelling which I so hated, I glimpsed behind one of the windows, the thin profile of Georges, hunched over some sewing. The child's hands flew backwards and forwards, tugging at the needle.

"At least he's useful!" observed my mother with reproachful emphasis while we waited in a dark, red-tiled corridor, in the far depths of which a stairway without banisters, practically a ladder, led to the Robins' rooms.

Some time earlier, Madame Robin had ceased educating her son. Stunted and sickly as little Georges was, she had decided that there was no point in counting on a future for him as any proper career would be forbidden him later on. So, what was the good of wasting money on an education that would be no use? Would he even live? She had her doubts. Meanwhile, his mother made use of him in the house, employing him as her servant, so to speak. She gave him all the dirty and unpleasant jobs which meant she did not have to employ a daily woman; he also washed the dishes, scoured the pots, swept the floors and waxed the boots. Then he spent the rest of the day sewing. He mended towels and sheets, darned old socks or knitted longjohns for his father. Seated behind the same window, constantly bent, his face ghastly, his poor body racked intermittently by coughing, he stitched the fabric, pausing now and then to watch children playing hopscotch on the paving-stones of the cornmarket, or to follow with his gaze the familiar flight of the pigeons and carts driving off towards main roads leading to greenery and the sun.

Madame Robin opened the door. She was wearing a baggy blouse; a pinafore of some blue cotton stuff protected her skirt, a black overskirt, only loosely fastened, which revealed her lower legs and her feet in their tapestry slippers. As soon as she recognised us, she quickly hid behind the door, ashamed of being surprised in this déshabille which put the finishing touches to her hideousness and made her blotchy complexion stand out the more.

"I can't receive you like this!" she cried. "I'm in the kitchen mincing the meat for a pâté. Let me put a dress on at least..."

"No, no!" insisted my mother. "We don't want to disturb, dear. I'll come into the kitchen with you. Albert can chat with Georges. I've some news..."

Madame Robin's face appeared round the door, a twisted mask of curiosity.

"It's hardly proper though ... Really, had I known you were coming..."

She continued to waver but my mother dragged her into the kitchen while I went to the room where Georges was.

A mahogany bed with white curtains stood in the middle of the room. The torn panels of a folding screen separated this conjugal bed from an iron bedstead, its head in the corner against the wall, Georges' bed. A walnut chest with grey marble top, an armchair in dark-red repp, an Empire-style tripod washstand and on the mantel, beneath a globe, a clock made of gilded zinc depicting Mary Stuart, comprised the total of the rest of furniture. Here and there were crucifixes, a holy water stoup, holy pictures yellowing in their wooden frames. Near the curtainless window opposite a pile of cloths and a wicker basket full of reels of thread, needle-rolls and rags, Georges sat sewing, bent double, his face obscured in blueish shadow, but rimmed with a line of bright light. The young invalid turned towards me, then, glancing fearfully towards the door and seeing I was alone, smiled.

"Mother isn't with you?" he whispered.

"No."

He dropped his work and, rising with difficulty, came over to greet me. His legs were too weak to carry his body, even puny as it was, and sagged at each step like the frail twigs of a shrub beneath the weight of a wren.

I had not often had the opportunity to spend time with him alone. The poor creature hardly ever went out and in his home or ours the icy shadow of his mother always fell between us. We did not speak on those occasions, but our eyes spoke and his eyes told eloquently of his suffering.

"Sit there, next to me," he said, bringing me a stool.

Leaning on my shoulder for support, he sat down in his chair again and then looked at me without saying a word. I said nothing either. A little embarrassed, a little chastened even, as one feels in the presence of someone one knows to be superior to oneself, I examined him. He had dull, blond hair, the dullness like the texture of the fur of sick animals; his bloodless, wizened face, was coloured only with a light, pinkish stain over the too prominent cheekbones. One guessed at the etiolated, skeletal frame and stunted limbs lost beneath the cotton overall which enveloped him down to his knees. His hands were astonishing, long and dry, hands the like of which I have never seen on any other child. And his dark-blue eyes were disturbing too, with their strangely intense stare and the precocity of the thoughts they revealed.

Georges' stare was still fixed on me and was becoming intolerable. It was as if something heavy were pressing on my skull. Suddenly he said to me:

"Have you never thought of getting away? Somewhere far away, really far?"

"No," I replied. "Why do you ask?"

He turned towards the window and waved his long, dry hand.

"Because the world must be beautiful, down there, beyond the roofs, the far-off lands beyond the forests. Yesterday evening, while my parents were at your house, I decided to leave and go farther still than that. I got up and I dressed. But the door was locked. So I went back to bed and I dreamt about all kinds of things. Tell me, is America far?"

"Why do you ask?" I said again.

"Because last year I read a book. It was about some children who lived on the plains, on the plains and in the woods. They ran about amongst lovely flowers and chased beautiful animals. In the trees were parrots and birds of paradise and wild peacocks. And they had no mother and no father! It was in America. Is it far?"

"I don't know," I said, my heart full.

"You don't know? Well, I'd like to go to America, or somewhere else. Sometimes I've seen children on the roads looking after cattle. The cows were grazing, the children gathered cowslips and made huge yellow bunches and they ate berries from the hedges. It must be nice looking after cows . . . Do you think cowherds have parents?"

"I don't know."

Georges looked irritated.

"Oh, you don't know anything," he sighed.

Suddenly he started again:

"Sometimes in the square I've seen the circus people go by . . . in big caravans, yellow, red, with little windows and a little chimney that smokes . . . And I want to go with them . . . Do you know where they go?"

"To the towns . . . far away . . ."

"To America maybe?"

"Maybe."

He thought for a moment; then he drew me to him and kissed me.

"You won't say anything . . . Well, when the caravans pass next time, I'm going down and I'm going to follow them and then I'll ask the circus people to take me with them . . ."

He broke off.

"So you've never thought of running away?"

Georges' words hurt me and shocked me in all my sacred childish beliefs, that animal attachment which rivets you even to the home where you have been unhappy, even to the family which denies you any tenderness. Deeply moved, I said:

"Listen Georges, what you're saying is not right, it's a sin and God will punish you. Do you not love your mother and father then, seeing as you want to leave them?"

The pale child shifted on his chair. A dark flare glowed briefly in his eyes, eyes which had become almost terrible in the face of such a fragile creature. Clenching his fists, he cried hoarsely:

"No! I do not love them. No!"

"Why?" I stammered. "Because they beat you, because they lock you up?"

"No, in the past they beat me and they locked me up but I still loved them."

"Then why do you not love them now?"

Georges caught his head in his hands and sobbed.

"Because they do filthy things! Filthy things!"

His tears suddenly turned to rage:

"Filthy things!" he repeated. "In the night, they think I'm sleeping and I hear them. At first I thought they were fighting, killing each other. The bed creaked, my mother yelled in a stifled, strangled voice. But once I saw . . . it was disgusting."

A dry cough stopped him. I had turned my eyes away from his, troubled by something I did not understand but which I sensed was terrible and shameful. The invalid continued:

"Why should I love them? They can beat me black and blue and throw me into the coal-hole day and night, I would love them anyway, but that! I can't look them in the eye any more. Just hearing my mother's dress swishing near me makes me blush, because I don't see them as they are when I see them, I see them as they are in the night. That's why I want to go away, far away, to a country where children don't have parents, where there are beautiful birds singing in the trees, like America . . ."

The sound of voices, followed immediately by steps came from behind the door. Georges picked up his work and hunched over to hide his emotion and my mother and Madame Robin came into the room.

Seeing us seated there, side by side and silent, she said, while Madame Robin behind her shoulder tossed me a glance of hatred:

"I see you've been very good . . ."

She went to Georges to kiss him. But suddenly, very pale, she pointed towards the window and cried:

"Ah, that's too much! Too much! Just look!"

Abbé Jules was crossing the square on the arm of cousin Debray. They were walking slowly, chatting like close friends, our cousin upright and gesticulating, the Abbé leaning on his arm with a contented air. At the corner by the Trois-Rois, they disappeared from sight.

My mother was speechless and Madame Robin, looked at her, very grave.

"That was all you needed. You know the Captain Debray is notorious for his scheming."

As for me, I had no thoughts for uncle Jules nor for cousin Debray. Still under the influence of Georges' words, I sensed a world of confused and fearful things unveiling before me, and my eyes went from Madame Robin, who now seemed less ugly, to the mahogany bed, above which some untold mystery hovered, entangled within the white drapes.

Chapter Two

Cousin Debray, apart from his army memories and his solid knowledge of the ways of polecats, did not have much in his head. Since leaving the regiment, he had only had one idea and had been obliged to give it up. This fine cousin of ours had decided to provide the area with a fire-fighting company, of which he was to be the commander. In connection with this he had written report upon report, memorandum on memorandum, drawn up plans, lists of statistics on fires and established an admirable set of rules. But he had constantly come up against the obstinacy of the town council, which refused to take on any financial responsibility, already in debt as it was. The captain took firmly against it and though he was a furious Bonapartist, flung himself wholeheartedly into the opposition – an opposition, I must hasten to say, that restricted itself to the occasional curse unleashed against local authorities. Owing to his status as a former soldier, he had a high profile in Viantais. He figured in full uniform in official processions but he also rendered various services to mothers who had sons in the army. When it was a question of obtaining leave, exemption from duty, any favour, it was to Captain Debray that people turned; he indicated the correct route to take, rephrased requests in the appropriate military terms, stormed the recruitment offices and war ministry with his recommendations. Extremely obliging as he was, he did enjoy some small popularity and in the end made up for not being a fireman by stuffing, furiously and with great conviction, all the polecats and weasels killed in the surrounding woods. Every family possessed at least one specimen of our cousin's skill and at that time we could not go into a house without seeing in its place of honour one of these animals, seated on its piece of wood, indulging in flirtatious gestures, generally in the style of squirrels. Owing to a tendency towards the ideal, which the elderly, retired military often display, our cousin adjusted and softened features in the animals' corpses which seemed too repellent or fierce. He lived a retiring life with a servant, Melanie, a fat, forty-five year-old woman, whom he referred to familiarly as 'my little tart'. The intimacy of the relationship between master and servant was known to all. Neither of them hid it and one day, when they had argued in front of several people, the captain had said, "Shout as loud as you like, my delicious little tart . . . You know very well that everything can be sorted out in bed." It was quite clear. However, according to the rules of polite bourgeois society, he could not be received, owing to the 'tart', but people continued respecting him because of the polecats, with which he was so generous and so prolific.

After the episode in the square, my mother decided that we should definitely not make an enemy of cousin Debray. It was preferable to humour him, to encourage him discreetly, direct him towards generous thoughts and actions and use him as an unwitting means of communication between ourselves and the Abbé, and later, as an instrument of reconciliation. So the captain was seen more often in our house and was even invited to dinner. He did not show too much surprise at this change of heart and, not being in the habit of looking for underlying meanings generally, he accepted. So, he was stuffed with good food and the best wine in the cellar. It was all a bitter disappointment. Our cousin ate, drank and said: "Ah, that fellow Jules is a damn fine rascal." His range of expressions of enthusiasm and his capacity for observation stopped there. That 'damn fine rascal' was the limit of his comment. It was impossible to draw him out further. There was no malice in it, he was as sincere as a dumb beast, the good captain. He simply kept coming back to that 'damn fine rascal' in connection with everything, modifying the tone of the exclamation depending on the degree of his enthusiasm, but never changing the form of his comment. My mother tried in vain to suggest ideas, sketch out replies for him, but he understood nothing, heard nothing and stuck with that 'damn fine rascal'. She sighed, attempting some complicity from him:

"Ah, it's so sad when families are divided. It would be good to be reunited and love one another. And he, all alone with such delicate health! We would look after him so tenderly. We are such petty people compared with him, with his intelligence, his eloquence. Lord, when one has his brains . . . when one has lived in Paris . . . We only have our hearts to offer!"

However, her voice and manner and gestures seemed to shout:

"Go and repeat that to him, idiot!"

To which, cousin Debray, mouth full, eye glassy, would reply:

"Oh Jules, he's a damn fine rascal. Sometimes when I'm chatting with him, I can't resist telling him, 'Jules, you're a damn fine rascal!'"

"And when you chat with him," continued my mother, desperately seizing on the few words pronounced by the captain that were not curses, "what does he say? Does he complain? Does he speak about Paris? About us?"

"Him? Ah! that devil of a cousin! He's a damn fine rascal, eh?"

At last he eventually admitted that he had been allowed into the library. He even added that he had seen some books, felt them, that Jules had shown him some very rare editions, very valuable they were. And he concluded, shaking his head:

"My dears, it's a damn fine library."

So, he alone of all the family had been invited to the Abbé's house! And not only had he been invited, but look, he had been into the library! In that library on whose door were written the words: NO ENTRY. In that library where no one until now had set foot, not even the Servières. And not only had he been inside, but my uncle had, with his own hands, shown him books, stressing their value and rarity.

"What about the trunk?" demanded my mother, in consternation. "Did you see the trunk?"

"No," said cousin Debray, who had been through a rosary of curses.

My parents were no longer listening to him but wrapped

in thought and our cousin swore into a void, stroking his grey moustache, greyer than ever against a face ruddied by poor digestion.

When he had gone:

"You see!" exclaimed my mother. "You see!"

My father spoke, pausing between each syllable:

"It is extraordinary. Who would ever have guessed?"

"You do understand, don't you? For the Abbé to have taken that vulgar person into his library and troubled himself to treat him so well, you do understand that he must have a high opinion of him . . ."

"I fear so!"

"And that our cousin will inherit everything!"

"It is possible, probable even. Because, if it weren't the case, the Abbé wouldn't have taken him into the library. The Abbé knows him well."

"Of course he knows him! He's possibly already made his will! How much is his fortune worth, exactly?"

My father made an evasive gesture, engaged in a little mental arithmetic, then replied:

"Now that is something I'd like to know. He paid twelve thousand francs for Les Capucins, not counting legal fees and taxes. From my mother's estate he had an income of six thousand pounds. Now . . . Has he more . . . or less? It's those six years in Paris which no one knows a thing about that bother me. What can he have been up to in Paris?"

"You haven't mentioned the library. Nor the trunk."

"Yes, but Paris, you see, that's what's annoying. What can he have been up to in Paris?"

He got up and strode about in the room, hands in pockets, worried. My mother abstractedly jangled a bunch of keys which made a pleasant metallic sound beneath her fingers, as of cowbells in the distance. After a few seconds' silence, my father said, not addressing anyone in particular:

"And here we are counting. What good is it going to be to us?"

My mother shook her keys harder and hunched her shoulders:

"A man that lives in sin and has no children. It's shameful."

"Yes indeed," concluded my father. "That's the justice of the world for you. What do you expect?"

My bedtime was long past. Absorbed in their thoughts, my parents had forgotten me and no longer noticed I was there. Besides, I was careful not to draw attention to myself, making myself as small as possible in my chair in the corner of shadow where I had been sensible enough to hide away. I was prodigiously interested, not in the calculations of the Abbé's fortune, which alone would have sufficed to send me to sleep, but by what was being said about my cousin Debray. I was hoping for revelations about his life, about the 'tart' in particular, who had been the subject of much comment at that time; for my parents, overtaken by events, had been somewhat relaxed in their style of language and the austerity of their observations. I realised there was a connection between the 'tart' and my cousin and Monsieur and Madame Robin. Since Georges' confidence, a new and still imprecise world had opened up for me; I was experiencing very strong sensations that involved my whole being, unfamiliar, heady sensations which had both the terror and attraction of the forbidden, an abominable but seductive evil, which I now felt I could read, without actually deciphering it, in the eyes of women. All this was confused, very uncertain, and I hoped that in a word or phrase about 'the cousin and his tart', my parents would disperse the mists veiling the mystery which I so desired, yet dreaded.

My father adjusted the lamp which had begun to smoke and came and sat down again. He had doubtless been thinking, for, seeing his wife still brooding and troubled, he patted her knee gently.

"Come along my dear. Don't worry your head about it. Let's just accept whatever happens. Thank Heavens we don't lack for anything and I'm good for a few years' more work!"

Cheerily he added as a kind of joke:

"Mind, we could do with a nice epidemic now and then!"

But my mother rebelled. In a hard voice, accompanied by a resolute gesture:

"No!" she said decisively. "I am not going to accept that it is settled that he is going to humiliate us so. I am determined to defend myself. First of all, you must go to Les Capucins."

"Me!" said my father, jumping out of his skin. "Me! Oh no! No indeed."

"Before you are so quick to say no ... good Lord, you really are of a piece with your family ..."

And speaking faster, she went on:

"You must go to Les Capucins. Listen to me. You will see your brother. Without abasing yourself, without snivelling, without begging for a reconciliation, you will ask him to take on Albert's education for us. Albert is his godson, for Heaven's sake."

"What about the priest?" interrupted my father. "He'll be offended."

"I'll sort out the priest. Once the little one is in place, you'll see that will alter things for us quite nicely. It's up to us to manage things cleverly. In any case, if he takes him as far as senior school, that's already a saving of four years of college in one stroke."

"He won't receive me," my father objected.

"How do you know?"

"It will cause problems!"

"What problems? Where are the problems? What could be more natural than for an uncle to give lessons to his nephew? Besides he's getting bored, it will distract him."

"And if he refuses?"

"Well, you will come home again and things will go on as before, but at least we can rest easy knowing that we tried."

My father scratched his head, hoping to make triumphant rejoinders spring from it. He had run out of arguments and no further objection presented itself. Thoroughly disgruntled, he agreed.

"Very well," he sighed, laboriously. "One of these days I'll go over there."

"Why wait? With health like his, he could die from one day to the next. Who knows. No, you will go tomorrow."

"Very well, I'll go tomorrow."

The following morning, my father prowled about the house, with an unfocused air. He was looking for pretexts to delay his departure, racking his brains to think of a suddenly pressing task, urgent visits which might have put off the fearful exchange for a few hours. He would never dare propose this absurd notion to his brother, so what was he going to say to him? Nothing, clearly.

"What if I took Albert along?" he wondered.

He felt the need not to be alone in confronting the terrible Abbé. He thought having me with him would give him more authority, more self-assurance. He also thought that in front of me, Jules might control himself more. He went from the kitchen to his study, from the study to the drawing room, shifting chairs, patting his pockets as if to check if he had forgotten anything. My mother pushed him towards the door.

"Get along with you! What are you looking for? What are you afraid of?"

"What if I took the little fellow along? That might be more proper."

"It would be madness. Go! And try to get him to receive you in the library."

My father was away a bare hour. When he returned he was joyful. His step resounded on the hard earth of the yard like a victory dance.

"Well?" asked my mother, tense and pale.

"It's done! He consents. From tomorrow Albert can go to his house."

"There, you see? I told you so!"

She threw herself into her husband's arms and kissed him.

"Wasn't I right? See? How did it go?"

He had to recount the interview. The Abbé had been very chilly, but polite. He was walking in his garden, wearing a sort of green greatcoat which was neither like a soutane nor like an overcoat. It was a real jumble of weeds, that garden, even the paths were disappearing beneath them. As soon as he spoke, Jules had smiled in a peculiar way, then he said: 'Good. I'll take him. He can come.' After which, he asked two or three questions about his pupil. What stage was he at? What had he learnt so far? As he led his brother to the entrance to the garden, he had said: 'I am anxious to warn you that this will not alter our relationship in any way, as I find it perfect as it is. I do not wish to see you or your wife.' Then they had separated.

"So you saw nothing of the house or the library?"

"Nothing. He did not ask me in."

"And what is he like?"

My father shook his head sadly.

"He has aged fearfully, the poor boy. I wouldn't be at all surprised if he has something wrong with his heart."

My heart was in my mouth when I, in my turn, took the narrow laurel avenue leading to Les Capucins. I did not think to look at the blackbirds which took off from clumps of greenery as I passed, nor the agile robins hopping about on the ground amid the low twigs, rustling like mice. A jay suddenly whirred up from a fir branch and gave a cry so loud I was afraid and my books fell to the ground. I picked them up and, as I stood up, spotted my uncle, straight, black, twenty paces in front of me in the avenue.

"Ah, there you are," he said.

"Yes, uncle."

I was trembling. My legs were giving way, wobbly and chilled.

He went towards the staircase, at the foot of which clumps of hortensias burgeoned, and sat on a step.

"Sit down, my boy," he said.

"Yes uncle."

"So you learn the flute? Or so your father says."

"Yes uncle."

"And Latin."

"Yes uncle."

"What are those under your arm?"

"My books."

He took them, glanced at them rapidly and threw them into the air, one after the other. I heard them fall heavily behind the little wall surrounding the yard.

"Do you know anything else?" he asked.

"No uncle."

"Right then. Go into the garden, you'll find a spade there. Dig the garden. When you're tired, lie down in the grass. Off you go."

That was my first lesson.

Chapter Three

"What should you seek in life? Happiness. And you cannot obtain it except by exercising your body, which makes you healthy, and by allowing as few ideas as possible into your head, for ideas trouble your peace of mind and always incite you to pointless acts, which are always painful and often criminal. Not hearing your ego, being an ungraspable thing, founded in nature, as a drop of water falling from a cloud is founded in the sea, such will be the aim of your efforts. I warn you that this is not easy to achieve and it is simpler to create a Jesus Christ or a Mohammed, a Napoleon, than a Nothing. Listen to me. You will reduce your knowledge of the functioning of humanity to the strictly necessary: One, man is a nasty, stupid beast. Two, justice is a lie. Three, love is filth. Four, God is an illusion. You will love nature. You will even adore it if you like, not to the extent that artists or scientists do, who have the idiotic audacity to try and express it in rhythms or explain it with formulae. You will adore it with the same adoration as an animal, or bigots, a God which one does not question. If you are gripped by the arrogant whim to try and penetrate its unfathomable secret, to probe its bottomless mystery, goodbye happiness. You will be ever prey to the tortures of doubt and frustration. Unfortunately, you live in a society with threatening and oppressive laws, amid hateful institutions, which are the reverse of nature and primitive reason. That creates multiple obligations for you, obligations towards power, towards your country, towards your peers – obligations which all engender vice, shame and savageries which you are taught to respect, in the name of virtue and duty. I would strongly advise you to ignore it all, but there are police, courts, prison, the guillotine. The best course is to contain the evil by reducing the number of social and personal obligations that you have and keeping as far away as possible from people, frequenting animals, plants and flowers. Live like them, a splendid life, which they draw from the very fount of nature, from Beauty. And then, having lived without the remorse which brings sorrow, without the passion for love or money which taint, without intellectual worries which kill, you will die peacefully. And everyone, ignorant of your life will ignore your death. You will be like those lovely creatures of the forest, whose carcasses are never found and which disappear, volatilised into matter. You see, my child, if I had known these truths before, I would not be where I am today. For I am a rogue, an evil being, the abject slave of vile passions. Perhaps I will tell you of that later. Do you know why? Because, from the day when I could make a sound, my head has been stuffed with ridiculous ideas and my heart with superhuman feelings. I had organs and they made me think in Greek, Latin and French that it was shameful to use them. They twisted my intelligence as they did my body and in the place of the natural, instinctive man, full of life, they substituted an artificial puppet, a mechanical doll of civilisation, with an ideal breathed into it . . . the ideal from which are born bankers, priests, cheats, debauches, assassins and the unhappy. Look, just now I told you God is an illusion. Well, I don't know. I don't know anything, for the consequence of our education and the result of our studies is to teach us to know nothing and doubt everything. There may be a God, there may be several. I don't know. Now, go and run about. No, wait. This morning I found a trap again, set for blackbirds. I forbid you to trap birds. A bird's life is to be respected. Do you know what you destroy when you kill them? You destroy music, a tremor, a life in fact worth more than yours. Have you looked into a bird's eyes? No? Well, take a look and you will not kill. Now, go and play. Climb trees. Throw stones. Off you go!"

It was by these vague, emotive and anarchic tirades that my uncle set about preparing me for a future baccalaureate, my parents' ambition for me.

Normally, lessons were limited to running about in the garden and violent and constant exercise of all kinds. Once a week at the most, beneath the acacia, the Abbé, wearing a floppy straw hat and his green greatcoat, which was gradually going yellow from exposure to the elements, initiated me into the secrets of his philosophy, which certainly frightened me a little, but which I did not understand at all. I saw him rarely. Entire days could go by without him appearing. He worked in his library or else locked himself into his mysterious room with the trunk. Sometimes Madeleine and I would hear him stamping his feet, shouting out, and the servant would sigh:

"Aah, listen. There 'e goes again in one of 'is rages. It'll end badly so it will."

On those days, Madeleine made use of me to draw water from the well or stack logs in the woodshed. Soon I started peeling carrots and doing some of her heavy jobs.

After a year of the Abbé's and Madeleine's bizarre schooling, I had completely forgotten the little Latin taught me by Father Blanchard. Spelling, arithmetic, French history were already mere memories, faded and old. My muscles and physical strength, however, were developing.

"How do you say *fire* in Latin?" my uncle might ask me as I came back into the house, sweating, panting and smelling of the fresh scent of grass.

"I don't know, uncle."

"Very good," the Abbé would say, rubbing his hands in satisfaction. "Perfect. And how do you spell *hazard*?"

I would think for a moment, then spell out:

"H...a...Ha...s..."

"S! Fine! Madeleine! Madeleine! Give Monsieur Albert a jam sandwich."

Very occasionally, he took me for a walk. Prompted by the slightest thing, a plant picked from the hedgerow, the bent back of a farmworker glimpsed beneath an apple tree, a sheep, a cloud, a spiral of dust caught up by the wind, he launched into theories about life, interspersed with reflections like the following:

"I don't know why I am telling you all this. Perhaps you would be better off as a clerk after all?"

It was rare that some extraordinary adventure did not

befall us. One afternoon, we met a little girl begging. She made her way towards us, her hand held out.

"Poor little creature," groaned my uncle, moved. "Look at her, that poor little girl. You must be kind to children and people who are suffering."

He spoke to the girl:

"Come here, my poor child, come to me. I will give you money. Would you be happy with ten francs?"

Astonished, pleased, the girl started to follow us at a discreet distance.

As we approached Les Capucins, my uncle turned round and caught sight of the young beggar, whom by now he had completely forgotten.

"What do you want?" he shouted. "Why are you following us, thief?"

Taken aback, she stared, wide-eyed, and said nothing.

"But it was you, uncle," I said hesitantly, "it was you who said to follow us."

"What do you mean, me? You're joking. Do I know her? A trollop that hangs around in bars, a carter's bit on the side. Get away! Off with you!"

Finally, just like cousin Debray, I was admitted to the library. This notable event took place one rainy day. Leading me into the redoubtable sanctuary, my uncle said:

"Look, these are books. These books contain all of human genius. Philosophies, world systems, religions, science, arts are all there. Well, my boy, it is all lies, foolishness or else criminal. Remember this: the naive emotion that a flower inspires in the heart of simple folk is worth more than the heavy intoxication and foolish pride that is drawn from these poisoned wells. And do you know why? Because the simple heart understands what the tiny flower is saying, something which all the savants, all the philosophers, all the poets, do not have the first inkling about. Savants, philosophers, poets, pah! They only serve to taint nature with their discoveries and their words, as absolutely as if you smeared a lily or a wild rose with your cack. Wait, wait, my boy, I am going to put you off reading. It won't take long!"

He climbed up on a ladder attached to the lower shelves of the library and took out a book at random.

"*Ethics* by Spinoza. That's just the job."

He came down and gave me the book, first slapping its cover several times with the flat of his hand.

"Sit down at the little table down there and read aloud from whichever page you please."

My uncle settled in his armchair and crossed his long legs, those long, thin, bony legs, whose knees almost touched his chin. His head back, right elbow on the armrest, left arm trailing, he ordered:

"Begin!"

In a faltering, doltish tone, I began to read out *Ethics*. Not understanding a word, I stammered and made stupid errors every line. At first my uncle sniggered, then gradually lost his patience.

"Pay attention, animal. So you've never even learnt to read. Take that sentence again."

Suddenly, he was keen. He interrupted me to add a comment or interject a roar of fury. His body leaning forward, two fists clenched beneath the arms of the chair, his eyes brilliant and wild, such as I remembered them when he arrived in Coulanges, he seemed to threaten the book, the table, me. He got up, tapping his foot irritably and shouting.

"He seems to think we haven't had enough of God. We've got to seek him all over the place! Imbecile!"

After this, when the weather was bad, and cold or rain condemned me to seek shelter in the kitchen, my uncle would call me. I would sit at the little table and read aloud. I read anything, from *Ecclesiastes* to Stuart Mill, from Saint Augustine to Auguste Comte. Every single time, my uncle lost his temper with the views expressed, as in the past he had lost his temper with people, with the same gestures, same words. He treated ideas like living people, shaking his fists at them, tossing at their incorporeal image his foaming rage, in the insult:

"Imbeciles!"

My parents were concerned by the way in which Abbé

Jules interpreted the idea of teaching. They did not like his system one bit and were very worried about the future he was preparing for me. For all that, they did not think for a moment of withdrawing me from the care of this strange teacher and even less of making the slightest comment to him. According to my mother, I was "on the spot", I was keeping an eye on the treasure and counteracting the influence of cousin Debray. Those advantages outweighed the disadvantages. Later on they would see to undoing the damage. Far from showing anger, they keenly devised insidious little phrases which they made me learn and instructed me to repeat and a series of delicate and diverting attentions which were all to lead to the conquest of the Abbé's heart. Often, my father's patients gave us gifts: fine, fat fowl, hares, woodcock, trout. I took them to Les Capucins and left them discreetly in the kitchen. My uncle never thanked me, never mentioned them, but ate them with an air of satisfaction. Even as I went to my lessons and met him on the way, his first glance was at my hands as if to ask "What have you brought me?"

My mother was annoyed by this silence. Whilst handing me a little basket containing four pots of strawberry jam, to which my uncle was very partial, for example, she would mutter:

"He could say thank you, rude man, but never mind."

The Abbé did not even think of it, having made himself a scornful rule of never uttering the name of my parents. The delicate hints in the sentences I had to offer him at the same time as I proffered the woodcock and the jam, were greeted with a whistled tune. Not one of the scenes set up by my parents succeeded.

"Do excuse me uncle, for being a little late. I'm afraid mummy is quite ill!" I might say, unable to prevent a blush spreading.

He turned away on his heels, and went off, hands behind his back. It was as if my parents did not exist for him. He did not even accord them the insulting honour of the epithet "imbeciles".

Despite the exceptional liberties which I continued to enjoy at Les Capucins, this obstinate silence eventually started to worry my mother a great deal. She no longer saw it as hatred, but something worse: irony. Today's silent irony frightened her more than yesterday's thundering rage, for she suspected that in it there lay the implacable chill of calculation, mixed with a desire to set a trap for the family after his death. After dinner, whilst awaiting the arrival of the Robins, she would remain silent for a long while, prey to painful thoughts which twisted her pale face with suffering, her tragic, bourgeois face. Doubtless, a battle was going on in the depths of her soul between her motherly love and her feminine greed. Remorse too, born of uncertainty, besieged her, breaking with little shudders the stiff immobility of her body.

One day I heard her talking to my father in a low voice, whilst he was gloomily polishing a scalpel:

"Do you think he really is so . . . so ill?"

"I haven't listened to his chest, my darling," he replied. And turning to me he asked:

"Have you noticed your uncle's legs getting swollen?"

"No, father."

"That's of no consequence," he went on. "I reckon it's some sort of heart disease or maybe a liver complaint. But, fortunately, I could be wrong in my diagnosis."

He placed his lips close to his instrument, whose blade dulled at his breath.

"I could be wrong," he repeated, nodding his head.

With a piece of an old leather glove, he polished the steel and delicately wiped it.

"So, you think he could go on like that for months, for years?"

"Good Lord! He could go on for a long time. He could die from one moment to the next. It depends."

He placed the scalpel in the beam of the lamp and turned it in his fingers, examining the polished surfaces which flashed, and repeated:

"It depends."

Then he slipped it into its sheath in the roll, whilst my mother, her eyes very vague, a deep crease in her forehead, murmured:

"What if we have sacrificed Albert's education for nothing?"

"Oh God. Have I not said so often enough? Well, let's send him to school!"

She thought for a few minutes.

"Let's wait a little longer," she said.

My father unfolded his newspaper and flopped heavily into his chair.

"Let's wait," he said.

A silence descended upon us, hideous and heavy as the lid of a sepulchre. The shadow hovering on the ceiling and trembling on the walls seemed to contain the terrible shade of Murder.

My uncle really was ill and declined each day. He had palpitations and fits of breathlessness which obliged him to spend entire nights with the window open in his room, his chest heaving, his throat constricted. He wanted to keep the spectre of death out of his mind and so would not consult a doctor nor change any of his habits or routines. He came and went and worked in his library, shut himself in the room with the trunk more often. His eyes kept their strange gleam and his body, knobbly with protruding bones as he grew thinner, seemed to be breaking in two. The only concession which he made to his sickness was to limit celebrating mass to once a week, on Sunday. Even so, on several Sundays his congregation awaited him in vain. The bells rang and the Abbé did not appear. Father Blanchard lost his patience. He decided that the illness was only a pretext since he had not given up his daily walks, and he had it out with him.

"I do what I like," declared my uncle. "If I am ill enough not to say mass but I am not ill enough to give up my walk, then that is a medical phenomenon that concerns me alone. Look after your vicars."

The priest took on an air of forbidding authority.

"Monsieur l'Abbé! If I have left you in peace so far, it is because you belong to one of the best families in the region, a pious family which I love, which I respect, which I esteem."

"Well, there you are then," interrupted the Abbé. "Esteem it, at your leisure. Play the flute to it. It's a fine family. You are a fine man, I am a rogue. That goes without saying. However, I have an income of three thousand francs, a small house, a large garden, I have argued with my family and have no heirs that interest me . . ."

He tapped the priest on the shoulder.

"What if I left it all to you in my will? Hmmm? What do you say to that?"

Looking at the Abbé with troubled eyes, in which the glimmer of greed flashed for an instant, Father Blanchard stuttered:

"Oh, Monsieur l'Abbé! Oh, my dear Monsieur l'Abbé! I am not worthy . . . I . . . I . . . I . . ."

"And you know I am ill, that I do not have long left . . ."

"Oh no!" protested the priest. "God would not wish . . . but really, I . . . I . . ."

An "imbecile", hissed mockingly, cut off his words and he felt himself propelled towards the door by Jules, who sniggered:

"Get out! So you believed me? Ha! Ha! Out!"

This anecdote amused cousin Debray a great deal, who thought he had read Voltaire once and felt Jules was more than ever a damn fine rascal. He visited Les Capucins often, braying, spitting, swearing, searching in the yard and amid the weeds of the avenues for traces of polecats or weasels. To flatter my uncle's ego, the captain enthused about everything, praised with a military precision and delicacy the trees on the property, the walls, the quality of the soil, the charm of the weather vane, the height of the ceilings, and each time he exclaimed as he waved at the meadow and the circle of trees surrounding it:

"I say, you have a damn fine view! It's damn peaceful

here! Bugger me, a man could be very comfy here stuffing polecats!"

More rarely, the Abbé received a visit from the Servières. When he was with pretty Madame Servière, his angularity softened, his conversation took a playful turn and assumed a witty, gallant charm which was astonishing in a man as excessive and surly, whose actions and words went from exaggerated enthusiasm to exaggerated rage. But his eyes belied the apparent calm of his manner, strangely lubricious eyes, when their gaze alighted on the back of the young woman's neck, on her bosom with its supple, vivacious curves, on the folds of her dress which those eyes seemed to lift, search and tear with the brutality of violating hands. And his nostrils flared, trembling, at the sensuality of the scents she exuded which rose into the air charged with lust. Madame Servière found it amusing, flattered at heart, by this adoration which undressed her and delivered her up to the obscene imaginings of a satyr in a black soutane.

I can still see in its tiniest, most insignificant details, the terrible scene which followed one of these visits.

My uncle is seated beneath the acacia, his back leaning against the trunk, his legs in the grass. He is over-excited, panting slightly, very grave, as if anticipating a crisis. His head begins to sag and loll on his chest like a too heavy ball. Sweat drips off his face. He tears off blades of couch grass which he chews and then throws aside. I am not far away, throwing stones, trying to reach the wall dividing the meadow from the garden. A little while earlier, Madame Servière was there, all in white amid the greenery: a white dress shimmering gently, a hat trimmed with white lace which trembled, a white parasol and her arms through the fine white fabric were rosy. She moistened her lips in a glass of Malaga wine, nibbled a biscuit. Monsieur Servière smoked a cigarette and spoke of the elections. My uncle was charming, said some delightful things which seemed singularly odd in his mouth. Picking a double poppy, whose faded petals like old silk fell one over the other in a pretty, gathered effect, he offered it to Madame Servière:

"Look at this flower! It's delicious, is it not? It's like a little dress in Louis XV style. All the passion, all the tenderness, all the grace, all the essence of a style, of an era, all that in this one little flower, whose garb a woman passing by one day must have envied . . . Gothic cathedrals were born of the look of love that a man out walking one day cast upon the great avenues of our forests. I wonder why dancers do not study the movement of animals, the flight of birds, the sway of branches."

"So you have seen dancers perform?" asked Madame Servière, laughing.

"I have," replied my uncle, "and they dance very badly." And the Servières left; and my uncle is beneath the acacia and I go on throwing stones. Birds fly by, birds sing.

"Albert!"

My uncle is calling me. Doubtless he wishes to teach me something; I foresee an anarchic diatribe on God, virtue and justice.

"Help me!"

He has a look in his eyes which terrifies me. I do not know why but I think that murderers must look like that when they kill.

"Help me, I said."

He grasps my hand, pulls on my shoulder and painfully drags himself to his feet. High in a pear tree nearby a bullfinch sings in full throttle.

"How old are you?" asks my uncle.

"Thirteen."

"Thirteen! Good. Come with me."

Without a word, we go towards the library. I settle into my usual place, at the little table where I have read the whole of philosophy at the age of thirteen! With jerky, impatient movements, my uncle rummages behind a row of large books. Perhaps he is looking for some philosophic work I do not yet know. And I feel, as I sit there, a vague fear. My uncle's back looks different in a way that frightens me; his hands really do worry me; they fly back and forth in an unseemly haste. At last he has found what he seeks. It is a book, smaller than the others, with a red, dirty, torn cover and pages falling out. It looks well-used ... My uncle turns the pages faster and faster, stops for a second, then starts turning them again, even faster. The sound is a kind of hiss, loud enough to drown out a thin stream of water falling onto pebbles.

"There! This is it!"

He smoothes out the page he has found, with an outstretched hand, places the book on the table, wide-open and indicates with a finger the place where I should start reading.

"Slowly. You will read slowly. When I tell you, start."

Whilst he goes to take his seat, his legs stuck out stiff and straight in front of him, I look at the title of the book and see: *Indiana*, by GEORGE SAND ... George Sand! Now I remember that my father often speaks about George Sand. He saw her once at the theatre. She is a bad woman who always dresses as a man and smokes a pipe. George Sand! I try to recall the details about her from my father's accounts. But my mother keeps on interrupting the anecdote he starts to tell. The name alone scandalises her and scandalises Madame Robin too. Evidently, *Indiana* is what in my family is known as a novel, that is to say, something forbidden and frightful, and I regard the book open in front of me with curiosity, mingled with terror.

"Start!" says my uncle. "And slowly, that's the important thing."

I glance at him. He has shut his eyes, his arms hang over the sides of the chair, his chest rises and falls like a bellows. I begin:

"Noun was choked with tears. She had torn the flowers from her brow, her long hair fell loose about her broad, dazzling shoulders. If Madame Delmare had not had the experience of her slavery and her pain to make her so beautiful, Noun would have infinitely surpassed her in loveliness at that instant. She was resplendent with pain and love."

"Slower," said my uncle, very quietly. "And don't fidget so in your chair."

"Raymond was overcome and drew her into his arms,

made her sit next to him on the sofa, and turned to the table laden with drinks, to pour her some orange-flower water in an enamelled goblet. Soothed by this act of concern, rather than by the calming beverage, Noun dried her tears and, throwing herself at Raymond's feet:

"Love me again," she said, passionately covering his knees with kisses. "Tell me again that you love me and I will be cured, I will be saved. Kiss me like before and I will no longer regret losing everything just to give you a few days of pleasure."

"Stop!" says my uncle, in a low, dull voice, rather like a child's groan. "Stop!"

I am feeling strange, my head is filled with a peculiar heaviness. Those words: love, pleasure; the sofa, the enamelled goblet, Raymond, Noun, those kisses, those dazzling shoulders, it all disturbs me. It seems to me that the writing in the book takes images of known things, dreamt things, divined things, and gives them worrying shape, so that they twist and grimace. My heart starts to race; my pulse thuds, a strange new fire circulates in my veins. I can hear my uncle's hoarse, uneven breathing. Why? I hazard a glance in his direction. His eyes are still closed, his arms still hanging and his body jerks now and then. Is he asleep? I am afraid. I want to run away.

"Continue."

I start reading again in a trembling voice.

"She wrapped her cool, brown arms around him, covered him with her long hair, her large, black eyes communicated to him a searing languor and that ardour of the blood, that wholly oriental voluptuousness which can triumph over all efforts of will and all delicacy of thought. Raymond forgot everything, his resolutions, his new love, the place where he was. He returned Noun's delirious caresses. He dipped his lips in the same goblet, and the intoxicating wines they found at hand finally made their loss of reason complete."

I think my uncle has spoken. I stop. Besides, I need to catch my breath. My throat is tightening, my hair is wet with sweat and sticks to my skull and I can feel a sharp pain at the back of my neck.

"Go on! What's wrong? Go on!"

Trying to control myself and keep a hold on my tottering reason and gather my thoughts which are darting everywhere, I continue:

"The two mirrors which reflected Noun's image from one to the other to infinity seemed peopled with a thousand phantoms."

I can see those phantoms. They pass by, fade away, reappear, incomplete, marvellous, with flowing hair, heads thrown back, limbs entwined ... And I read and read. The lines slide away before my eyes, leap out of the book and slip off the table, fly into the air and fill the room around me. I keep reading. Stunned, panting, I recognise amid the terrifying hallucinations the Robins, the Tart, cousin Debray, Madame Servière, all displaying shameful nudity and a multiplicity of strange postures. All my memories take shape and come to join this diabolical ronde. I read on:

"It was she who called him and smiled at him from behind the white muslin drapes; it was of her, too, that he dreamt, on this bed, when, succumbing to love and wine, he carried off his tousled Creole girl."

Suddenly I fall silent. My eyes have been blinded by a rush of blood. My ears buzz, my heart fails me, I am drowning in a sudden wave of adult instincts. I can no longer see anything or hear anything. I want to cry out, call, for I believe I am about to die.

Then the silence of the library strikes me. I can no longer even perceive my uncle's breathing and I dare not look at him. A minute, a slow minute passes. Not a sound reaches me, not the slightest breath or creaking of the armchair where he sits. What is he doing? Very quietly, I call him.

"Uncle!"

He does not reply.

"Uncle!"

He has not moved. I listen. He has not breathed.

Then a terrible doubt assails me. I remember what my father said the other night when cleaning his scalpel:

"He could die from one moment to the next."

"Uncle!"

This time I have shouted with all my strength, panic-stricken. Nothing.

I get up, trembling, teeth chattering. He is there, stretched out, lying almost flat, in the pose he held beforehand. But his face is very pale. My father's question comes to mind:

"Have you noticed whether his legs swell up?" Yes, they look enormous! And he is not moving! A fly circles over his forehead, then runs across his eyelids, goes down his nose and back again. He does not move. I take his hand. It is cold. A white foam flecks his closed lips.

"Uncle! Uncle!"

But now his fingers start to move; the flecks of foam flutter on an exhaled breath and his lips feebly release a cry, then another, then yet another. Gradually the tense muscles of his face relax; his jaw shifts and clicks, his chest swells and respires, his eyes open a little; and from his mouth, now wide open, gasping for the air of life, a long sigh, a long groan escapes.

"Uncle! Uncle!"

This is no longer a cry of distress but a cry of joy. He is alive!

My uncle is looking at me, but his eyes do not register his return from the abyss, from hell. He does not yet know where he is, he does not yet know who I am. His eyes brighten, register astonishment. Then his glance passes back and forth from me to the table where the book still lies. His eyes seek, enquire, show shame, imploring. In the space of a second they translate all the sensation that the return of consciousness brings to him, his memory regained.

"Albert, it's you!"

"Yes, uncle, it is I."

With an expression of pain and such compassionate, deep sadness that I will never be able to forget it, my uncle mutters:

"Poor child, leave now. Poor child."

"No, uncle, you are sick. I will look after you."

"Go now, poor child. It's over now. Please go, it is my wish."

The following day I found my uncle in the yard, seated before a blazing bonfire. By him lay a heap of books. He took them one by one, tore them up and threw them into the flames.

"You see," he said to me, "I'm burning them."

He placed his hand on his breast and added with profound disgust:

"But it is this other fearful book we should be destroying, the book of my heart."

I watched the smoke mounting in the air in blueish spirals and vanishing, and followed the little pieces of burnt paper, fluttering, pursued by the wind, like dead leaves.

Chapter Four

Dusk was falling at the end of a mild April day. My uncle and I were leaning out of the window of his room, resting on our elbows and looking at one another. It was still light but a finer light, more drained of colour, duller was spreading over the landscape. Behind the hazily sketched wood, dusted with ashy green, the sun was going down; and the sky was without a cloud, calm as a summer sea, its charming pallor quickened with a blush of rose on the horizon. There was a renaissance occurring, life swelled the branches with buds ready to burst. The trees seemed to take pleasure in spreading their fertile limbs. Already a Judas tree displayed the red pattern of its florets; further off, a chestnut tree flourished its broad leaves of a tender green. A strong scent of germination rose from the soil in its labour of love; on a pear tree, opposite us, two sparrows chased one another and coupled, feathers blending, wings fluttering.

"Do you know what they're doing?" asked my uncle all of a sudden.

"No, uncle, I don't."

"Well, they are making love. It looks simple, brief and gentle, doesn't it? That is because animals are fine creatures who arrange their lives honestly and know the value of things, never having had philosophers or scientists to explain anything to them. There! They've flown off. They never have regrets, they don't."

Pausing between each sentence, to draw breath – because at that stage he was wheezing a great deal – he said:

"We are not animals, unfortunately, and we make love differently. Instead of preserving the character that love has in nature, of a normal, peaceful and noble act, indeed the character of an organic function, we have introduced an element of fantasy. Fantasy created unappeased desire, and unappeased desire created debauchery. For debauchery is nothing other than the deformation of natural love by the ideal. Religions –

and the Catholic religion above all – have set themselves up as the great pimps of love. Under the pretext of softening the brutal side of love – which is in fact its only heroic aspect – they have developed the perverse, unhealthy side, by the sensuality of music and perfumes, by the mysticism of prayer and the moral onanism of adoration . . . Do you understand? They knew what they were doing, you know, those courtesans! They knew it was the best and surest way to brutalise men and enslave them. So, poets have sung only of love, arts have exalted only love. Love has dominated life, like the whip dominates the life of the slave it lashes or the murdering knife the chest it pierces. As for God! God is merely a form of debauched love. He is the supreme, inexorable moment of pleasure towards which we all direct our overworked desires and which we can never reach. In the past I believed in love and I believed in God. Often I still believe, for it is a poison one is never quite cured of. In churches, on solemn feast days, stunned by the voice of the organ music, weakened by the intoxicating scents of incense, overcome by the marvellous poetry of the psalms, I feel my soul exalt. It trembles, is moved in waves of delight, all its unspoken, unformulated aspirations, just as my flesh trembles, shaken to the marrow, before a naked woman or even merely before an imagined image of one. Do you understand?"

"No, uncle," I replied timidly.

He seemed astonished and shrugged his shoulders.

"Well, is there anything you do understand?" he said.

"It is also true," I ventured, "that you always tell me things that frighten me, uncle."

The Abbé exclaimed:

"That frighten you! That frighten you! Because you're an imbecile, because your parents, who are imbeciles, have given you a deplorable education."

He stopped again, his throat constricted, suffocating. Sweat dripped down his face. He opened his mouth wide and drank in the fresh, garden air in a long, painful breath.

"That frighten you!" he went on. "It's obvious. Fathers and mothers are guilty, put that in your head, boy. Instead of hiding from a child what love is, instead of falsifying its essence, troubling his heart, describing it to him as a fearful mystery or a vile sin, if they had the intelligence to explain it to him clearly, to teach him it, like they teach him to walk and eat; if they guaranteed for him its free exercise, at the decisive moments in puberty, well the world would not be what it is. Young people would not come to women with their imaginations already rotted, all their abominable curiosities already exhausted in degrading fantasies. What about you? I wager..."

My uncle stared at me, I felt myself blush, without knowing why.

"I wager," he continued, "that you have dreamt of ... things ... of things ... Answer me!"

"No, no, uncle!" I stammered, blushing still more.

"Come along, don't lie! Answer."

I did not answer.

"Why are you blushing? You see, little rascal."

At that moment, Madeleine, who had not heard us come back in, called out, running through the garden:

"Monsieur l'Abbé! Monsieur l'Abbé!"

"What is it?" asked my uncle.

"You must go straightaway with the good Lord and 'is 'oly oils! There's a man awaiting in the kitchen."

"A man!" yelled my uncle. "Is he making fun of me? What is he to do with me? Am I the parish priest?"

"The man says," explained Madeleine, "that Father isn't in the presbytery. Monsieur Desroches is sick, and then the other vicar's away. It's for a young girl who's more than 'alf dead already!"

"Very well, I'll see this man."

He grumbled as he left the room:

"Huh, well, first of all, I'm ill myself."

The wood was an expanse of dark blue and red masses, pierced here and there with brilliant orange lights. It was not yet night, but the greenery was already draining of colour beneath the evening sky, objects took on an indistinct shape, their contours dissolving into the denser air. A sense of mystery flooded the plain whose silvery green mingled with the pulverulent mist; and against the paling gold of the walls, the trees in the garden twisted their tormented silhouettes, harsher now. The birds had fallen silent. And I thought sadly that a young girl was about to die.

My uncle came back unhappy, breathing more heavily. He had to sit down for a few minutes to get his breath back. He complained:

"At this time of night. It's madness. And I'm ill too!"

His chest wheezed and panted, groaning like a steam engine; his sides heaved and occasionally one could see the fleshless outline of his ribs beneath the soutane.

"Extreme unction!" he muttered. "How should I know how to administer that? Little one!"

"Yes, uncle."

"You're coming with me. You can be the altar boy. Frélotte. Do you know the village Frélotte?"

"Yes, uncle."

"Is it about a mile from Viantais?"

"Yes, uncle."

"A mile! I can't make it that far. And my ritual, where's my ritual?"

He had to search for his ritual and eventually found it at the bottom of a drawer amid scraps of candle and rusty nails. While he rapidly scanned the pages dealing with extreme unction, he grumbled:

"What about the parish priest? No doubt he's stuffing his face at some official dinner somewhere. Ugh, *ad manus, ad pedes*, the symbolism is ludicrous. And when I've daubed her . . . *ad lumbos* . . . will the poor girl be purer? *Ad aures* . . . So people can't be left to die in peace then."

The Abbé closed his ritual, put it in the pocket of his soutane.

"Right, let's go," he said.

As we walked, he kept repeating:

"*Ad pedes? Ad manus* . . . A mile! God, I'm suffocating."

A wan light that gave no illumination, the glimmer of the pale night sky entering through the broad picture windows of the church, broke the shadows in the aisles with its mean, dubious gleam. Our footsteps echoed on the flagstones and the sound rose towards the vaulted ceilings, fading into the dark depths of the chapels and the nave, where columns, indistinct arches and dim patches of whiteness could be made out very vaguely, shadows amid the shadows. A comma of light, the invisible chancel lamp suspended in space, was as sad as a solitary star, lost in a firmament veiled with black clouds and moonless.

The verger had been forewarned and was already awaiting us in the sacristy. Guttering candle ends in tall candlesticks of yellow brass cast a weak, funereal glow over a room paved with black and white tiles, a range of gleaming cupboards and right at the end, a little confessional whose carvings shone between the two curtains of green serge. A sour smell of melted wax, mingled with the scent of incense, caught the back of our throats.

"Let's hurry," said my uncle to the verger, who bowed his head respectfully.

He was a small man, pale, round, very clean, with long, thin hair sticking to his temples, and that affable but sly manner typical of lay brothers. He was a baker by trade, but also had charge of the town sewers, of the market tolls and the church pews. On important occasions, he served at table for the priest. Punctual, meticulous, and marvellously conversant with all the sacraments, Baptiste Coudray was a distinguished verger, so distinguished that he was respected almost as much as a vicar. He spoke very quietly and very slowly, in well-chosen and careful terms. He had already prepared his box and lit the red lantern with its long handle, which I was to carry.

"I thought I had best put a communion cloth in the box," he explained. "Those kind of people on the whole never have anything suitable for the holy viaticum."

"Put what you like in there. Hurry up!" replied my uncle.

Whilst he donned the surplice and the stole, aided by the verger, he asked:

"And where is the parish priest?"

"Father is at a conference in Saint-Cyr-la-Rosière."

"And the vicar?"

"Today I was told that the reverend vicar would be marrying his sister in another parish."

The verger handed my uncle his cappa magna and with a combination of concern and protectiveness added:

"I notice that Monsieur l'Abbé is not well . . . and Frélotte is quite a walk."

My uncle moaned:

"A walk! You've forgotten the maniple, Baptiste."

"In these circumstances, the officiant never wears the maniple. Monsieur l'Abbé can check it in his ritual."

This said, in a reproachful and slightly shocked tone, he disappeared to light the altar candles.

My uncle did not delay before the altar, despatched as quickly as possible the *oremus* and the genuflections, then, having covered the ciborium with its gold-fringed cloth, came down again. We set off.

The verger walked in front holding the box with the holy oils in one hand and a bell in the other. I came after, carrying the lantern. My uncle followed us, panting, ill, heavily encumbered by the ciborium, which he raised, lowered, leaned to the left and then the right, trying to find a comfortable position for it, so that he could draw breath more easily.

"Not so fast!" he cried, when we came out onto the avenue of elms which led from the church to the village.

At every twentieth step, the verger shook his bell, *dring, dring*! People came to their doors, leaned out of the windows, took off their hats, crossed themselves. In the street, women genuflected, heads bent, hands joined. A little line of people formed behind my uncle and swelled at every crossroads until it became a real procession. The bell sounded, *dring, dring*, at regular intervals. I was proud of my rôle and every time we passed beneath a street lamp, I amused myself by looking at my shadow and the shadow of the lantern getting larger, lengthening along the road surface, onto the pavements, onto the white façades of the houses, with the dancing glow of the red light reflected at the bottom. *Drrr* . . .

in . . . gg! As we left the town, my uncle stopped, his breath giving out.

"I am suffocating!" he said to me. "My head's swimming . . . And this . . . this . . . this thing is causing me terrible problems. Here, hold it."

He handed me the ciborium, wiped his sweat-soaked face with a fold of his surplice and for a few seconds greedily gulped in lungfuls of air, then we set off again.

The night was deep, silent, disturbed by our steps alone and by the hoarse wheezing escaping from my uncle's chest. The verger now only rang his bell if he could hear distant voices or the wheels of a cart. And we kept walking, beneath the low, dull sky, invaded now by livid clouds, we walked between the great sheets of shadow covering the countryside, between the great shadows skittering along the ever-narrowing horizon, amid the twisted, untidy, demonic shadows of apple trees. Sometimes, edging the road, we saw terrifying silhouettes of oak trunks, short, bare, branches lopped, like a flight of embryonic monsters in the gloomy darkness, a gallop of fat, hunched larvae, emerging from the void. Sometimes, treeless, shadowless, verge-less, the road ascended, paler between the abyss of uniform shadows and, hanging above it, a high wall of wan sky without space, distance or depth, which closed it in within its leaden mass, the extreme limit of the earth and the firmament. I was afraid and even the verger coughed ostentatiously to reassure himself a little.

Weakened by exertion and exhausted by pain, my uncle had to stop again. His legs were trembling and refused to support the weight of his body, so he sat down on a milestone and stayed there a long while, in a state of collapse, the ciborium between his feet, his head in his hands. In that mournful darkness it was sinister to hear him gasping, rasping, snatching life from the gusts of wind passing by.

"Just ten minutes to go, Monsieur l'Abbé," offered the verger by way of encouragement. "I can see the lights of Frélotte down there."

"Ten minutes! I'll never make it. I'm suffocating. I'm dying."

He tried to get up but fell back and the ciborium rolled along the ground and dropped into the ditch with a clang.

"Holy Virgin!" cried the verger. "Our Saviour's body in the ditch! The good Lord may well be lost!"

A white pebble gleamed in the shadows on the verge. He thought it was the host shining.

"I can see it," he babbled. "It's shining!"

"Well pick it up then, Baptiste," ordered my uncle in a strangled voice.

Baptiste was seized with terror.

"I, Monsieur l'Abbé? I? Touch the good Lord with impure hands when my soul is full of sin? No, no, never! I would be struck down!"

"Imbecile!" swore the Abbé. "Help me, child."

He managed to stand up and we searched for the ciborium. The verger had put his box and his bell down on the ground and, quite pale, his eyes wide, he was holding the lantern tilted at ground level and running it along the edge of the ditch. Soon, in the red glow spreading over the grass, we could see the ciborium, intact, still covered with its cloth. I picked it up, not without a shudder. The covering had not shifted. My uncle raised it slightly and seeing the host at the bottom of the holy receptacle said:

"Right, no harm done. Let's go."

On the right now could be seen the dark outline of several houses, and a few lights pierced the darkness. My uncle's wheezing was quieter now and his step firmer. Still terrified by the scene with the chalice which he interpreted as a profanation, a sacrilege, the verger mumbled prayers under his breath. From time to time he turned round, his face pallid, his eye fearful, horrified that a priest could treat the good Lord so cavalierly. As we entered the village, he shook his bell: *drr ... ii ... nnggg!* Doors slammed, clogs clattered, shadows passed, faces appeared in the rectangles of lighted windows. *Drr ... iii ... nng! Drr ... iii ... ng!* Two dogs started up a lengthy chorus of barking, others replied. And the bell kept on: *ddrr . . . i . . . nggg!* We crossed yards, walked alongside manure heaps, beside low walls above which tousled shocks of tree branches shook. And the bell went on: *ddrr . . . ii . . . ngg!*

In front of the sick girl's house, a carriage was standing and, by the light of a lantern held by a farm labourer, I recognised my father undoing his horse's rein. He moved the carriage so as to leave the roadway clear and I heard him say in astonishment:

"Look! It's Albert! It's Jules!"

Then he melted into the crowd of passers-by and people drawn by the sound of the bell.

On a high bed draped with heavy cotton, amid white sheets upon which flashes of light played, the sick girl lay motionless, her face waxen, her teeth clenched. Her hands, thin and yellow, did not move, extended on the fold of sheet. With her pinched nostrils and stiff eyelids, she looked dead. At the bedside, a woman sobbed, bent forward, her face in her apron. Between the door and the gloomy bed, neighbours prayed, the women on their knees, the men standing, heads bowed, turning their hats sadly in their hands. Between the hearth, where gorse roots were burning, and the bed, against the smoke-stained wall, a little table had been prepared. In the centre of this table, covered with a white cloth, was a rough crucifix, flanked by two candles, and a vase full of holy water where an aspergeoir made of birch twigs lay soaking. There was also a plate containing a roll of tow, some bread and, next to the plate, a bowl of water for the priest's ablutions. Any light in the room was directed onto the bed and the face of the dying girl, and shadows crowded overhead in the cotton draperies.

My uncle paused on the threshold and, faced with the spectacle of death and of prayer, his face all of a sudden was transfigured. Pain and pity moistened the lips which earlier had blasphemed; an almost noble serenity appeared in his eyes, which earlier anger had narrowed horribly. With a brusque and powerful effort of will, he silenced the pain which ravaged his chest and tore at his throat and extending his hand in a noble, calm, kind gesture, he walked into the wretched room.

"*Pax huic domui,*" he said in a soft, compassionate voice.

The verger replied:

"*Et omnibus habitantibus in ea.*"

Having placed the ciborium on the table and sprinkled holy water on the people present, he said:

"*Dominus vobiscum!*"

The verger responded:

"*Et cum spiritu tuo.*"

The Abbé took the crucifix and brought it to the lips of the dying girl, but the lips remained motionless in contact with God. She could no longer see, hear nor feel anything. Her eyes already gazed on infinity. So he bent over her tenderly. A feeble, gentle breath like the soft breath of a flower falling, wilted and exhausted, exhaled from between her clenched teeth. The sheet over her chest did not even rise. And the child, beneath the pale mask of death, retained the look of youth and a touching beauty.

"This is God coming to meet you," said my uncle. "Do you not feel his presence?"

The young girl remained motionless.

So the Abbé turned towards those present, towards the women kneeling, their white caps skimmed by the light, towards the men standing, who turned their dark faces in the shadow towards him.

"She is dying," he said.

He pointed at the chalice gleaming on the table and the holy oils in their silver cruet and added:

"What's the point? Let us not disturb her. Pray, you who love her."

He knelt down next to the bed and in a voice full of emotion that sang the sad epithalamion of death:

"Poor child, you came to us on one day and the following day you left us. Of life you have known only the first smiles and you fall asleep at the time when pain will be inevitable. Go into the light and into rest, little soul, sister of the fragrant soul of flowers, sister of the musical soul of birds ... Tomorrow in my garden I will scent your fragrance in the perfume of my flowers and hear you sing in the branches of my trees. You will be the guardian of my heart and the invisible solace of my thoughts."

He stood up, placed a kiss on the forehead of the dead girl and once again stretching his hands over those present, who were stunned by this unusual prayer:

"*Dominus vobiscum*," he said.

But the verger did not reply. Astonished, horrified, he did not understand anything that had just happened. Not only did he not understand, but he did not know whether he really was alive, if this house, these women, the chalice on the table, the dead girl, if all that surrounded him was not a dream. In his disturbance, in his confusion, he did not follow the Abbé who was making for the door, and stayed in the room amid the people, his eyes wild, his arms loose, his mouth wide open.

My father was waiting for us outside.

"Good evening, Jules," he said, going towards his brother, his hand outstretched.

"Good evening. It is you?"

"Yes, I was leaving the house, I recognised you. It's late, you're ill, would you like me to drive you back?"

"Yes indeed," said my uncle.

"And the chalice? You had the host with you, I think."

"Oh yes, oh dear, I've left it behind. Never mind, Baptiste will sort it out."

All three of us huddled into the carriage. Soon my uncle started to gasp.

"Are you ill?" asked my father.

"Yes, yes! I'm suffocating. I feel I'm suffocating, then my head spins and then I shiver with fever."

My father wrapped him in a blanket and took from his pocket a little bottle of ammonia which he made his brother sniff.

"Why do you not want to see me?" he asked with gentle reproach. "I would look after you well. I would cure you.

Listen Jules, I am your brother, damn it! And I have never done anything to harm you, never!"

So my uncle replied in between painful intakes of breath:

"Yes, I'd like that. Come. And your wife must come too. I'm suffocating!"

The following day, my mother and father came to Les Capucins. They found the Abbé in his bed in a fever. He had tried to get up at his usual time, but had suffered a fit, followed by vomiting. After that, stunned, his head spinning, his body racked by shivering, he had been obliged to go back to bed. My father listened to his chest, examined him with the greatest of care and faced with the seriousness of the illness could not hide his concern.

"It might be nothing," he said. "But would you mind if I asked for a second opinion? You know, I'm a stickler . . . and anyway one never quite knows how to cope when it's a member of the family . . ."

My uncle replied with resignation:

"What's the use? I can feel I'm going downhill, that I don't have many days left to live. What I would like is to be left to die in peace the way I wish. If I am in too much pain, relieve it a little. That's all I ask."

With sorrowful melancholy, he added:

"My death is of no importance. It's always sad to see old houses, old trees, old towers fall. But I have never sheltered anyone, I've never given anyone fruit, no one has ever sung in me of faith or love. If I die well, if I go on my way, calm, without regrets or hatred, my death will have been the only good thing in my life, and perhaps the only thing that redeems it."

He stopped, for the weight in his chest cut his breath. Then a few moments later he started again:

"What I would like too, is that my bed be taken to the window. I love my garden, I love my trees, I love this sky, this great sky . . ."

My father was very moved, my mother looked at the garden, impassive, hard. She said, with a chilly smile:

"Indeed, it is a pretty sight."

The Abbé suppressed a grimace, extinguished a nasty light that gleamed in his eye and sighed:

"Oh, I love it for things you cannot see, hear or understand, my sister."

He turned his face towards the wall, staring at the pale flowers on the paper and spoke no more.

I spent most of the day in the garden neither playing nor running about. I was no longer in the mood. Everything looked gloomy, sad; the greenery was in mourning; even the birds were sorrowful, the acacia reminded me of the sombre shrubs people plant on tombs. However, I stayed out there, seated where my uncle liked to sit, his long legs in the grass. I imagined his green greatcoat, his straw hat, his jerky walk, his strange conversations which had frightened me but which now frightened me less, for at that particular moment, they confused me, I felt a kind of abstract pain, which perhaps some act of tenderness might have soothed. I loved him, yes, I really loved him, and I considered how he in his turn, prone to anger as he was, had never once acted towards me with impatience. Anguished, I was constantly drawn back to the house. I questioned Madeleine, trying to reassure myself; or else I quietly tiptoed to the bedroom door and stayed there for long minutes listening to the noise of my uncle's breathing and the swish of my mother's dress as she walked across the parquet.

Towards evening, cousin Debray arrived:

"Well, what's up?" he cried. "A damn fine fellow like you?"

He was astonished to find my father and mother there, installed before him at the bedside of the invalid and he glanced at the tables and chests of drawers with the tense curiosity of the potential heir.

We left the room; it was nearly time for dinner.

"Well?" asked my mother.

"He's finished," said my father. "It's not just the heart disease, it's the fever. Poor Jules."

That evening, my father went back to Les Capucins and

watched over the invalid, whilst my mother checked over all our black clothing with the calm, meticulous care of a good housewife.

Chapter Five

My mother had been at the Abbé's bedside for three hours and had just come out. She was going to Viantais where, she said, she had some errands to do. I stayed alone in the room with my uncle. The illness had further ravaged his face, scoring with pitiless claws new furrows on the withered, dried-out skin. Fever splashed the protruding cheekbones with two purplish stains and his huge eyes shone with an already superhuman light from large, dark-blue ringed sockets. From time to time, his trembling hand, with its knotty protuberances, carried a cup of some refreshing drink to his lips and his furred tongue made a constant, pitiful, clicking sound against his palate. He was breathing with difficulty. On the marble of the bedside table, phials, symmetrically arranged, exuded pharmaceutical odours and the kettle sang, placed on the hot ashes of the hearth.

"My child," my uncle said, "lock the door so that no one can come in and come here, next to me. I need to speak to you, all alone, just you. For you are the only person who has ever really loved me."

The gentle sadness with which he said this moved me so much, I could not hold back the tears. I immediately burst out sobbing.

"Come along now," the invalid consoled me tenderly. "Don't cry, my child, and do what I ask."

I bolted the door and went over to the bed. My uncle smiled at me, then drew back for a few moments.

Outside in the garden, cousin Debray was walking about, spitting. He too had settled in at Les Capucins and would not leave, watching my parents with disquiet. His presence was a source of irritation for my uncle, though he occasionally joked with the captain.

"You know, cousin, when I am dead you will stuff me and put me on a pine board with a nut in my paws, like one of your polecats." To which the captain would reply:

"What a joker you are Jules. I've never known a damned invalid like you."

Nevertheless, the cousin had been persuaded that he should enter the bedroom as seldom as possible. He spent his days walking around the house or else passed long periods in the library trying to find the very expensive, rare volumes the Abbé had shown him before. Then he roamed through the rooms apparently making an inventory of all the objects and throwing furtive looks about him.

My uncle wiped his lips to clean off the sediment from the fever, drank another mouthful of tisane and in a halting, painful voice began to speak:

"My dear child, I made my will some months back. I have left nothing to you nor to your family. Your mother will be furious, but you are of an age not to attach any importance to questions of money. I hope you won't hold it against me later on. Will you resent it?"

"No, uncle," I stammered, a little embarrassed and blushing.

He thanked me with a nod and went on:

"If I have disinherited you, do not please assume that I do not love you. You will have money enough without mine adding to what your parents leave you. For a long time now I had a peculiar idea, a psychological experiment to try out which you will find out about the day after my death. So, you don't resent me? Is that really true?"

"Really true, uncle," I replied.

"Now, listen to me. Like all people who have lived a bad life, I have feared death for a long time. But I have reflected a great deal in latter years and I have grown used to looking it in the face, questioning it. It holds no terror for me any longer. Last night as I dozed, I dreamt that it was like a huge lake, without horizon or limits, a lake on which I felt myself gently drifting between the whiteness of waves, the whiteness of sky, infinite whiteness. At this moment, I can see it as this great sky there in front of me. It has wonderful, deep clearings."

The Abbé lifted his head off the pillow and craning his

neck towards the window, intoxication in his eyes, he let his gaze wander in space.

Clouds of silver incandescence floated obliquely across the blueness washed with pink in places and in places iced with the pale green of crystal. They climbed above the wood, piled up, lengthened and dispersed into the infinite firmament.

"Yes," he repeated, "death is like that great sky."

He stayed silent a moment, tracing with his eyes, in a kind of ecstasy, the luminous ascent of the clouds above the wood; then he turned back and settled his head onto his pillow, stretched out in the bed and in a melancholy voice said:

"I wasted my life, little Albert, I wasted it, because I was never able to dominate fully the filthy passions that were in me, the repressed passions of the priest, inherited passions, born of my mother's mysticism and the alcoholism of my father. I did put up a fight though, really I did! But they conquered me. I am dying as a result of that battle and that defeat. When I decided to come back to this peace and this solitude, I promised myself I would forget the past and live happily, work, because I had enormous projects. I have not been able. Here, as everywhere, I found myself face to face with the monster. I endured terrible tortures. It is good that I am dying therefore. But though I have lived in an evil haste, in fever, in that permanent disproportion between the dreams in my head and the appetites in my flesh, I want to die in serenity; I want, be it only for a day, to taste that luxury I have never known; the fullness of repose for my mind, my heart, my senses."

The invalid gave a long sigh; and, crumpling with feeble fingers the handkerchief he held in his hands, for a few more seconds he uttered not a word. Then he went on in more clipped tones, a grimace distorting his lips.

"I know where your mother is. At least I can guess. Your mother is with the parish priest. That was inevitable. She wants the priest to see me and bring me what people call the consolations of religion. She wished it not for me, whom she could not care less about, but for herself, for your father, for the pious reputation of the family. Now, I do not want that priest to set foot in my house. I do not want it. What he would say, I know as well as he, and the visit of that fat imbecile would annoy me, irritate me and compromise the peace of my last hours. If God exists, imagine if he would present himself to me in the vulgar form of that oaf, that ignoramus . . . If I want to pray, I need no one. Let me be left to die in the way I see fit. I make you the guardian of my repose. Promise me that if the priest tries to force his way in, promise me that you will drive him away. You will explain to him that I refuse to see him, that I desire neither the deceit of his prayers nor the sad farce of his exhortations, nor that ridiculous and sinister comedy which is acted out around the beds of the dying. Will you promise to do that for me? Will you promise to defend me against all the violators of the final agony, even against your mother?"

He took my hands, and look at me almost begging.

"Will you?"

"I promise, uncle," I said, my heart breaking.

"Good, my child! I thank you."

Then, speaking to himself, he muttered in a quieter voice:

"Isn't it strange, this thing that is taking place in me? The calmer my soul becomes, the dimmer the image of God becomes in my mind. I don't understand any more. God! God! When I lived a bad life, I believed in God, he terrified me. Now, I seek him in vain. I cannot find him any longer. He has gone. Is he maybe the theoretical embodiment of remorse?"

He mused a few moments, then turned towards me:

"And now, stop being sad, my child. Whenever I look at your little face there are tears there. Smile for me. There is no need to cry when someone we love dies. It is Catholicism that has turned death into a grim, fearful event, whilst it is but the deliverance of man, the return of the prisoner from life to his real home, to the sweet, kindly void. Ah! Instead of tears and mourning, I would like there to be only be music and joy in the rooms of the dying! I would like . . . I would like . . ."

He stopped, apparently searching for words and thoughts that evaded him.

"I no longer know what else I would like," he mumbled, "I no longer know. If I speak to you like this, it is because I sense I am near the end. There are moments when life drains from my limbs, dries up in my heart, when my head spins, my mind becomes confused, blends with space, when I feel I am already floating on the huge lake, the lake that is infinite in extent and profundity ... Before leaving, before disappearing into the radiant whiteness, I would like to give you something which is worth more than money, the secret of happiness. I have thought about it a great deal, a great deal. Love nature, my child, and you will be a fine man, and you will be happy. All earthly joys are in that love, all virtues also. Whatever turns away from nature is a perversion and leaves only incurable pain and a remorse that ever taints. I would like one more thing, I would like you to read me Pascal. Go and find me Pascal, you will find the book in the library on the third shelf on the left, near the fireplace. It is a little red book, with gold edging. Go on!"

I came back with Pascal and for more than an hour, I read to my uncle. Sometimes he fell asleep; his breath came in shorter, faster, weaker rasps, so I would shut the book and fall silent. But he, not hearing my voice any more would wake with a start and look at me as if trying to recognise me, remember. He would murmur:

"Ah, yes, it is you. Go on, my child, your voice lulls me to sleep, I can hear what you are reading. The words, the ideas reach me very softly, very faintly, garbed in delicious dreams. They come to me like fairy beings, they come through rosy mists floating over dazzling seas; they reach me in bedizened robes and long silk trains, covered with jewels and perfumes. What magic have thoughts glimpsed through a fever. How they gain new life and colour in the bright light of death. One should always be dying, always! Read, child. If I fall asleep, do not stop."

Sometimes too, all of a sudden, his gaze haggard, he interrupted me:

"You know what you promised! The priest ... your mother ... God! Stop! You are tiring me. The words now have strange faces; the thoughts pass by, black, shapeless, like shadows ... And that trumpet that sounds down there, on and on, ah! It is tiring me so! Have it stop, my child, I beg you! And that bell, make that bell stop. It is the priest making all that din. It is droning in my ears like a swarm of hornets. Drive it away. I want to sleep ..."

When my mother came back, the Abbé was very agitated. He was shifting about in his bed, pushing the covers right down to his belly, often uttering incoherent words. My mother went up to him.

"Don't say anything to me!" he exclaimed. "I do not want the priest to come. I do not want anything to do with his God. I do not want it! I want to die how I see fit! Why are you tormenting me like this?"

She pulled the sheets up over his chest and spoke softly to him.

"The priest was passing by, dear brother," she explained. "Knowing you were ill, he came. He is in the garden."

My uncle sat bolt upright, terrified.

"No! No!" he repeated. "I do not want it. Let me die in peace."

My mother insisted with tender words and a caressing voice, supplication in her eyes.

"He will only stay a minute, brother, you know ..."

But the Abbé let out a roar of fury.

"Leave me alone, you! Leave me alone!"

And grasping my mother's hand, he bit her ferociously on the thumb.

"How you enrage me, vile woman! I would love to kill you, old harpy, kill you in some atrocious way!"

During this, Father Blanchard had half-opened the door and put his red, shiny head round it. My uncle glimpsed him, turned to face the wall and would not move. It was impossible to get a single word from him. He did not reply to the priest's questions and, his teeth clenched, his cheekbones splashed with a brighter red, his eyes fixed on some vague

216

point on the wall, he remained motionless and grim. Only his fingers tightened on the sheet, twisting it spasmodically. I could sense his heart beating fast in his chest and hear his teeth grinding. The priest threw his hands up in a gesture of resignation and, led by my mother, eventually left the room, muttering in a scandalised whisper.

"Would you like me to go on reading, uncle?" I asked, a little ashamed at not having kept my promise and hoping to divert attention from the painful scene that had taken place.

The invalid did not move. I heard him crooning to himself in a low, shaky voice:

> *The priest asked her*
> *La, la, la*
> *The priest asked her:*
>
> *What have you beneath your skirt*
> *La, la, la*
> *What have you beneath your skirt?*

"Uncle! Uncle!" I implored. "Speak to me! Look at me!"

He went on, weaker still, not moving, whilst his hand scratched at the sheet like a crab's claw:

> *What I have beneath my skirt*
> *La, la, la*
> *What I have beneath my skirt*
>
> *Is a little plump pussy*
> *La, la, la*
> *Is a little plump pussy*

Then he fell into a painful sleep, punctuated with sudden wakefulness and sobs.

He was prey to an extraordinary level of excitement and passed a bad night. His fever strengthened. His heart beat like a clock with a broken spring. His life seemed to be draining away in a wild ringing of bells. The delirium gave his eyes a terrible, demented look and his gestures looked murderous. My father, who was watching over him, helped by Madeleine, had great difficulty in restraining him. He tried to get up and let out savage cries, attempting to hurl himself against an imaginary being whose chaotic movements he followed with mounting fury from minute to minute. He thought it was Father Blanchard.

"You are lying in wait for my soul, bandit!" he yelled. "You do not want it free and dispersed around us, thief! I want it to be happy, but you will not have it. It is here!" (He pointed to his throat, constricted by a fit). "It is here. It is hurting me, suffocating me, but I will not spit it out. Get out! Get out!"

And when my father bent over him and tried to calm him.

"Drive him out!" he commanded, "He's hanging onto the cornices now, his wings outstretched, all black! Ah! There he is, flying . . . flying . . . listen to the drone of his wings . . . there he is! Kill him! Ah! Kill him now! Look! He's hiding under my bed, he's lifting it up, he's carrying it off! Ah! Kill him now! Kill that vile priest!"

At another point, he was crying and, completely terrified, huddled under the blankets, in a corner of the bed, like a small child.

Towards morning, he calmed down. The agitation of the night gave way to grim exhaustion, dull prostration of his mind and body. For three hours, he dozed, shaken by nervous jolts, his poor head haunted by horrifying nightmares which tore from him cries of terror. When his gaze rested upon us in the intervals when he was awake, his eyes were deep as a chasm, and had that disturbing, alarming, overwhelming fixity of the mysterious gaze of animals newly dead. They no longer reflected anything of life in their glassy convexity, no sign of recognition of the life around, no sign of an inner life. The lids seemed to have swollen out of all proportion around the dead pupils, empty of light, inert and pale orbs. At one point he seemed to recognise me, but it was only a fleeting glimmer which was immediately extinguished.

"Uncle," I said, "uncle, I am Albert, your little Albert, can you not see me?"

He went on staring at me and in a painful voice, without articulating, the words falling from his lips like sobs, he intoned:

> *What I have beneath my skirt*
> *La, la, la*
> *What I have beneath my skirt . . .*

From this point on, cousin Debray no longer took his walks in the garden. He stayed in the library, his ears pricked, appearing in the corridor at the slightest noise emerging from my uncle's room. Every time my father or my mother came out, he was there, ever before them opposite the door, his eyes bulging and suspicious.

"Well then? Still just as bad?"

"Worse, yes."

"Ah! You know, we'll have to put seals everywhere."

Every morning, the Tart brought him a bottle of cider, a big loaf of bread and slices of cold meat. He ate in the library and slept there too at night, stretched out in my uncle's large armchair, waking at all hours to come and listen at the door and gauge the progress of the illness. One evening he had an argument with my mother which began in very low voices, then gradually blew up into angry, violent, threatening tones. The captain kept saying:

"We'll have to seal everything up."

And my mother, impatient at this sentence uttered at every turn, replied:

"What is it to do with you? Why are you here in any case?"

"Why, for Christ's sake? Why? To stop you stealing, carrying stuff off to your house!"

"I? I?" cried my mother. "You are the one rummaging through drawers! You are the thief! What are you doing here? You are only his cousin."

"There is cutlery and silver missing. I am going to inform the police."

"And I will have you thrown out by the police."

My father had to come and insist that the captain hold his tongue as he was settling down to a litany of oaths.

As my uncle's condition deteriorated, cousin Debray became more insolent. He had the aggressive defiance of a slave master. He watched over my parents, stooped to the lowest of spying tricks, and did not attempt to conceal his cynical hopes. He kept mumbling:

"Damn it, have to get those doors sealed, damn it. I'm in the will, you're not, you lot. The Abbé didn't give a cuss about you, damn it."

He eventually decided that the library was too far from the dying man's room. He installed the large armchair in the corridor and thenceforth passed all his days and nights there, on watch duty, his heart warmed by the yelling, rasping and panting that reached him from the bed of pain in which my uncle suffered a terrible, nightmarish, final agony. We could hear him walking about, spitting, swearing.

"Chrissake! Have to seal the doors."

One Sunday morning, I remember, my father and my mother had left the bedside to go to the early mass in Viantais. Madeleine and I sat with my uncle. Over the course of a week, he had only recovered full consciousness two or three times – moments of clarity that soon passed. And in the brief flashes of intelligence, battered by the tortured madness of the fever, nothing was more painful than to hear him say:

"I am happy. I am happy to die so peacefully. How sweet it is to sink like this, rocked on the great lake of light. Why do you not read to me, my little Albert? When I am asleep, it acts like a charm on me, it chases the fever away. Read me a little Lucretius."

His delirium on bad nights had on several occasions assumed an erotic nature, a sexual excitement of a surprising and troubling intensity. Just like when he had typhoid fever, he pronounced terrible words and abandoned himself to obscene acts. At those moments, my mother did not dare go near the bed, fearing some unexpected attack or a sudden shameless embrace, such as on one occasion, when she had great difficulty breaking free. The Abbé had grabbed her by the waist and drawn her brutally towards him. She had felt on her lips his diseased, burning, fevered breath. That Sunday, Madeleine and I had only been alone in the room for about half an hour, when the Abbé flung sheets and covers far from him and suddenly rose up in front of us, an obscene display. Then, before we could prevent him, he got out of bed and, staggering on his long, fleshless legs, his nightshirt raised, belly bare, he cowered in a corner of the room. It was a vile scene, impossible to convey in all its terrifying horror. His carnal desires, now suppressed and overcome, now exacerbated and increased by the imaginings of a brain that never tired, spurted from his whole being, emptied his veins, his marrow of their accumulated lava. It was like the vomiting of a passion with which his body had always been tormented. Head against the wall, knees bent, haunches rutting, he opened and closed his hands, as if palpating impure, naked forms hunched over him: raised haunches, hanging breasts, stained bellies ... Letting out hoarse cries, roars of frightful desire, he simulated terrifying fornications, terrifying vice, where the idea of love mingled with the idea of blood; where the fury of the embrace was increased by the rage of murder. He thought he was Tiberius, Nero, Caligula.

"Whip them! Tear them to pieces!" he yelled.

His fingers curled into claws, he tore at the air, imagining he was tearing at living female flesh; his lips pursed in monstrous kisses, sucking blood from streaming, red wounds. And it was horrible, in that frenetic paroxysm of dying flesh, to see those two empty eyes, staring without a glimmer of light or thought, those two eyes, already dead, staring between the shrivelling lids. At last, he fell heavily onto the wooden floor and his hands, groping and leaping around him, sought their prey for the act of love.

At first, petrified by terror, I did not move an inch. My mind paralysed, my limbs numb, with the sensation that I had suddenly dropped into a corner of hell, I longed to flee. A heavy, painful emotion held me there, before this lamentable, hideous, damned man. However, when I saw my uncle fall, I cried out, and called for cousin Debray, who was still on guard in the corridor. The Abbé allowed himself to be picked up without offering any resistance.

"It's over," he said. "I can sleep."

Back in bed, he uttered little sobs, little whimpers, amid which I recognised the tune of the song returning in the midst of his delirium like an ironical, melancholy obsession:

> *What I have beneath my skirt*
> *La, la, la*
> *What I have beneath my skirt*
>
> *Is a little plump pussy*
> *La, la, la*
> *Is a little plump pussy*

From then on I was forbidden to stay in the room. I too settled in the corridor, with cousin Debray who never once spoke to me. The cousin roamed from one end of the corridor to the other, his hands behind his back, preoccupied, discontented, doubtless finding the death agony prolonged beyond convenience. He was tired and dirty. So clean normally, his clothing was covered in dust, his beard too long, a black scarf twisted around his neck. Sometimes, he went into the library, where I heard him patting the books, then he came back and sat in the armchair, grousing, muttering things I could not understand beneath his moustache.

In the room, the attacks succeeded one another, each more terrible. Through the wall came wild shouts, stifled cries, gasping, groans. There were sounds of struggle, creaking of the bed, shifting of furniture, something vague and agonising which sounded to me like someone being killed. From time to time my father's voice begged:

"Jules, please, please, calm down, old fellow!"

From time to time, Jules' voice screamed:

"Come here! Ah! Whore! Beat her!"

Father Blanchard came, stayed a half-hour then came out again, accompanied by my mother. They were whispering:

"It is terrible, terrible! He doesn't recognise anyone any more," my mother was saying.

"Fortunately," replied the priest. "Otherwise, he would never have agreed . . . Ah well, that's that now. People do not necessarily need to know everything."

For the whole day, with the comings and goings, there was panic, haste, a madness which increased. The captain narrowed the scope of his watch, his eyes permanently fixed on the door, through which that poor, accursed soul was about to fly away and disappear.

The agony went on for two days more, two atrocious days which felt to me like two centuries. In truth I do not know how I avoided going mad myself. I lived in constant horror, my reason wandered, I was prey to unexpected dizzinesses. My senses could not function properly, shaken by too much violence. The most ordinary objects took on threatening, abnormal, supernatural aspects. When my father and mother crossed the corridor, they appeared to glide by, carried on a great mass of shadows, like insubstantial beings in a nightmare, containing something of the terrifying madness of the Abbé. The priest came back several times and he too seemed like an extravagant and incredible dream, created by a fevered brain. Like my uncle, I saw him fluttering by on strange, black wings, a huge, sinister carrion crow. Though I did not enter the room in those terrible days, I could not blot out the terrifying image of my uncle Jules, hideous in his lust. Rather, it obsessed me, multiplying, amplifying into spectral images of debauchery. Every roar, every choked gasp, every rasp which I could hear distinctly through the wall, took on physical representation in my mind, assumed visible and tangible forms, forms of an incoherent dream, motions of a parodic and monstrous life, whose macabre terror grew and grew. I wanted to run away and could not. I stayed there, listening to that voice spewing out in its last breaths of life blasphemies and obscenities; I stayed there, listening to the last rebellion of that cursed intelligence, the last spasms of that damned sexuality. And I recalled the desolate words of my uncle: "How sweet to sink, rocked on the great lake of light. " There were times when I thought I was dying too, when I felt the suffocating shades of eternal punishment crowding in on me.

Towards the end of the second day, the noise stopped, the voice fell silent. An hour perhaps went by like this in silence. Night fell; a yellow light shone through the cracks under the door. I was all alone. Cousin Debray had shut himself in the library. My father came out and called me.

"Go and say goodbye to your uncle, my son," he murmured quietly. Two huge tears rolled down his pale cheeks.

I went into the room. My uncle was resting peacefully, his head sideways on the pillow. His face was twisted and horribly yellow, his body motionless, he seemed to be sleeping. Now and then, a spasm shook his jaw, and his hands lying flat on the sheet. From his barely open mouth, a little, soft, musical sound emerged, like the sound of a bottle emptying. His beard made harsh shadows on the skin which was orangey where the bones protruded and leaden where the shrivelled muscles sank back emptily. At the foot of the bed, my mother prayed on her knees. Was she really praying?

I went up to him: my heart missing a beat, I placed a kiss on my uncle's forehead. In that brief second when my lips touched his unfeeling skin, with an extraordinary clarity, the whole life of that poor creature came into my mind; since the day when he had taken my school books and flung them over the wall in an amusing gesture, to the moment when he had crouched, obscene and terrifying in the corner of that room. I burst into tears. My mother stood up, crossed the hands of the dying man across his chest and inserted between his fingers a little brass cross which she had brought; then she went back to her prayers.

Despite my suffering, I could still hear the tune in my head; that tune kept coming back through all other sounds; it was in my mother's whispering lips; it was in the ever fainter, feebler rasp, saying as it expired, just like a kitten's gentle purr:

> *What have you under your skirt?*
> *La, la, la*
> *What have you under your skirt?*

And I responded to myself, choked by tears:

> *A little plump pussy*
> *La, la, la*
> *A little plump pussy*

When I went into the library, cousin Debray was standing on a ladder, a candle in his hand, inspecting the books. For a long time he had been trying to find the very rare and expensive books the Abbé had shown him once.

"Well?" he asked, "Jules? I can't hear him bawling."

"He is dead," I said, bursting into tears again.

The captain nearly fell over backwards and had to grab onto a shelf.

"Christ!" he swore.

He climbed down quickly, grabbed his polecat-skin cap which he had left on the table and ran out shouting:

"Seal the doors!"

Chapter Six

The Dervelle family had gathered in the solicitor's office for the reading of my uncle's will. First, the solicitor held up and circulated a large, square, yellow envelope, sealed with five, very large, greenish, wax seals and inscribed with the words: "My Last Will and Testament". Then he pointed out that the seals were intact, broke them and drew out of the envelope a piece of stamped paper, folded in two, and read in a slow, solemn voice the strange document which follows:

Les Capucins, 27th September, 1868

I have never believed in the sincerity of the vocation of country priests, and I always thought they were priests because they were poor. The job of priest in the main attracts lazy men who dream of a life of crude pleasures, without work, without self-sacrifice, vain and bad sons disgusted by the labourer's smock, who deny their fathers, backs bent by toil, fingers calluused. For them, the priesthood represents a life as the comfortable bourgeois of the presbytery, waited upon at table, indulging their pride, being bowed low to by passers-by. Most of these pathetic beings, envious and rebellious peasants as they are, if born rich would never have dreamt for a moment of taking orders, and if they came into money all of a sudden, almost all would quickly leave the priesthood. I wish to make a startling and public demonstration of this.

This then is my will, and my will consists in that demonstration.

To the first priest in the diocese after the day of my death who chooses to be defrocked, I bequeath in sole ownership, my goods, land and property, as follows:

1. My house Les Capucins, with its outbuildings and all the furnishings contained within, from cellar to attic, with the exception of my library, which I allocate below.
2. Three thousand five hundred francs of income, in various securities, the title deeds for which, all registered, are held by the notary in Viantais.

3. *Any moneys, cheques, bills of sale, etc., which might be found in my house at the time of my death.*

I have no doubt that, once this legacy is made known, a great number of priests will leave the church and will greedily hasten to claim my house, income, money and furniture. For this reason, I charge my executor to verify that the title of "first defrocked" be properly and duly established — this will be a source of hatred, ferocious jealousy, impudent deceits, false testimonies and hideous passions, which will prove what the soul of a priest really is. If it should happen that twenty, fifty, two hundred priests were to be defrocked the same day at the same moment, fate will decide which of these co-defrockees will inherit the legacy I make in this document, freely and joyously, of my entire fortune. They will take their chance, either drawing straws, or tossing a coin, under the surveillance of my executor.

This unknown, worthless heir must keep my servant Madeleine in his employ and pay her a hundred and twenty francs per year or, if he prefers, grant her an income of four hundred francs until her death.

I ask Monsieur Servière, landowner in Viantais, and friend, to be so kind as to fulfil these duties as the executor of my will; I beg him too, in memory of the good relations we have enjoyed and in compensation for the trouble I will cause him, to accept the legacy I make him of my library, such as it is on the day of my death. I call careful attention to the following paragraph.

Monsieur Servière will find in the room facing the library, a very old trunk, painted black, the lid of which is bound with leather straps. I charge Monsieur Servière, on the fourth day after my death, to burn this trunk in the yard of Les Capucins, this to be done in the presence of the magistrate, the notary and the police superintendent.

Finally, I wish my burial to be simple and brief; no mass is to be celebrated, no candle burnt during the religious service, which should be that reserved for the poor. Moreover, I declare that no part of my legacy is to be used for my funeral, and, in so doing, ensure the disappointment of Father Blanchard, the parish priest.

JULES-PIERRE-DERVELLE
Priest

The notary had finished reading. Shaking his head, he went over the piece of stamped paper several times, examining it with contrite attention.

"That's all," he said, waving his hand evasively. "That really is all there is."

He stood up and asked:

"Would you like me to have copies made for you?"

At a nod from my father, the notary went into his study with the will.

There was total astonishment, a crushed silence. Cousin Debray had not moved at all; his eyes fixed on the floor, he looked like a block of stone, so still was he, so heavily did his stupefaction weigh on his body, reducing him to an inert heap. However, after a few minutes, he stood up in his turn, and breathed out heavily:

"Ah! The damned bastard!" he muttered dully.

Without looking at anyone, he left, uttering horrible oaths.

As for my father, certainly, he had always dreaded some final joke on the part of the Abbé, but he could never have foreseen such a will. The will went far beyond anything he could have imagined as a bourgeois fearful of the terrible power of an irreparable sacrilege; the will perpetuated even in death that life of impiety, ingratitude, disorder and mystification which had been his brother's; the will was like a last eructation of that impenitent soul, the last rictus of that diabolical spirit, and from now on he would never ever be free of their effects. What afflicted him most cruelly, was the outrageous indifference of my uncle towards a family which had cared for him, which had devoted itself to him in the inferno of his death agony. My father felt sorry for himself and for me; he kept saying to himself, a sob in his voice, his eyes wet:

"Not a word for me! No small memento for Albert! My wife, I can understand, but me! The little one!"

When the notary came back in, carrying the copies, my father felt moved to express something of his feelings, and sadly, quietly, he said:

"I must say, something like that is quite hard to take. My

God! It is not so much his fortune. He was free to dispose of it as he wished, though, in truth, that will is an infamy . . . Well . . . No, it is the way he did it! Not one memento for Albert, his godson, poor child. Look, he might have left him just his library, that wouldn't have been too much, would it? In that case, no one would have had any objections! And to think that before, in Randonnai, and lately, at Les Capucins, I abandoned my own patients for him! Ah! People are going to have a field day!"

The notary nodded, adjusting his expressions and gestures according to those of my father.

"Yes, yes," he kept saying. "Very distressing. I must stress this is not advice I am giving you, but, it does seem to me to be contestable, extremely contestable. I do not know how far . . . Well, anyway, you must do what you wish."

"Legal action!" groaned my father. "Oh no, no, and it would be no less wounding for all that . . ."

However, he tucked the copy into his briefcase and hurried back to the house, where Monsieur and Madame Robin were waiting for him.

When my mother heard the will she had difficulty containing herself; Madame Robin uttered cries of protest; Monsieur Robin exclaimed:

"It is null and void, null and void! It is an altar to imtiety and immorality . . . It is null and void . . . How can such a legacy de given to the first defrocked priest! It is null and void!"

For three hours he quoted passages from the *Code Civil* and judgements from the Appeal Courts. In my mother's eyes was a terrifying, dull gleam of hatred. My father quietly continued his lament:

"Not one memento for the boy! And if you knew how we took care of him! The child read to him . . . His godson, Madame Robin, is it conceivable? Ah! Servière must be having a good laugh at our expense! The library to Servière? I ask you . . ."

The burial was simple and brief, exactly as my uncle desired it. It was even almost cheerful. Not one priest came from neighbouring parishes. As was the custom at paupers' funerals, there was no drapery over the church door nor the high altar, and no organ music. But following the coffin, the crowd was enormous, a whispering, insolent crowd, discussing the Abbé's will. Cheeky, disrespectful comments passed from one group to another; the tale of the trunk went from mouth to mouth. The length of the procession could be heard a chorus of stifled laughter, ironic laughter which imitated the cadence of the *dring, dring* of the bell, and every other moment, the grating voice of the cantor. At the cemetery, the crowd swelled and pushed forward, jostled round the grave. Perhaps they were expecting my uncle to lift the lid of the coffin and show his grimacing face, give a final pirouette in a last act of blasphemy. When the hole had been filled, the assembled company slowly drifted away, disconcerted at not having seen anything supernatural or comic. No one came forward to throw a little holy water on the freshly turned earth, nor was any wreath or flower placed upon it.

The fourth day after the death of my uncle, my father and I made our way to Les Capucins. Monsieur Robin, who had to be present at the incineration of the trunk, had insisted that we accompany him. The notary, Monsieur Servière and the police superintendent had already arrived. In the middle of the yard, a kind of small bonfire had been prepared, a bonfire made up of three very dry logs and tinder to feed the fire. Monsieur Robin had placed seals everywhere in Les Capucins. It was established that the seals on the trunk had not been tampered with, then Monsieur Servière and the police superintendent carried the trunk into the yard and lodged it carefully on top of the logs. This was a moment of great emotion, an emotion close to fear.

The mystery lying at the bottom of that trunk troubled everyone. And it was about to go up in smoke! Everyone dreaded it, but wanted to know. We all kept our eyes fixed on the trunk, straining to see through the pieces of wood, the terrible worm-eaten, warped pieces of wood which concealed from us . . . what? The magistrate went up to my father and said, his face very pale:

"What if it is full of explosives?"

My father reassured him.

"If that were the case, he would have asked that I should be the one setting fire to the trunk."

Monsieur Servière inserted plugs of blazing straw between the network of logs. At first, thick columns of smoke rose into the calm air, barely drifting eastwards, borne by a light breeze. Gradually, the fire took, crackled, the flame grew, twisting the dry branches, a yellow and blue flame which soon licked the sides of the trunk! And the trunk caught fire, slipping, sinking into the furnace. The sides, worm-eaten and very old, split and suddenly opened up; a surge of papers, strange etchings, monstrous drawings escaped, and we saw, twisted by the flame, enormous female haunches, phallic images, incredible nudes, breasts, bellies, legs in the air, thighs entwined, a great muddle of bodies pell-mell, satanic rutting, extravagant acts of pederasty, to which the fire, which was shrivelling the paper, lent extraordinary motion. We had all drawn closer, our eyes wide at this unexpected spectacle.

"Off you go, off you go, son!"

Thus my father, who had taken me by the arm and propelled me far from the blaze.

"Off you go, off you go, son."

I stepped back, very troubled in my mind, and positioned myself at the beginning of the avenue of laurels. For a quarter of an hour, all five stayed there hunched over the flames, craning stretched necks, with curious faces and devouring eyes.

The fire died down, the smoke dispersed. Still they gazed at the heap of ash as it grew cold.

The return to Viantais was silent. In the square, as we left Monsieur Robin, I glanced up at the house of the Misses Lejar. Behind his window, little Georges was sewing, more bent, more wan, more bony than ever. His hands flew back and forth, drawing the needle.

"This evening then!" said my father to the magistrate.

"This evening!" replied Monsieur Robin.

That evening, life went back to normal, as in the past. Several times my father cried out:

"But what can he have been up to in Paris?"

And I thought I could hear mocking laughter in reply, distant laughter, a stifled sound, emerging from somewhere below, beneath the earth.

Kérisper, July 1887, January 1888